London Bridge is Broken Down

A Tale of Two Londons

Written by S. G. Lee

SB

An imprint of *Shillelagh Books*

London, Ontario, Canada

Acknowledgments:

Sincere thanks to Jodi and Sydney, without your constant support and encouragement, this book would not be possible. You are the best friends a writer could have. I dedicate this book to my daughters, my son-in law and my husband who have all supported my writing endeavours with encouragement and love. Special thanks to my beloved mother and my beloved sister Robin, in heaven, who taught me dreams, can come true with hard work, perseverance and patience. Special thanks also to my friend, ***Shuki Raz*** who contributed an original picture of London Bridge, in London England. which I used in the cover art.

ISBN: 978-1-987977-51-6 (paperback)

ISBN: 978-1-987977-52-3 (e-book)

Preface:

London Bridge is Falling Down are the usually remembered lyrics, but the original lyrics to this song/ poem used in a game were (as printed in Tommy Thumb's Pretty Song Book (c.1744) actually the listed below. What most people don't know is that the lyrics actually refer to the numerous repairs to the bridge and how they watched Anne Boleyn in her imprisonment. I thought this rhyme appropriate for the title; as we delve into Heather's background and why she took Clover.

London Bridge Is Broken Down

London Bridge is broken down,

Dance over my Lady Lee.

London Bridge is Broken down

With a gay Lady

How shall we build

It up again,

Dance over my Lady Lee, and company

London Bridge is Broken Down
A Tale of Two Londons

Build it up with Gravel and Stone,

Dance over my Lady Lee and company

Gravel and Stone, Will wash away

Dance over my Lady Lee, and company

Build it up with Iron and Steel,

Dance over my Lady Lee and company

Iron and Steel, Will bend and Bow

Dance over my Lady Lee and company

Build it up with, Silver and Gold,

Dance over my Lady Lee and company

Silver and Gold, will be stolen away

Dance over my Lady Lee and company

Then we'll set, a man to Watch

Dance over my Lady Lee

Then we'll set, a man to Watch

With a gay Lady.

~0~

The watcher stared. It was her! She'd gained a few pounds; but he'd recognize her Heather anywhere, from his dad's descriptions, and the picture he still carried in his wallet. How he wanted to tear the picture up, but his dad had said it was to remind him, that women could be treacherous. She was the reason his father had forsaken his half- brother and why his mother and sister and died. She had been allowed to continue her life and now she had a child. While he'd fix that! Did she really think she could sail through life happy, while his family suffered? He'd make her pay; but first she had to suffer a little; victory would not be his until she did. A few scares then the finale. He could hardly wait to begin; but this would require careful planning and time, He would succeed and his father would forgive his half-brother, but crown him, the good son.

~0~

Chapter 1 - No Never Again

A week ago

Heather adjusted the blanket on the baby, tears streaming from her eyes. How could her little baby be dead? Okay, so Lily wasn't a baby any more, but she still thought of her that way. Lily was so young... had been so young…much too young to die. Eileen Jones would pay for what she did to Lily. She would hire someone she knew to take care of that evil, little bitch. Heather was due a few favours and she still had contacts, no matter what the agency might think.

That evil Eileen Jones would drop dead unexpectedly, in her cushy mental health cell. She wouldn't live a normal life while Lily had none. Because of Eileen Jones, Clover would never know her mother. The best of Lily. Her sweet Lily, was dead. That kind generous woman. Lily who never saw bad in anyone. How that girl became a prosecuting attorney, Heather could not understand. Lily had a hard time seeing that anyone could be bad when she was young and she hadn't changed that much even though Grandma Katha had raised her from the age of nine, instead of her mother. Grandma Katha had poured all the love that she hadn't given her own daughter Florence, or her granddaughter Heather, into Lily and Amelia. Did they know how lucky they were? Amelia must. Now, that damn Eileen, she was unlucky, now that Heather knew what she had done, Eileen would pay for taking Lily's life.

She couldn't leave Clover, in Canada, with Emmett Rogers. The damn man hadn't even married Lily even knowing that she was having his baby and he brought havoc in his wake. How many murders had he exposed Lily and Rose to? Okay, so a few had been nutjobs; but being crazy in Heather's book did not excuse murder of innocents. Gerhard Brandt was on Heather's tail. How had he discovered that she was Lily's mother? Had she had exposed Clover and Lily to him? Heather would have spirited Lily away to safety with the baby and Rose. She'd allowed Katha to take Lily away out of the country and be raised without her mother hadn't that proved love? Instead, Katha considered that desertion would Lily have thought her mother abandoned her if she'd known. No put those thoughts behind her Heather had to deal with the here and now. If only her mind was so foggy at times, but if she took her medicine, it would be okay, she could protect hem both.

Clover would never be safe as long as Gerhard was alive. Gerhard wanted to make her pay for killing his wife and daughter. They weren't supposed to die; but he was.

Heather remembered how she'd been under orders at the time to tell them where Gerhard would be and at what time. Heather had hesitated but she knew it was her job and Gerhard was a dangerous man to the world. His plans for terrorism in the U. K. could have killed the monarchy. Heather was loyal to Queen and country she couldn't let the fact that a man could die enter her work. She knew when she joined that people could die; as long as it wasn't her family member, she could live with it.

She had heard on the news that Gerhard's wife and daughter had arrived unexpectedly.

Gerhard had gone to the market to collect food; when the bomb went off killing the wife and daughter. Lily not been directly involved with their demise. She had consoled herself that maybe some other agency that had placed the bomb; but she had questioned her own role in it. She had reasoned that she was a low-level spy and she had no control over agency business; so why was he blaming her? It was irrational but grief often was. This was a cold-blooded business and so was being a terrorist did he think there would be no after-effects because of his actions? Yet he was so arrogant he probably did and all he wanted was vengeance.

All hell broke loose, Heather's mother, Florence who was living with them was killed while crossing a street; then Lily and Heather were snatched out of Lily's car. Heather blamed herself for not thinking about how they would retaliate against her and grab Lily and herself. After all actions have consequences.

That fateful day she had been driving Lily to school. Lily happily chatted about the play she would be in, when a car came out of nowhere and started banging her bumper.

Heather speeded up and so did the car. Heather had driven defensively trying to lose them. Until they drove her into a lamp post. Suddenly, Heather was fenced in,

Two cars were in front of her and the car behind her became two as well. Four cars against one; boxed in so Heather couldn't move. Men at all the escape routes so they couldn't escape. Guns trained on her and Lily. What else could she do to protect Lily, she surrendered.

At first, she thought it was Gerhard Brandt coming for his revenge; but before she surrendered it occurred to her that she and Lily would already be dead, if it was Gerhard. These were other people who had turned their sights on Heather and her spying that she had been doing for the English crown. Paperwork, that's all she really been doing recently, so why target her? Okay so she freelanced a little business with Gerhard for them; but nothing else. Heather had racked her brains, but had not come up with a reason, except perhaps leverage, or mistaken identity.

She begged them to leave Lily, but that was her mistake. That made Lily her weakness. She should have remembered her training;

but with Lily at risk, everything had gone out the window. The agency had promised her family would never be at risk, that they would be protected… foolishly, Heather took them at their word.

The villains took them both in the back of an unmarked van. Heather and Lily were driven to an unknown location, hustled into what looked like an abandoned building. It was there the torture began on Heather. Heather held out strongly; but when they hit Lily and blackened her eyes, then threatened to do more evil things to Lily, Heather started to bend. She offered up some information; none of it was good enough for them, they wanted what she couldn't divulge; or didn't know.

A week had passed and still they were prisoners something had to give. Heather knew if she gave in, they still kill them both she started planning their escape. Unfortunately, things got worse, one of the kidnappers started getting over familiar with Lily. Heather found one of them stripping her to her underwear. Only intervention from another kidnapper saved Lily from his tendencies.

Heather waited for two of them to leave living only the abuser. She hit the abuser over the head and wanted to kill him; but then another kidnaper came out of nowhere. He was new and seemed nice if that was possible, he was a kidnapper though and she had to protect her daughter, the job wasn't finished. Heather knew there would be no escape...unless...she offered up herself. The kidnapper locked Lily in a room and then he had taken Heather to another bedroom. Heather had offered herself willingly anything for Lily's safety. Heather had endured it all with a smile pretending she liked it. The kidnapper told Heather his name was Jake. It probably wasn't his real name; but it felt like they were bonding. She got him to agree to help Lily escape and get her daughter to safety. Heather didn't care what happened to herself as long as Lily was safe.

The man had stabbed the abuser spilling blood everywhere. He then took bags of stored blood out of the fridge and poured it on the floor. Blood didn't come from nowhere. What had he been planning and for how long? Would he take Heather and Lily somewhere they didn't want to go? He'd promised to help Lily escape; Heather would do anything to make that happen.

"What was that for?" Heather had asked.

"You haven't been a spy long, have you?" he answered.

"I'm a low-level spy. I've been a spy for ten years. I married Peter, he's an attaché eight and half years ago. He has no idea what I do."

"You've only been married for eight years? But the child is nine! How long did you know him?"

Heather was appalled how she could have revealed so much to this kidnapper, she didn't know. No one was supposed to know about Lily's father, that she'd never reveal, not only for Lily's sake but her father's. Heather could say that Peter and she knew each other longer that was the story they'd told everyone.

"Peter adopted her," she admitted and she didn't quite no why.

"You have shown such trust with me, I will help the little girl escape. They should never have taken my child."

"Thank you, Jake. Wait a minute, *my* child, why are you calling Lily, your child?"

"I can't believe you didn't recognize me. Do you sleep with every Peter, Tom or Harry, my Scottish flower?"

Heather had remembered how Jacob had called her that and how he'd vowed to protect her and they'd said he was dead but why did he look so different?

"Jacob? They said you were dead."

"My darling, I've looked high and low for you. I couldn't find you. I came to rescue you and Lily.

My face had to be reconstructed after my so-called death so it's now wonder you didn't recognize me. Still, I had hoped that you slept with me because you recognized me…"

"Jacob?"

“We can get away from these criminals; but for now, we have to spirit our daughter away to safety, for Lily, is my daughter correct?’

Heather found herself nodding.

Jacob then helped Lily out the basement window and told Lily where the police station was.

“Wander into the police station Lily look lost and be vague. Your mother and I must leave, but one day we will be back. Just remember we love you.”

“I don’t know if she can do this Jacob.”

“Then you need to take her as far as the station, direct her in, and disappear.”

“I need to be away, before the police raid comes. Meet me at the Prague Astronomical Clock in one week’s time. If you’re not there I’ll understand darling, that you can’t, or won’t meet me. If I’m discovered, I’ll tell the others, including the police that you are dead. I’ll explain everything then. I promise, “Jake insisted.

Heather had agreed thinking she be safe and so, would Lily. She'd leave Peter and be with the love of her life. The father of her child; but none of this had worked out, everything was ruined; when the men had grabbed her and spirited her to a Russian gulag.

Heather had done what she could to save Lily and hoped that her daughter wouldn't be traumatized; but she had heard that Lily didn't remember what had happened to her after her stay in the hospital. Heather knew Lily's psyche was fragile and it was therefore better if she thought Heather was dead. Katha had whisked Lily away to Canada, believing that Heather was dead. Heather had hoped to come to Canada, a retired agent and be reunited with her daughter, but she'd been grabbed again and taken to Russia. Two of other kidnappers and some others from the Soviet government had grabbed her and she'd languished in Siberian prison. At first, they had tried to break her and take all the secrets she knew. She hadn't given in after a year and they had then sent her remote prison camp, Petus, in the Siberian region of Russia.

Breaking rocks and doing menial labor, with little food, Heather slept on the floor and longed to be free. She waited her chance and had succeeded too late to be with Lily, Lily was young adult, studying to become a lawyer. Grandma Katha probably thought she'd abandoned her daughter, but Heather would have never left her daughter willingly how could Grandma Katha have thought so badly of her. Heather had thought Grandma Katha loved Heather but she had been proven wrong and yet Heather had trusted Grandma Katha with her greatest treasure.

Heather saw here was no place in Lily's life, that her presence could harm Lily at least that's what Lily's shrink had told Heather. She felt guilty how she had held that shrink at gunpoint and yet the psychiatrist had held her ground and actually told Heather the truth about Lily. Lily had been scarred by all the traumas; she had suffered. Lily, however had overcome them had pulled herself together in order to become a good mom to a little girl that needed one, because that little girl. Rose, too, was scarred. The psychiatrist felt though that if she were to see Heather alive, that would be too much and that Lily would recall her ordeal, that Lily might not be able to handle what had happened to her when she was nine. Someday the trauma would be handled but Lily couldn't have handled then.

So, Heather hadn't come forward but she kept an eye on Lily through her network. She felt like she knew her daughter that way, but it wasn't enough, especially now that Lily was gone. She'd never get back that time with her little girl, or see her daughter in person again to tell her how sorry she was.

Heather had given up all rights and ties to Lily to protect her; but no one knew that. Grandma Katha just thought she was selfish. Who cared what that old bat thought! She didn't still care, did she?

Poor little Rose, but she had Grandma Katha, Rose would be okay. She couldn't take the kid away from everyone she knew. That would traumatize the child.

Rose had bonded with Grandma Katha. The woman wasn't all bad, even if she irrationally hated Heather and had grossly, misjudged Heather. Okay, the truth was Heather hated Grandma Katha, too. She hated her for judging her without talking to Heather. Grandma Katha had no right she herself had been responsible for some of the troubles in Heather's life by abandoning her to her mother, Florence. She hadn't helped mother when she begged for help from her terrible choice of an abusive husband. Grandma Katha wasn't perfect so why did she expect others to be?

As for the man who called himself Heather's father. He wasn't though, was he? Grandma Katha and Florence knew that. She'd overheard her mother begging Grandma Katha for help n the phone…just a little money to get away from her husband and when Grandma Katha had refused, mother had said that she would tell Heather the truth, that Heather's real father was her grandfather!! Talk about family secrets…now admit that Grandma Katha!!

Rose wasn't Heather's flesh and blood, either, but Clover was. She wasn't about to try and raise an almost full-grown teenager like Rose. Rose was a kind sweet girl, but Grandma Katha would do a much better job of that. Grandma Katha had to be better the second or third time around; she done an okay job with Lily and Amelia.

As for that Emmett Rogers, the father of the baby; men were nothing but trouble. It was his fault, his and Grandma Katha's that this cretin Eileen Jones had come into Lily's life.

Sure, Emmett had served in Afghanistan and got a medal... Who the heck cared? That didn't make him father material! Clover needed lots of love and affection. She needed her mother Lily, but she'd never have her, so Heather would give her the next best thing her grandmother's love and affection. Heather would be the best mother to this baby girl she could be, a better mom then she'd been to Lily. She'd be a wonderful mother to her granddaughter. She would make up for all the love she should have given Lily.

She'd get to raise a little girl. That alone made her smile through her tears. Lily had been taken away from Heather when she was only nine years old.

Lily had a wonderful childhood (with Grandma Katha), unlike Heather. Heather hadn't seen Grandma Katha for years, not until she was an adult and she had suffered living with her mother and the man she called Heather's father.

Heather's mother, Florence had suffered as the broken, battered wife. Heather had felt sorry for her. Heather's childhood was traumatic and filled with only bruises and broken bones from her father. Heather had retreated into books. Her eidetic memory made her memorize all sorts of useless facts and situations. Unfortunately, with her synaesthesia everything, even bad situations became remembered in vivid colours. Sometimes, Heather could use this to her advantage, barely even glancing at the books to remember and score A pluses in all her courses. The intelligence tests they gave her showed her scores as off the charts. These scores were sent on and someone who finally noticed Heather. Barely sixteen years old and they recruited her for government work in England where she lived. Florence thought it was just a prestigious government job Heather was being trained for some kind of secretarial job Florence had thought. The complexities of the job were only explained to Heather who readily agreed then she got Florence to agree to Heather's training as schooling at such an early age. Heather left her home and didn't see her mother again; until she found herself pregnant with Lily.

Heather had been devastated at first, to find out she was expecting. How could she raise a child? She was a spy, and a spy needed no encumbrances; that and the fact that the father (the love of her life) had disappeared. Heather couldn't believe that all she had left of Jacob MacAulay was a note that said he was sorry, but he had to say goodbye.

How could the man she'd given her heart against all her brain power telling her this was wrong disappear without a trace? She tried all channels to find him and had ended up with nothing. The she'd gone to a doctor under an assumed name to find out she was pregnant. How could she raise a baby? She'd thought about abortion, but she couldn't bring herself to do it. Days went by and it was too late for an abortion. Heather was told she was being transferred to Paris. She should have been happy; but the agency didn't know about the pregnancy and she feared what they would do to her once she began showing more.

Heather decided she only had one choice. On a cold, snowy, April morning at 2 a. m., she decided to take action.

Heather climbed the span of the Pont Neuf (the oldest standing bridge across the river Seine in Paris, France) This was the heart of Paris in medieval times and in her mind the right place to jump into the Seine.

As she was about to put her foot forward and leap, she heard a voice.

"Nothing is that insurmountable. Talk to me, tell me, how I can help?"

Heather had turned around and saw an older man, somewhere between about thirty-two and thirty-five years old. He was dressed in a double-breasted suit that she recognized as from St. Jacob of London. This man had money she categorized and then wondered, why she did. What did it matter? She needed to gather her strength up and take that final step.

He had red hairm graying at the sides and warm blue eyes. As he talked his smile met his eyes and hers. He was charming and compassionate. He listened as she found herself revealing how Jacob had left her and she was alone. She told him she was working a clerical job and that she didn't know how she could do it and raise a child alone.

Peter was a marvel, a hero in suit. He told her, he too had a problem that he couldn't quite solve. He needed a wife in name only, because the rumours about him were getting too intense. He'd come there to jump too, but had changed his mind.

"You have a mistress? Is that the rumour?"

"No, I've never said this aloud. It's very hard and if anyone found out, I'd lose my job."

"You're gay," Heather stated, suddenly understanding.

"I am," Peter had admitted.

Peter had talked Heather off her perch and they talked in his car. Peter in a matter of moments, had come up with a solution to both their problems, which made sense.

Heather could have financial stability, a loving father for her baby (and although Peter didn't know) a cover for her spying. Peter after all worked as an attaché for the government of Canada, in Paris. Later they moved to Prague. Peter had no idea that he was harbouring a spy. Peter needed a wife and family so he asked no questions, and Heather needed not tell any lies.

Heather could even provide a home for her mother, Florence who had been released from prison after spending a year in it for killing Heather's father, shortly after Heather had left home. For nine years long years Heather had looked after her mother seeing that she had what she needed and then just like that, Florence had been killed in an accident. At least it looked like an accident… at first; until her contacts told her they were really looking for Heather and had killed Florence by mistake. All that plastic surgery Heather had paid for to reconstruct her mother's damaged face (from her abusive husband) hadn't helped anyone; but Heather.

Heather felt guilty and devastated to realize that the surgery had made her mother look so much younger, that they had mistaken Florence, for Heather. Her mother had seemed a different person though, confident happy, vibrant, so. maybe Heather should stop blaming herself for her mother's death. No, it was her fault they killed her mother because Heather was a spy. No, Heather could never forget that *she* was the reason, why Florence was dead.

Then of course Heather and Lily had been kidnapped and her life had spiralled once again into sadness and bleakness. She had continued with her career spying, after she escaped from the Russian prison. Heather really had been offered no other choice as the agency had rescued her from that prison. She thought about coming back to Peter and Lily, but it was too late, they had moved on with their lives. Peter had continued with his career and to Heather's surprise (in Heather's absence) had long ago abandoned his daughter to Grandma Katha and a country far away.

Still Heather had managed to watch Lily from a distance, watched her grow into the attorney she became. She continued her work with the agency and did their bidding. Heather had even met Horace (Lily's dead husband) once and threatened him if he ever harmed Lily, or took Rose away. Heather had believed Horace had been frightened, he hadn't revealed to anyone that Heather was alive, but he obviously hadn't believed her as at the time of his death, for he'd plan to take Rose and divorce her. That cop Brad

Owens had fixed that problem. Heather hadn't even had to lift a finger to get him to do that either. Luckily for her the agency (although they heard about the murders) knew Heather wasn't involved. She had been busy in Turkey (so she had the greatest alibi) when that all went down. Heather felt guilty that someone had gotten so close to Lily without her knowledge; but she understood that this Brad person, was now locked up where he could harm no one.

Lately though, the agency seemed to think Heather was a little unstable. Heather worried that they would either imprison her in a mental facility, or sanction her. She knew she was a little off; but if she stayed on her secret medications that she got in her Lady Lee name she could function.

She had convinced them she was stable and they were off her back for now; but when they found out about Clover, all bets were off. They'd try to take Clover and give her back to Emmett. No, she wouldn't let that bastard have Clover; he couldn't protect her not like Heather. Look how little badly he'd protected my Lily.

Heather could never get back that time with Lily, thanks to Grandma Katha. Grandma

Katha had threatened to inform those same Siberian people; where she was if she didn't stay away from Lily. How had Grandma Katha known about them? Had Grandma Katha known all along? No, it was probably her husband, Terrence. The man was a former judge and a terrible busybody. Grandma Katha and Terrence hadn't even told Lily what had happened to her mother that Heather was alive.

Heather hadn't been able to stay away. Lily was her little girl, even grown up and Grandma Katha had no right to keep her from her. Grandma Katha would have seized the baby, Clover and tried to raise her like she raised Amelia and Lily, but that cow was too old now and that damn, Gerhard had found Heather. Heather had revealed too much with a recent lover who had drugged her. He had been sent to find out information about her. she realized too late, and she had told him of her attitude about the others. Gerhard who had probably sent him knew she only cared about Lily. Gerhard would be after Heather's family next. Katha could fend for herself but Clover couldn't.

If she ran, he'd know she didn't care about Rose and Katha and he'd leave them alone. They'd be safe. but little Clover? Clover was at risk, because of her connection to her grandmother.

This was Heather second chance; she could raise Clover in one of her secret London flat. Her flats all had different names the one she was living in with now was for Sarah Crouse. She had another that was sold to Amanda Lee (the same she used for her doctor appointments and treatments. No one would find Clover and Heather. Heather would do what she needed to do, to protect the two of them.

Rose would be content and happy with Grandma Katha; after all she was only two years away from adulthood. Grandma Katha was old now and probably wouldn't live too much longer than that, Heather reasoned.

Clover deserved a mother who was young enough to raise her. Heather could be that mother; she knew she had the tools. Clover's father had put her in danger, as had Grandma Katha picking that fake nanny, Eileen Jones. That evil bitch, Heather would make her pay for killing Lily. Her time was coming. Eileen had better enjoy her time now, because sometime in the future, when Eileen least expected it, karma would bite her on the butt. Heather would see she suffered as much or more than Lily had.

As for that Emmett Rogers; he didn't deserve to raise Clover, so Heather would step in. She wouldn't let Lily down. Not again …no never again.

"This is my promise, Clover, darling girl; I will protect you," Heather vowed.

~0~

Chapter 2 - Bitter Waters

One week later

Lily lay in her bed recuperating and talking to Grandma Katha.

"It's over, Grandma Katha. I'm moving back to my house. He can stay at his home, while I stay in mine. He hasn't been to visit me in days."

"Are you giving up Lily? Or do you want to spend your life with this man?" Katha asked.

"You're blaming me? I'm not in this relationship alone. He is never there when I need him." Lily complained, "When that woman attacked me and I almost lost the baby; where was he?"

"Clover is gone. You have to stop thinking she isn't," Katha uttered; but Lily went on choosing to not to hear Grandma Katha.

"Rose isn't speaking to him either."

"Lily, you have to decide what's more important. Do you love him enough to reach out to him; or do you want to continue to wallow in self-pity?" Katha asked.

"Eileen Jones has much to answer for, but where was Emmett, when our baby needed protecting?"

"It wasn't Emmett's fault. It was Eileen's. She is getting the care she needs. Poor Dafydd, he had no idea that his sister was posing as the nanny," Katha replied looking guilty herself.

"Dafydd knew about his unstable sister. I also blame him."

"I'm sorry I should have known somehow. I should have known!!"

"It wasn't your fault Grandma Katha. You went to a reputable agency. Emmett should not have lashed out at you like that. He acted like it was entirely your fault. He lived with her, he should have known what she was about, but he didn't see it either. What did he expect? That I was going to cut off ties with you on his say so? Blame you for Eileen's deed?"

"You are both grieving for that baby. You both said things, you didn't mean. You have to go speak with Emmett, if you want to patch this up."

"I don't want to. He should make the first move. It's not like I can leave the hospital," Lily declared stubbornly.

"*Cross Patch, draw the latch, sit by the fire and spin; Take a cup, and drink it up. Then call your neighbours in.*"

"You used to say that when I was little; when I was being stubborn," Lily replied surprised.

"It's an old English nursery rhyme, but it still applies my pet. Don't be so stubborn you cut off your nose, to spite your face," Katha continued.

"I know you are right, Grandma Katha; but I'm just too angry at him," Lily explained.

"It will get better. Anger is a natural reaction on both your parts, you want to blame someone. Emmett is blaming himself too, for not knowing who Laura… I mean Eileen really was," Katha explained, "I can never forgive myself for hiring her; but we all have to put our anger aside and deal with the grief that is eating us up inside."

"I know logically that he is; but I also find myself blaming him for not being there when we needed him the most."

"Rose isn't over her trauma either. She's pretending not to be angry trying to put aside that anger to support you; but under it all she's still mad and hurt that we didn't tell her about Cordelia's breakdown."

"You know why I didn't tell her, number one I made a promise, and two, the shrink didn't think it was a good idea. The information might traumatize and harm my daughter."

"Harm we harmed her!! She's angry with both of us, for keeping this secret and she's mad that her mother is in bad shape. We have to help her."

"I keep hoping that Cordelia will get better and then maybe some day Rose can have a relationship with her."

"That's big of you."

"You almost seem sarcastic. I'm sure you didn't mean it in that context. I'm not saying there wouldn't be a little jealousy; but Rose's needs always come first, before any feelings I might have. You taught me that, Grandma Katha, because you always put me first."

"Ah…" Katha began then she seemed to change what she wanted to say and commented, "It will take time; but you will heal from this. Both of you and Emmett, too."

"I can't see that happening anytime soon. Emmett wasn't here for us. Do you know I had the weirdest hallucination when I was giving birth… my mother was here and she held out papers for me to sign she said she said she was there to help me and take my baby, just in case I died in childbirth. What a weird dream!! It must be, because I needed someone there and of course my head injury just conjured her up...I just wish they would have let me see my little girl, before they kept her in isolation so long. I know I've been ill; but I want to see my baby girl. No, I need to see my little girl!!"

Katha looked alarmed and tried to hide it.

Lily just kept talking, "You've seen her, correct? Clover is eating, okay? She's gaining weight, right? She must be missing her mother; but at least she has had you and her father."

"Lily, I've tried to tell you over and over again," Katha began.

"Is there something wrong with Clover? She was too early, it's entirely my fault. Is that the real reason, they haven't let me see her? She's having her own health problems?"

"I told you over, and over again, Clover's dead."

"Clover is not dead! How dare you say that to me!!"

"Listen to me, Lily. Clover died and I'm sure your mind brought your mother to you in spirit."

"It just seemed so real. I miss my mother so."

Lily saw something in Katha face and suddenly she knew the truth, "My mother is alive? That wasn't a dream?"

"She's alive," Katha admitted.

Lily stared at Katha long and hard. Her eyes widen and her mouth dropped open.

"You evil, old bag!! You knew my mother was alive and you never said a word? You let me congratulate you on what a wonderful job you had done raising me and yet you knew my mother was alive? How long have you known?"

"Just since your shooting last year."

"Since my shooting? You've known she was alive since then and didn't say a word? How could you do this to me? To Clover!!"

"I'm sorry Lily. I felt I protected you, but what's worse is Rose believes your mother was there when Clover died. Even if Heather was there, Clover s dead. The doctors said they pronounced the baby dead."

"Clover is not dead. I would know if my baby was dead and I don't feel that… not like when George died."

"They are both dead."

"How dare you. George was such a tiny baby six months formed and way to early, but Clover…"

"Clover is dead, you have to believe me. They've issued a death certificate."

"It's a fabrication. If my mother faked her death, she could fake Clover's too. Rose did see her with Clover. Where is Rose and where is my mother?"

"I wish I was lying Lily, but Heather didn't take your daughter. As for Heather's employers, they are no one to tangle with."

"You are telling me that my mother is alive, but my child is dead?"

"Yes."

"Why wouldn't she stay then? The mother I remember loved me. She wouldn't leave me to grieve my daughter by myself. She wouldn't hurt me like this."

"I believe Heather was here; but I don't believe she took Clover. Heather could have taken Clover. Heather is delusional. Her employers think she needs help."

"If I had known…the description that Rose gave Emmett fits her to a tee. You told them all this? You told the authorities my mother is alive and that she took my daughter?"

"She didn't take your child! Clover was declared dead. You have to accept the truth, Lily!!"

"Then you saw Clover? You know this because you investigated it thoroughly?"

"No," Katha admitted.

"Then how do you know she's dead? I'd know if Clover was dead; they haven't shown me a body! I don't feel that; so, the only logical explanation is that my mother took her. I don't know why she'd do that unless… she thought I was dead? You did you tell the authorities Heather was here? Didn't you? That she faked her death?"

"I didn't know she was here. I still don't," Katha explained.

"Get out of my room!! I never want to see you again," Lily yelled at Katha.

"You don't mean that," Katha protested.

"Oh, but I do. You left me open to my mother's attack; by not letting me know she was alive. I grieved for my mother… all this time and she was alive!! You kept vital information that could find my own daughter to yourself. I never want to see you again. Get out!" Lily repeated coldly.

"When you are ready to apologise, I'll be back, missy," Katha stated.

"That will be a cold day in hell. Thanks to you, Emmett, and my evil mother, any hope of finding my daughter is gone," Lily exclaimed colder still.

"Your daughter is dead. I'm grieving too. I was responsible for hiring Eileen, so as I've said over and over again, I take responsibility for that. How can you blame Emmett for any of this?" asked Katha.

"Just go away. Get out of my sight, you liar and don't come back, ever!!! Rose can take me home."

Katha left reluctantly walking straight into Rose standing outside Lily's hospital room.

"What did you do to my mother?" asked Rose having heard the last sentence Lily yelled.

"I told her the truth. Sometimes the truth hurts."

"Here's a truth for you. You did the wrong thing and now you aren't admitting it. At least Lily admitted to me that she kept where my mother was from me to protect me. She didn't tell me she was dead. If you value your relationship with my mother, you'll make it up to her," Rose explained.

"Something things can be fixed right away, this can't. This will take some time."

"You always say that family is so important to you. Being a Kelly is important to you; so, find my sister, Clover and she'll forgive you."

"Clover is dead; the hospital says so."

"I don't believe that and neither does my mother.

"I will find your Grandmother ***Heather*** and she will pay for her misdeeds. I can't find a baby that is dead. I can't bring back someone from the dead."

"Heather? My grandmother took Clover? So, she thinks that woman was Heather? Is that why Lily was yelling at you?"

"Quit calling her Lily, she's more of a mother to you than Cordelia ever was. I believe Heather, Lily's mother was there, I don't believe ***she*** took Clover."

"Mom's mother is alive? That's what she was talking about."

"Yes."

"Explain to me how Heather (for I refuse to call her my grandmother) … how she is alive. I thought she was kidnapped and possibly murdered, when my mother was nine years old," Rose replied shocked.

"There is a lot more to the story. Your grandmother Heather was kidnapped; but escaped and ran away leaving everyone to think she was dead."

"But why would she do that? I thought she loved my mom?"

"I'm going to tell you something… maybe I shouldn't!"

"Secrets, you have more secrets?"

"You're right it's time for all the secrets to end. Heather was a spy and it she may have been playing both sides; but they just haven't been able to prove it."

"A spy? A double agent, a spy? Are you freakin' kidding me?" Rose exclaimed.

"Okay, so, maybe, she wasn't a double agent; but Heather was a spy for her home country, England and possibly the U. K. .Up until now, I thought they kept her on a short leash away from us."

"You don't like her much, do you?"

"I loved Heather and sometimes I still do; but she is hard to love."

"So, why did I know and why didn't mom say anything? I mean I knew the whole story of the kidnapping, when she was nine; but wasn't she declared dead?"

"Heather was declared dead; but the story your mother tells isn't quite accurate."

"Was mom ashamed? Why did she lie to me and everyone? Or didn't she not know that her mother was alive and a spy?"

"She not only didn't know she was a spy, but she had no idea that Heather was still alive."

"How could she do that to Mom? .... Oh, so that's why she's mad at you. You knew and didn't tell her. Did you think you were protecting her?"

"I've been protecting Lily for years."

"So, that's the only reason, she's mad at you?"

Rose looked at Katha and saw the truth.

"Oh no, poor mom! Of course, Heather was the nurse who was suspicious. Why didn't you tell us? We've wasted a week! Because of you, that woman was able to come and take my sister! And you expect my mom to forgive you?"

"Rose, please! Your mom was mistaken. Heather wasn't there."

"I saw her! I saw the woman who took my sister. I could have saved her. No wonder she looked familiar. I've seen pictures of her that mom kept…"

"Don't persist in this delusion. It will only harm your mother. Clover is dead; the sooner you, and your mother believe that, the sooner we will all heal."

“I’m delusional? Do you expect anyone to forgive you? My sister has been taken and you had the information that could have stopped it; or at least helped us find her in the last week.”

“I made a mistake, one that is costing me,” Katha replied, “Can you find it in your heart to forgive me?”

“You know what? This isn’t the time for forgiveness. This is the time to lay all the cards on the table, we need all the information you’ve been holding back on Heather. Tell me, why do you think Heather would want my sister? She obviously didn’t want my mother, or she would have come out of hiding and claimed her. My mother suffered terribly from her so-called death. She still grieves for that evil woman. How could a mother do that?”

“I have no idea why she would have done this, if Clover is truly alive,” Katha protested.

“Don’t tell me, tell my sister that,” Rose exclaimed turning her back on Katha.

“I’ll find her. As God as my witness if Clover us alive I’ll find my granddaughter and great-great-granddaughter and bring Clover home to Lily."

"You had better. Even if you do, I'm not sure either my mother, or I will totally forgive you. Now I may, or may not talk to you later, so, get cracking on finding my sister and then I might."

"I'm going home to research some of Heather's past; maybe that will give me a lead. I'm also going to speak to your Grandpa Terrence."

"Grandpa Terence knows too?"

Katha nodded.

"Oh, crap that's not good. Don't let mom know. She needs someone to lean on."

Katha then went home.

Rose's cellphone rang, just as she was about to enter Lily's room. "Drat, I forgot to turn this off, sorry, mom."

"Just answer it." Lily insisted, "It could be someone about Clover."

Rose obeyed and answered her phone.

"Rose, it's Emmett."

"Does Emmett have any information on Clover?" demanded Lily.

"Let me hear, mom and then I'll let you know."

"Put it on speaker phone, so I can hear too," Lily ordered.

"Have you found my sister?"

"The hospital is till insisting Clover is dead."

"I just had an interesting conversation with Grandma Katha. She says my so-called grandmother, Heather, may have taken Clover.

"Heather is alive?"

"Yes, and she fits the description of the woman I saw. The woman dressed as a nurse whose badge said Candace."

"I knew someone must have taken her. I knew I'd feel it in my bones if Clover was dead! This is great information but we can't get your mother's hopes like this."

"Then go find Heather and find out if she has Clover. Prove me wrong."

"Give me that phone," demanded Lily putting on the speaker phone.

"Clover is alive, and my mother probably took her. Emmett, you have to go where Heather is," Lily insisted speaking into the phone.

"I can't. I want to, but I can't,"

"Why? Don't you want our baby, Clover back?"

"Of course, I want Clover back. She's my little girl. I love her as much, as I love Rose. She feels like my daughter too. I had hoped that you might consider me a good step-dad for Rose. However, I just got a call from my attorney and my sister. My attorney tells me that Henrietta Parsons has successfully gotten temporary custody of Deirdre and Rebecca and she wants full custody of Joseph when he gets out of juvenile detention."

"But what about Clover? She needs you, too."

"Some friends of mine, that I know owe me a huge favour. Thomas Mancini, served with me in Afghanistan and I saved his life. Another two men I met afterwards say that I helped them too; though I don't remember it. They are George Gagnon, Henri Cote. They'll help us."

"You were in Afghanistan? When?" Rose demanded.

"Years ago, I served after 911 and then came home after four years. I don't talk about it. It was a difficult time."

"I thought I knew everything about you. I don't want you to lose Deirdre and Rebecca, but if Clover is alive, she'll need her dad, too," Rose said.

"We can trust these guys to find my mother and our daughter?"

"These guys are like my brothers; they won't rest until they find Heather and if necessary, they can retrieve Clover from her as well. Once I win this case against Henrietta Parsons, I can join them. I promise you. Lily we'll find our Clover; or at least get answers from your mother."

"I can't Lily. Those kids can't be raised by that evil woman. I have to handle this too. I have an obligation to my sister and my nephew and nieces."

"Your daughter should come first!!" Lily and Rose both shouted together.

"We don't know that Heather has Clover. Someone else could have taken her."

"I know my mother has my daughter. You should be going to get our daughter. Now what will your friends do?"

"Turn Heather over to the proper authorities and bring Clover back to us.... if she's alive but what will you do if she isn't? what if your mother did something? She doesn't sound like she was in her right mind I mean she took Clover!!"

"I'll grieve if my daughter is really dead; but I know in my heart of hearts she's not; my mother would never harm her granddaughter."

"Lily…"

"Don't Lily me. You need to go find Clover."

"I can't Lily."

"Because of the court case with Henrietta Parsons?"

"Yes."

Emmett felt bad about lying to Lily, about his health; but he wasn't ready to share it with her. He was getting better slowly, but Lily still had a long way to go with her own health; he didn't want to add to her stress.

"I hope you beat Henrietta Parsons in court. Those kids deserve a good life; but I need you to find our daughter. My doctor won't let me travel, or I'd go myself. If there is one chance in a hundred that Clover is alive. We have to find her, Emmett."

"I'll get my buddies to help us. They owe me and they really are good friends. But what's going to happen with you and I?"

"We will see when we get Clover back."

Rose hung up the phone as Lily begged her to find her a wheelchair; so, she could go find Clover herself. Rose just shook her head. Lily needed to stay in bed a little longer to get stronger. They'd have to trust Emmett's friends to find Clover, for now she reassured mom that everything would be okay, soon because she had to believe that it would be so. Clover was okay and safe.

"Mom, surely former soldiers can find Heather. They are trained to handle difficult situations and this qualifies. If you can't do it yourself than this is the next best thing."

"They are former soldiers; but your Grandma Katha says Heather's a spy, or maybe a former spy. I'm not quite sure, what she is. I only know we have to find her and bring your baby sister home. If her employers think she's so unstable; how safe could Clover be with her?"

"They say she's unstable? Then why didn't they do something about her, before she took Clover? We have to make sure someone who knows how to find dangerous people finds her. If she was a spy she'd know how to hide. She could be really treacherous and life threatening to everyone, but especially my little sister!"

"I agree; but I feel so helpless. I'm her mother. I should be recovering my baby, on my own. She needs her mother now. I want to call that woman my mom, (because I remember when I was young that she gave me love and so much joy) but how could my mother do this? From now on to distance myself, I refuse to call her anything but Heather."

"I can understand that mom; I don't want to call her grandmother. So, we trust the soldiers; until we can go to wherever she's taken Clover and retrieve her?" Rose asked.

"Yes, we trust the soldiers. I swear though if Emmett really cares for Clover and our family, he'd better drop everything then and come with us. He needs to go get our baby, when they find her."

"He will mom. I know he loves us all."

"He'd better start proving it."

~0~

Chapter 3 – Family Surprises

Lily grabbed her cane (and as she

waked from her a to the front room); she had heard someone come in. Grandma Katha coming to apologise yet again, she thought. Three months had passed and there was no sign of Clover. Lily was still trying to recover and do therapy every day; but it was taking way too long. She still had a huge roll in her middle section from giving birth. Ugh she was fat, she thought. She should have lost some of this baby fat. Baby, the word on her lips hurt and she wanted a sweet to make the pain go away, if only for a moment. They said it takes nine months to birth a baby so expect at least nine months to lose the weight but I bet those people had their babies with them. If she just stuck to her diet, no call it nourishing choices so, she would be healthy when they found Clover. If they found Clover…

Lily needed to search for Clover on her own. Emmett's friends still had no signs of Heather. Was mother that good at hiding? Of course, she was, but Lily felt she could use her bloodline to find her, sort of a like psychic thing.

The Kellys had a muted Christmas. For Rose's sake, Lily had been with Grandma Katha's for the day; but she hardly spoken to Grandma Katha. All Lily could think about, was the fact that Clover was missing her first Christmas with her family. Lily knew that Clover being not quite three months old would not have known the difference, but the ache in Caleb, Rose's and Lily's hearts were palpable. Yes, she'd left Emmett out. Lily knew he was probably hurting; but he didn't show it outwardly and Lily was tired of being the only hurting parent. Lily had tried, but she couldn't be anything; but sad on Christmas. Emmett had acted like she was bringing everyone down. What the heck did he expect? Lily had not really enjoyed any of the day and she felt bad for being the Killjoy but she really couldn't help it.

Lily couldn't forgive Grandma Katha at least not yet; after all Grandma Katha had kept the secret that her mother, Heather was alive all these years. Even now, it didn't make sense. Lily knew her mother loved her. Why would mom have kept away from her for so long, and why would she have taken Clover? Had Lily's mother lost her mind?

None of this matter the only thing; that mattered at this point was getting Clover back and proving to everyone else that Clover was alive. Sometimes, she believed that the only person who truly understood that Clover was alive was Rose and Emmett. Rose had been rock and yet, Lily knew she hadn't completely forgiven Lily for not telling her about her biological mother. Rose had put her feelings aside of anger at Lily and had tried to comfort Lily.

Rose couldn't be anymore in Lily's heart; then if she sprung from Lily's womb. Rose had put her anger aside and now forgave Lily. How she loved that little girl; while not so little girl anymore; Rose was a young woman, a determined young woman who wanted her sister back, too. Should she be worried about Rose? Rose seemed a little thinner. Was she too thin?

She'd made Rose go to school; but she wasn't happy about it. Maybe, this was Rose coming home early?

Lily turned the corner and spotted Grandma Katha; but as she rotated, she spotted a man standing behind Grandma Katha. He was tall broad shoulder and he had gray hair with a neatly trimmed beard.

"Daddy? Is that really you?"

"Hi, pumpkin."

You're really here?"

"I'm sorry it took so long, baby-doll. I should have been here. I'm so sorry."

"Where were you?"

"I…

"It was my fault," said another man stepping into the room with suitcases, whom Lily recognized immediately as her father's major domo/ butler, Charles.

"Oh, it's so great to see you, Charles. I missed you," Lily commented.

"It really was my fault."

"Now Charles," protested Peter, Lily's father.

"I'm just glad you're both here daddy. I've come to think of Charles as family; so, I'm glad you're both here."

Peter crossed the distance and took Lily in his arms and she began to sob. A few minutes later they sat at the kitchen table, Peter reached out to her with his hand.

"You're wearing your wedding ring again. daddy? Have you seen mom?"

"Your mother is dead and this is not the wedding ring that I wore with your mother."

"I don't understand."

"I got married a week ago," Peter said quietly.

"To whom? Where is she?"

Peter looked at Charles, as if besieging him to tell Lily something.

"Lily, I've always loved you like a daughter. I hope you can forgive me for not including you. Peter and I were married a week ago."

"What? I must have heard you wrong. Did you say you and daddy got married? You mean you were at his wedding. Where is the bride? Who is she?"

"There is no she; it has always been Charles for me; since I met him."

"But you were married to mom, when you met Charles."

"Your mother knew I was gay when we met. She wanted to save my career and be my beard as they say. I never acted on my feelings, while I was married to your mother and I never would have… but times were different. In the diplomatic core it was frowned on to be a homosexual. You could be subjected to blackmailed they believed."

"I had no idea you were gay, daddy that you and Charles….

"Did I really hide it that well?"

"I don't think I ever thought about it. I knew you and Uncle Charles were close friends but…"

"I know it's probably a shock; but I truly love Charles, baby. I've loved him for a long time; but I never wanted to be disloyal to your mother's memory. I loved her too, but in a different way."

Lily was surprised, no make that shocked but she thought quickly, did this really change anything that she thought of her father? He was still the same man she called daddy. Nothing had really changed except for him admitting his true self. Lily took a deep breath, smiled at the two of them who looked at her with expectation.

"I'm sorry daddy, that you felt you had to hide a piece of yourself from all of us. It should have been different. I thought people were more open here in Canada; but I guess I was living in a bubble, thinking that we'd made such strides. I'm glad you can be yourself now, daddy. I want to welcome to the family, Charles. Though it's always felt like you were a part of it. Can I still call you Uncle Charles?"

"Of course, I'd love that." Charles replied and then hugged Lily.

"You've been on honeymoon? For three months?"

“Yes,” Peter admitted, “I broke my cell phone and I just didn’t want to leave the wilds of Scotland to get it fixed. I wanted to have the life we’d missed and I stupidly thought you’d be fine with your Grandma Katha that I could keep my real self away from you and nothing would then change with us.”

“Daddy, I love you. This is a surprise; but it shouldn’t be. You are a wonderful person dad and grandfather and your sexuality is just a part of you that’s always been there.”

“I’m sorry honey I should have trusted that you’d be excepting but I’d hidden myself for so long… I thought nothing would go wrong in your life, so, I delayed and delayed getting my phone repaired. Charles said what if I was needed by family. I needed to be myself with the world starting with my family. I finally overnighted a new phone and synced it with my old one and I found all those messages from you all. I’d planned on calling you but when I heard those messages, we got the first flight here. I’m so sorry, I wasn’t here for you sweetie.”

“You’re here now, Daddy.”

"I'm sorry for not realizing how you felt about Charles and making things harder for you both. You said mom knew?"

"I did love your mother and she knew I was gay, but I never ever, cheated on her, not as long as she was alive."

"As long as she was alive? Daddy, she lied to both of us; she is still alive and she's got my baby."

Peter looked worried and stared at Grandma Katha s if he thought Lily had lost her mind.

"I'm not crazy. My so-called mother, Heather is alive and she took Clover."

"Nonsense if she was alive, we would have known. I know you are having a hard time now Lily and it's understandable…" Peter began.

"I'm not crazy!!! I thought she would have come forward too, but Grandma Katha has known awhile. Ask her!!"

"This isn't true, is it, Katha?"

Katha looked embarrassed and tried to look away.

"How long have you known Katha? How could you have kept this a secret? Why didn't you tell me?" Peter demanded.

"I've known since the year before last, when Lily was shot. Heather was at the hospital. She wanted to see Lily; but I stopped her."

"What? But how? Heather was declared dead."

"Did you get a legal divorce Peter?"

"I divorced her absentia; but I still thought she was dead and all this time…"

"All this time Heather was alive, but she did run away at first (she claimed) to save you and Lily both," Katha commented.

"Why didn't you tell Lily and I as soon as you knew she was alive?" Peter shouted.

"There was too much water under the bridge and I was so angry. I didn't want her near Lily."

"I entrusted you with my daughter. How could you keep this from us?"

"I… I'm sorry."

"It's a good thing, we are staying," Charles declared.

"How? Don't you have to go back to your job, daddy?"

"I've retired and now that I'm retired, I've decided to come out of the closet, as the kids say. I want to be nearer to my daughter and granddaughters."

"We've looking at a house in Brighton Bay just outside of Happy Valley, or possible London. London has some reasonable housing prices and a major hospital," Charles announced changing the subject.

"Reasonable for who, Charles? Do you need a hospital Peter, or Charles."

"We're both getting older and I 'm thinking of the future. It's good to have a major hospital with great health care nearby. How's the Happy Valley Hospital?"

"It's okay but we are a smaller centre. A lot of major medical care is sent out of town to London, Ontario."

"That's what I thought. We'll find a nice home but it's a consideration," Charles said.

"We'll be close by anytime, you need us, not an ocean away anymore," insisted Peter then turning to Katha he asked, "Katha, Lily claims she has Clover. Do you think that it is possible that Heather could have taken the baby?"

"It's quite possible Grandpa Kelly. I'm sure that I saw Heather with Clover; the night she was born. I believe she took Clover," Rose claimed walking in the room.

"You are supposed to be at school," Lily exclaimed exasperated.

"I'm also supposed to have my little sister here at our house. I can't stay in school, while Clover is missing. If I need to, I'll go to summer school to make up the time; but I have to find my sister. Caleb believes me. He says if he didn't have to attend classes at Western he'd be here or where ever Heather was getting our sister safely back to us."

"Is Caleb, okay?" Lily asked.

"None of us are okay, mom, and we won't be until we have Clover here. Personally, I don't think Heather can be in her right mind. No mother would take her grandchild, from her own child…not a loving mother like you. The only thing I can think is she heard someone say Lily Kelly was dead and she though the baby would be better off with her. Like I did! You know I thought you were dead mom."

"So, Caleb is Emmett's son? Clover's half-brother?"

That's right dad."

"I'm sorry Rose; that must have been traumatic for you. I'm glad this Caleb was there for you to speak with. I believe you, too," Charles declared.

My…Heather took Clover." Peter stated, "Heather can't be in in her right mind. The Heather I knew, wouldn't do this!"

"Heather was troubled all those years ago. I thought at first that she run away," Charles stated.

"But they said she was dead. The embassy said she was dead. They had me declare her dead! Why did they lie to me? They must have known!!" Charles blurted.

"Do you want a divorce?" Peter asked.

"A divorce? Never! I love you, Peter."

"I love you, too!"

"But that doesn't explain why she would keep Clover, from you and I," Katha objected.

"I think it makes perfect sense. She hates you, Grandma Katha, for not letting me know she was alive. You were the one who kept her from seeing me, weren't you?" Lily asked.

"Lily, I was protecting you, please forgive me, I'm begging you…," Katha protested.

"I'm not listening to you, anymore," Lily stated.

"I understand you are angry; but I have to go to a meeting at the hospital. You're in good hands with your father; so, I don't feel guilty leaving you. Please, think about why I did this. I really believed I was protecting you. We also have to talk about Rose."

"Now we don't. Grandma Katha. Don't you worry my mom," Rose whispered.

"I have to we can't let this go. Did you tell her the other reason you aren't at school? That you collapsed?

"Grandma Katha, I'm warning you," Rose cautioned.

"I don't want to talk to you; so, please leave now," Lily stated in anger; not hearing Katha's comments about Rose.

I'll leave for now. Your father can watch out for you, for now," Katha replied. "But I'm only a phone call away and I love you, Lily and Rose. Now Peter and Charles take care of them both."

"I will Katha," Charles and Peter answered simultaneously.

Katha then left.

"Your Grandma Katha loves you, Lily. You may feel she made a mistake; but it was one done from love. She gave up her entire life to take first you, and then Amelia in," Charles said quietly.

Lily felt guilty for still being mad. Charles was right. Her father fell apart after her mother went missing and when the authorities thought him responsible, Grandma Katha and dad had done everything they could to shield Lily, even to the extent of spiriting her to Canada in the middle of the night. This protected Lily from the unrelenting press, the endless authorities' questions and the other children's taunts. Was Grandma Katha's actions any worse than, Lily keeping Cordelia away from Rose?

Yes, it was! Heather had taken Clover; because none of them had been aware of her being alive. She would not forgive Grandma Katha ever.

Lily then felt guilty again for being mad at Grandma Katha. Grandma Katha had done so much for her. Lily knew she had blocked some of that time out; maybe there was more of a reason than she knew, for Grandma Katha protecting her? Over the years Lily had talked about it to a psychotherapist. She wanted to remember that time better; but the psychologist had thought her mind was blocking it out because it scared her too much. Maybe Lily didn't want to remember her mother's disappearance because there was more to it? Now that she was hearing (what almost sounded like an outlandish story) of her mother being a low-level spy in danger, she wondered did her mother fake her death to protect Lily, or had she just left simply because she really didn't want to be a mother to a nine-year-old anymore? Should Lily go to her shrink and get the answers? Was she brave enough? If it would help Clover, Lily would do it. Would it help, or take her away from Clover? That is if she managed to get Heather to give her child back.

"Mom? You haven't said anything for a few minutes are you okay?" asked Rose worried.

"I just want my baby back and I can't even travel yet to find her."

"Grandpa Kelly has connections. Don't you? You can help find Heather? Can't you?"

"I'm certainly going to try. I love both my granddaughters and I'm going to see them both happy healthy and with their mother, if it's at all possible. Now I'll make some calls, but Lily I can't promise that it will end anytime soon. Your mother is very good at hiding," Peter declared.

"Thank-you Daddy for believing in me and Clover. I know you'll find her."

"I always believe in you. As your Grandma Katha says *"From your lips to God's ears"*. Now Rose why don't we see your mother rest and you and I can talk. You can help me strategize on how to get Clover back and then when you wake-up Lily we can share the finalized plans with you."

"Oh, daddy. I love you."

"Don't you worry honey. We're going to get Clover back.

~0~

Chapter 4 – Hiding Out

Heather adjusted her short, ugly black-haired wig in the elevator. Glancing at Clover in her pram, she noted that the little girl was still asleep. Heather knew she needed to get the little girl's vaccinations up to date. Clover was three months old now and needed her first shots. She should have had them last month; but Heather was weary of the authorities searching for Clover, on Emmett Rogers' behalf. So far, her fake identification (that she set up so long ago) was holding. Sarah Crouse owned a posh apartment in London England; a three-bedroom flat. Heather had to use her Sarah Crouse credit card barely three months ago (with its $50,000 limit) to purchase the finest crib and baby accessories for Clover and it had held since then, solidly. No queries for Sarah were noted by her contacts.

It had been easy to take savings from her Sarah Crouse bank account and pay the bills immediately. Sarah Crouse had an *A* one credit rating and Heather wanted that to continue.

The story that Heather had concocted was that Sarah was on maternity leave from her job, as an advertising executive. Thirty-nine paid weeks was the average in the UK; (unless your partner took twenty-six weeks after you did.) Heather had kept that information in her head in case anyone asked. The devil was in the details after all, every good spy knew that could trip you up.

Heather should have changed Clover's name; but somehow, she couldn't; it was her last tie to her dead daughter, Lily. It would hurt too much to change Clover's first name, and Clover needed that tie to her mother. Someday, Heather would explain who Clover's real mom was, and how she died, maybe when Clover was an adult. Heather would also have had to explain why she'd had kept Clover away from her father to protect her. Would Clover understand? Heather hoped so.

"Good morning, Ms. Crouse. How is the little one today?" The doorman asked, as

Heather stepped off the elevator pushing the pram.

“She’s teething a little. I think Clover is getting her first tooth.”

“Poor little one and poor mom. Can I get you a cab, Ms. Crouse?”

“Please, call me Sarah, Henry and yes, we could really use a cab. Clover needs to get her vaccinations today.”

“Did you give her some Paracetamol, or Ibuprofen, like Nurofen for babies? She’s over three months, now, right? The wife always gave our boy some, before the vaccinations and it kept the reactions down to a minimum. You have to keep track of the dosages though. You don’t want to overdose and some babies can’t have it that young.”

“Thank you, Henry, I’ll do that,” Heather said smiling at him.

Henry hailed a cab and Heather noted the man standing under the awning at the apartment across the way. Was he spying on her? Should she do a midnight move? She could easily leave everyone and everything behind? She still had an identity, no one knew about, and she'd seen another apartment here in London, an address near London Bridge for long term rental. She'd rent it in Amanda Lee offer them an exorbitant amount so that she could get it today. She made a quick call on a burner phone and the place was theirs.

She had Clover's favourite toys with her; she could reset up her apartment. They didn't need to come back. Clover's vaccinations would wait, she couldn't take someone to her doctor, although Clover needed those vaccinations at some point. They couldn't wait forever.

Henry would empty the fridge for her and she'd give up the lease quietly in a few months, sending all her furniture to charity. Heather would book two tickets to Canada and send a woman with a baby in her stead. That would fool whoever was spying on Heather. They wouldn't find her. She would become Amanda Lee. No, she didn't need to move yet, she'd wait just a little longer because she was a little paranoid. This apartment was good for Clover and the man could be quite innocently standing there. She glanced over again. Maybe it was innocent? The man had gotten into a cab;

but Heather would stay vigilant and move if necessary to London Bridge Apartments.

She'd keep Lily safe... no… not Lily she was confused again. It had to be stress that her mind kept wondering and she kept mistaking Clover for Lily. Of course, they looked so much alike and she was grieving… she was too young for dementia.

Gerhard, or the agency must never find them, Heather would see to that. She hoped that Peter wasn't too worried about Lily; but she was protecting her. No, her mind had wandered again this was Clover, not Lily. Emmett Rogers was Clover's dad, not Peter. Maybe some day she'd let Clover see him when Clover was all grown up… Emmett that was Clover would see, not Peter of course if he could forgive Heather. If Clover wanted to see him...

Heather tried to think of anything; but the fear she had of Gerhard finding them and without warning (memories that she thought she'd blocked) came rushing back of Jacob, dear Jacob… how she missed him even after all of these years. Jacob was a saint at least in her memories.

Heather had been eighteen-years old, when she met Jacob MacKay in a nightclub. Jacob stood all by himself near the bar. He was a dashing figure in a tight pair of jeans and a red silk shirt. He was about five feet ten inches and his blonde hair streaked with red short and military cut. He was a little older than Heather (she'd guessed he had to be about twenty -seven).

Jacob told her that he was single, a student and they began to talk the night away. She'd fallen hard for him that night and they'd soon moved in together;(while sort of) he had his dorm room and she had her apartment and they'd spent as much as time possible together.

She remembered Jacob's smile; the way he'd look at her and she'd melt into a puddle of goo. Being near him made her reach out and touch his arm, just to feel him. She felt safe and loved for the first time in her life with him. He told her that he never met his father had no idea who the man was and that his mom had raised him all by herself in Canada. She had told him about how her stepfather had abused her and how she had left to save herself and make a life. He thought her brave.

He had no idea she was seventeen, when they met, as she lied and said she was nineteen years old, to his twenty-seven years old. He told her he was a Rhodes Scholar, attending Oxford University in England, fifty- six miles away from her home base London; but they made the relationship work. She told him she worked as a secretary (she couldn't tell him she was a fact checker for MI5, and that she was hoping to move up.)

They rented hotel rooms spending all their time there; since he lived in the dorms and he stayed at her apartment weekends. She'd questioned none of it; but maybe she should have; as in many aspects of her life; maybe it was too good to be true.

No, she'd dare not dwell on the memories, because if she did, she'd remember how he disappeared and that would kill her. She didn't want to think it had been her fault, but even after all this time she wasn't sure that she hadn't been responsible in some way. Had the agency killed him or had some other spy agency killed him? Or had he run away from her; because he couldn't handle their relationship anymore. She didn't know.

She'd tried everything to find out where Jacob had disappeared to with no success. At one point she'd decided that he just didn't love her anymore. If only he had known about Lily but she hadn't had a chance to tell him and then it was too late. She received a note in his handwriting in the post saying Jacob was going away and she'd never see him again. She'd been so sure at first that it was a forgery; but as she examined it over and over, she knew it wasn't.

For two years they had a relationship, and then one day she came home to find that goodbye note in the post, saying it was all over. This had been both astonishing and perplexing. Heather had been so certain that Jacob loved her. She gone to Oxford to find him. They told her Jacob had left without a forwarding address. She searched fruitlessly for him, no trace of him anywhere. She'd even tried some of the agency's contacts in Canada; but there was no sign of him anywhere there. It was if he didn't really exist. Was his name really Jacob Mackay, or had that too had all been a lie? She who had prided herself on her wealth of knowledge, had taken Jacob totally at face value. He wasn't a Rhodes scholar and he didn't go to

Oxford. The room she had been in many, many times… that she thought was Jake's girlfriend… had been a friend of his. Even his 'friend' Adam didn't know where Jake had disappeared to. Jacob had paid Adam to use his room and have Heather stay overnight. He'd even paid him to pretend to be his friend. Since Adam need the cash, he'd been willing to pretend as it paid his room fees. He didn't know him from Adam!!

If Heather hadn't been so profoundly sad, she would have laughed at that. Heather really hadn't known him, yet she loved him and maybe that's what had driven her to that Paris bridge and Peter.

Heather had spent nine years with a man who had been her best friend, who had been all about family. Peter had met and hired Charles his butler /major-domo, when they'd been married two years. Lily saw the sparks between them and felt bad, that Peter couldn't reach out for love. Peter however insisted he was in the closet and his job could be at stake. He wouldn't act on this love he vowed, for he loved his job more. So, Heather had insisted he hire Charles, as their domo and keep him close to him.

Charles was one of their family, when no one else was around. Lily called him Uncle Charles. They hadn't even consummated their relationship; because Peter took his marriage vows seriously and wouldn't sleep with the man he loved if it meant betraying his vows to Heather. Heather had considered leaving Peter to give him his happiness. She even considered giving him most of the custody of Lily; since Lily believed he was her father. Peter was the best father; a little girl could have; but selfishly she liked being his wife and had put those thoughts away for some time in the future.

Then the worst had come stripping away that life, which had made her feel human and then came the years in the Russian gulag. She'd thought about coming forward and having a relationship again with Lily; but too much time had passed and too much danger could still be transferred to Lily she thought. Heather had assumed one day they could be together again as a family. Then life had played its evil game and sent that love crazed bitch to kill Lily. She must put all these thoughts behind her. It was too bad she'd never be able to tell Lily about her real father. Heather knew that she could ever never now ever get the chance. If she ever found Jacob again, she would have to tell him their daughter was dead. What a terrible legacy how he would hate her for that. Sometimes Heather hated herself for that.

No, her focus had to be Clover. Clover was her world now. Clover needed Heather and Heather had to get her head on straight and protect her granddaughter. Heather still kept tabs on them and knew that Charles and Peter were now married, at least someone was happy. Peter was visiting Happy Valley he would comfort Katha and Rose. Katha had judged Heather; but that didn't mean Heather didn't feel bad that Katha too was grieving. Katha had raised her beloved Lily, she owed her a great gratitude for keeping her little girl safe. Now Emmett Rogers was a different story Heather hoped he was suffering for not keeping Lily safe from that woman.

Heather glanced at Clover, the child was so like her mother, Lily, that it was like having Lily, all over again. The grief that she felt at Lily's passing almost ripped her apart; if it hadn't been for Clover, she felt she would have died. Clover was her only link to her daughter and she would keep her safe and happy. She owed that much to Lily. She'd lose this spy and they'd start all over again. Lily would grow up happy with her mother…no, she done it again. Clover would grow up happy with her grandmother, who would tell her all about her wonderful mother, Lily. She had a scrapbook of Lily's life she could share with Clover. Clover would know how much her mother would have loved her.

Was that someone watching at the corner? The man standing under the awning at the apartment had been looking her way. She wouldn't go back to the apartment. She lose this tail and change her appearance becoming another person. She'd be Amanda Lee with an apartment near London Bridge, after she lost her tail. She didn't have another option if they were wise to Sarah.

"Driver, please take me to Harrods' Department store."

"That'll be extra money, that's in Knightsbridge you know."

"I am well aware. I shop there regularly," Heather replied in an upper crust English accent.

The cab soon dropped her at Harrods, where Heather went into the washroom. Making sure there was no one there she then removed her black –haired wig and removed her nose prosthesis wiped off the bright red lipstick that bled around her lips and the heavy eye make-up, as well as the pancake make-up that changed the shade of her skin to olive tones and made her look of Italian origin.

She removed a long auburn-haired wig from her bag and placed it on her head. She then did her make-up with an expert hand and was surprised to find that she now looked like a thirty-year-old. They'd never guess it was her she decided. She shaved off Clover's blonde curls and left her bald putting her in blue clothes befitting a boy. People were foolish and felt there were girl and boy's clothes, a glance of the colour should convince most his was a boy child. This should fool Gerhard's minion. She'd hate to shave off such beautiful hair; but Clover's hair would grow back in a short time and they needed to be safe.

Heather went to the baby department and had soon, bought enough had to replace everything Clover had and more, to be set up Amanda's new apartment. She made sure that that information was made secret, with a little cash and a story about a dangerous abusive ex.

She took what she would need immediately, ordered a cab from a restaurant down the street and then after switching to two new cabs she walked three blocks (carrying Clover who babbled animatedly). Heather on alert, hyperaware of her surroundings and any cars or foot traffic, noted that no one had followed them. They'd be secure, Heather would see to it.

The apartment was spacious. Using the telescope, she had bought years ago (along with some upgrades to it) she used it to scan the surroundings. It didn't appear anyone was watching the new apartment. For the first time today, Heather felt sheltered and safe. She breathed a calm breath. No one was watching for now; she was sure of it, but what would tomorrow bring? Heather would keep Clover safe, even if she had to sacrifice herself to do it.

Months had passed and she felt safe. A year passed and Covid had broken out. Everyone moaning about restrictions and permissions being taken away' but it had suited Heather fine. It had been easier to hide in plain sight in a face mask. COVID was terrible of course there was no doubt about that and she had to keep Clover safe from COVID. She kept her six feet away from others and had even got the smart little girl to wear a mask to protect herself. It wasn't fair however that she had no playmates except Grandma to play with. The child would be anti-social when this was over fearing strangers but was that a good or a bad thing? If Emmett Rogers guessed the truth and came looking for her, or Clover, he would find Clover had changed into and unrecognizable child, and Heather was a chameleon; Emmett couldn't travel her easily because of travel restrictions however so she felt safer for it.

Clover was two years old now, precocious and possibly because he'd only had adult company her language skills were far advanced. Clover's blond ringlets and her blue eyes, echoed Heather's own. Clover looked like Heather's child (or Amanda Lee's child, the name she had sustained for all this time since the scare).

Clover was thriving her teeth had come in early and her toothy grin, greeted Heather every morning as well as the words from

Clover's lips of Gramma. Heather couldn't allow Clover to call her mom, after all. Even if Lily had passed away, Clover only had one mother.

Heather was content, it would be some time before COVID restrictions eased and Heather would use that to her advantage. No one would see them and they could stay in this safe little world watching the same princesses' movie with the snowman over and over again…ha, ha. Clover never seemed to tire of that movie, though Heather had introduced her to a few other classics, she still demanded the snowman movie.

~0~

Chapter 5 – Bad News Comes in Threes

It was the middle of the night. Emmett

wanted to stay wrapped in the cocoon of the dream he'd just been in, (with Lily beside him in the bed bouncing Clover; as she laughed on her chest) but he started awake shaken out of his sleep by some unknown sound. His dark thoughts wouldn't allow him to go back into that wonderful dream.

His eyes burned with the unshod tears. He'd yet to cry for his daughter and for the tatters of Lily's and his relationship. She hated him for not going at once to where Heather was. He'd had word from his army pals, but nothing definite. They hadn't seen the baby only what they thought might be Heather; but if Clover was alive, where was she? It had been so long since Clover's birth. Lily was so sure Clover was alive and it made him think it might be true; but his heart wouldn't let him go there. One of them needed to be prepared in case that wicked grandmother of hers had done something unforgivable.

Besides he had done so many unforgivable things in Afghanistan, that surely, Eileen's obsession with him and subsequently all that had happened, including Heather taking Clover (when Clover came too soon.) would cause something… no he shouldn't go there. Lily had to be right; because he couldn't bear to lose both of them. He still had hopes of getting Lily to forgive him, but he wouldn't be able to forgive himself, if Clover wasn't returned to them both.

Emmett's doctor said not to travel, for at least two more months by plane, or car; was he ever going tog et better? The damage done by the carbon monoxide poisoning had been long lasting and he was getting better, but not quick enough to search for his daughter himself.

Lily had no idea of this, maybe he should stop keeping this to himself? Lily thought Emmett was working; but he hadn't been back to work since before the poisoning (except for the deposition he'd had to give to the Special Investigation Unit of Ontario, about the police officers who had committed crimes in Happy Valley.)

They'd all been tarnished with the same brush thanks to the corruption of those officers. Sometimes, Emmett was glad he wasn't at work when Kendall called him and told him what was happening. It had to be awful with the public and the Special Investigation Unit of Ontario suspecting everyone of being in league with those cops. Kendall was ready to quit and find another policing job in another city; maybe he should consider the same once he was able to work in full time policing again.

This business of what had happened in Afghanistan was also weighing on him. Everyone had walked away just like the war had been nothing and maybe it had to them; but Emmett had lost too much, and too many people this just felt like a death over again. Everyone leaving and leaving those most vulnerable behind what had it all be about?

What about all those that had been lost? His mind wondered back to that day so long ago. Cadet Tommy Harrow, Lieutenant Fred

Aswad, Cadet Helen Bowman and Cadet Peter Paul Mancini and Captain Campbell had been captured by the Taliban. They had tortured all of them and then killed Helen right in front of them all. Emmett had loved Helen and maybe he would have left his wife, Jenna for her. They could have made a life and now all the sacrifices that they had all made... the lives lost Helen, Fred and Pete and Captain Campbell had died as well. Tommy had artificial legs now; all because of a war where they were supposed to be helping the Afghans.

Now, the people were leaving them off worse than before. The women who had freedoms like never before, were now under Taliban rule and laws that took all their hard-won freedoms away… girls couldn't even go to school and for this Helen had died?

He had watched on the news almost a year ago as Afghans climbed on the wings of the A U.S. Air Force C-17 Globemaster III which had evacuated some 640 Afghans from Kabul. Those poor souls on the wings are obviously dead he had reasoned with deep sorrow. He tried to console himself with the fact that the Globemaster III had carried a lot more than he ever thought they could fit on the plane; but it was near enough. What would these people do? Canada was offering to resettle some loyal Afghans who had helped the effort; but would that help? How many really would be resettled? Time had passed and he hadn't seen that many Afghanis settled. Their excuse COVID; but that was just it, it was an excuse.

He held his head in his hands. He felt like burrowing under the blankets and staying there permanently. Maybe, he should call his shrink? Instead, he reached for his water and took one of his pills for PTSD.

The phone rang at Emmett's bedside.

"Uncle Emmett?"

"Who is this?" Emmett asked not recognizing the voice.

"It's Austin Spriet, your nephew."

"Of course. Sorry I didn't recognize your voice, Austin. It's really deepened."

"Uncle Emmett, mom needs you and so do I."

"What's happened?"

"Dad died. He had a heart attack right out of the blue, while they were evacuating. He couldn't even die a F... en hero."

"I'm so sorry, Austin. Where's your brother Greg?"

"Didn't mom tell you? He broke her heart and joined the army, just like dad a few months ago. He's over in Germany."

"Does he know about your dad?"

"Yes, he knows; but he's not coming home. They offered him leave but he's not taking it."

"Sorry Austin. I'm sure you'd have liked your brother there and so would you mother."

"Maybe mom would; Greg is so much like dad. I'm glad he's not here. He'd be making this all about him."

"I'll get in my car and be there in a couple of hours."

"Good, because they are taking me to a foster home."

"What? Why?"

"Mom has cracked up. They had to section her."

"When did they take her?"

"This morning! Dad died a week ago and the funeral, I arranged is supposed to take place the day after tomorrow. I can't postpone it again."

"Why didn't you call me sooner.?"

"I know how much you hated my dad. I also heard last year that you were injured, when that crazy lady took Lily and her daughter hostage and then your baby died. So, I didn't want to trouble you. I'm so sorry, Uncle Emmett."

"Good grief, Austin; this is the time you call your uncle. We're family and family, helps family!"

"I just need to be kept out of foster care. You'll do that right?"

“I’ll do more than that. I will tell them I’m coming and you’ll stay with me, until your mom is better.

“We’ll talk about that I don’t want to leave London and mom.”

“We’ll talk about that; but don’t worry, I’ll be there soon.”

Austin told Emmett the address they were taking him to and Emmett promised he’d be there soon.

When Emmett got off the phone, he worried how he would tell Lily that he was going to London, Ontario; but he couldn’t travel to wherever Heather had gotten to, to find out if she had their daughter. He was a lot better but the doctor forbid long car rides and plane rides were completely out.

Maybe, he should be sharing that he had side effects from the carbon monoxide poisoning and they felt he couldn’t travel especially by plane?

His doctor had made an appointment in London, Ontario with a specialist and coincidentally the appointment was tomorrow. His doctor in Happy Valley had said to deal with the after effects of fatigue;

maybe they could also help with the memory problems and stomach problems he'd been having and the specialist had set up an MRI for tomorrow morning to look at his brain. He'd asked the doctor why and they said they were ruling anoxic brain injury. Brain injury? It sounded scary. It couldn't be permanently disabled he was a strong police officer.

The doctor had cautioned that Hyperbaric oxygen therapy could help some; but he'd had that when he first came to the hospital. Surely, that had made a difference?

He needed a driver. He shouldn't be driving if were stopping someone in his condition (while they were driving); he'd throw the book at them. Who would do this favour for him? Dafydd of course. Dafydd and Emmett could visit with Caleb at Western University after his classes today maybe take him out for supper.

He'd phone Lily and let her know about his brother-in law, after he had retrieved Austin and saw that Paula was being well-cared for. Lily would understand after all Paula's husband had died. The news of his health could wait until he had definite news, maybe

Lily wouldn't want a disabled father and husband.

As he got in his car and pointed it toward London, his mind pondered a lot of baggage from the past and now what the future held. He wanted Lily. He needed Lily. She was his present and his future he just had to make her see that his refusal was not because he didn't love their little girl; but because of his health. He would have to tell her; but he waited and do it in person. If only his nightmares would go away, maybe, it was because he felt so helpless because of Eileen that he was dreaming of Afghanistan again. Last night he'd dreamt of her again. Helen Bowman, the woman he'd been responsible for and let down. The Taliban had taken them all and tortured Helen Bowman right in front of them and they hadn't been able to fight back. Instead, they had had to hear her cries and endured a week of their own torture. Somehow Emmett had managed to get free and then he saved the others as best he could. Cadet Tommy Harrow, Lieutenant Fred Aswad, Cadet Peter Paul Mancini and Captain Robert Campbell. Fred and Captain Campbell had died from their wounds despite Emmett trying to save them. So had

Pete, as Pete had burns on most of his body. Fred had died under torture.

Emmett had found some comfort in talking about this in therapy. Emmett had met some really good soldiers who also suffered from P.T.S. D. They would help him find Clover. His friends George Gagnon, Henri Cote, and his friend Tommy who had grown-up after his brush with death.

Emmett had thought Captain Campbell was alive once before and it was happening again; either the man's ghost was haunting him, or he was imagining him again. Emmett suspected that latter; it was his imagination, he was hallucinating Captain Campbell again. It had to be the poisoning and the stress of losing Clover. He wanted to believe as Lily did that Clover was alive, but he didn't want to get his hopes up. If Clover was dead, then Lily would need him, he couldn't follow apart like this maybe he needed to see Doctor Rétrécir again. Doctor Rétrécir was in private practice now. Doctor Rétrécir had left the service. He had a practice in London, Ontario and Emmett had an appointment in London with a neurologist maybe if he was lucky, Emmett could get Doctor Rétrécir to fit him in.

Emmett would also have to get Austin; but maybe he could hang out with his cousin and Dafydd.

Emmett would fit in a session and pay for it outright so there was no record. He couldn't let anyone know about his P, T.S.D. and let it get back to the police department. They might think he was unfit for duty ever. It was bad enough, that they were waiting for the doctor's report for his return to duty.

No wonder he was losing his mind everything was stressful, COVID wasn't even on his mind what with his health, Clover's disappearance; and now his sister's own mental health issue; but it was on everyone else's' and on their faces with the masks everyone was wearing. He had been told he was fortunate that the neurologist would even see him in person, maybe Doctor Rétrécir could talk to him over Zoom over something if he couldn't see Emmett in person. He had to calm down.

His friends were searching in England (thank goodness because the skies were closing to travellers over COVID) for Clover but they had no success so far Heather had covered her tracks a little too well.

As for Paula's situation losing her husband, he would have to dig deep to pretend that he was sorry that Jason died. Okay, so he was sorry for Paula, Greg and Austin; but he'd never taken to Jason. Paula claimed that Jason had never raised a hand to her again after Emmett had spoken with him. Even if Jason wasn't physically abusive, then he was mentally abusive. Emmett had tried in the early days to get his sister to leave Jason; but she declared she loved him and that he wasn't abusive. So, Emmett had given up and had stayed in touch with his sister only by phone and video every once in a while.

Would Paula even welcome him there? He didn't know; but they needed him so he was going to make this work. He had to and maybe, he would get Paula and Austin to move to Happy Valley; where he could keep an eye on them.

His life was really screwed up, but he'd fix it and maybe, just maybe, Clover was alive and his friends would bring her home, then Lily and Rose would be in his life again too. He could fix everything and even get the children, Dee and Rebecca back from their grandmother. Joseph would finish his sentence for the shooting of his father in seven months and they'd all be together again.

~0~

Chapter 6 – Pulling Off the Band-Aid

Lily wanted to do the exercises. She was getting better; but too slowly and she needed Clover.

Was Clover, okay? Did Heather treat Clover properly? She refused to think of this woman as her mother; not after what she had done. How could she have taken Clover even if she thought Lily was dead? Emmett was her father and Rose was Clover's sister. They would have needed to be with Clover too. Was Heather even in her right mind?

Had this been Heather's plan all along, because she didn't raise Lily, she thought she could just snatch her granddaughter?

All this time alone with her grandmother Clover probably thought Heather was her mother, not Lily. Lily was missing too many milestones in Clover's life.

Emmett claimed his friends (George Gagnon, Henri Cote and Henry Mancini) were searching for Clover. but it had almost fourteen months since Clover had been taken and she heard nothing. Okay, so they thought there had been a few leads but they never petered out. Fourteen months, so many missing milestones. even if they found Clover today would she accept Lily?

The COVID outbreak hadn't helped either. So many restrictions on travel had slowed down the information and even if Lily hadn't wanted to travel, she couldn't have. Her first vaccination was this afternoon though. She was getting earlier than most because she'd had a stroke; but what about Emmett? Was he at risk?

Grandma Katha and Grandpa Terrence had their first vaccination yesterday. Lily tried to change her thoughts, she was acting like she had made up with Grandma Katha but that hadn't happened and she felt a little guilty. She still hadn't forgiven Grandma Katha for not telling her about Heather being alive.

Grandpa Terrence had begged her to and she almost relented.

Her dad and his new husband had been nice to have around. They had taken her to their new rental home, since they were still looking for their permanent home; but real estate prices were increasing and they had been out bid too many times to count. Peter and Charles had paid for a regular therapist to come in and Lily was doing the exercises; but she had to admit all she could think about what her baby. Clover occupied her mind at all times.

Dad and Charles were still in the throes of their honeymoon and she felt like a third wheel. They understood her grief, her anger, and her burning desire to find Clover, but she felt like no one was really doing anything and she was losing all her bonding time with Clover. Daddy had tried to get his contacts to help him; but because of COVID it had been like pulling teeth to cut through bureaucracy and get the government to look too.

If Lily found Clover today, would Clover even know her? Lily thought again. No. she'd be a total stranger to her baby.

Something else she had Heather to blame for.

She picked up the phone. Maybe, she could forgive Grandma Katha? She really needed her now and she had done so much for Lily over the years. She had been there when Lily had nightmares from the kidnapping that she had endured with Heather, and when both Lily's husbands had died. Amelia had begged and pleaded for her to forgive Grandma Katha and Lily did miss her, so much.

Yet something held Lily back. She wanted to forgive; but would Grandma Katha understand though she was forgiving she hadn't forgot what Grandma Katha had done. Keeping her mother's existence made Lily vulnerable to her kidnapping Clover; Lily thought as she put down the phone. She should have forgiven Emmett by now she still loved him but she was holding back from him. Like it was his fault Heather had taken Clover. The truth was Lily blamed herself Heather was her mother and Heather took Clover, because ***she*** was her grandmother. She should speak with Amelia it had been so long since they'd spoken. The anger that she had at Amelia over her treatment of Rose had passed. After Grandma Katha had explained Amelia's loss, she had understood how Amelia's bitterness had clouded her senses. After all wasn't Lily's loss of Clover clouding her own?

Amelia had apologised and Rose had accepted her apologies, so Lily had done the same. They were good again, or so Lily thought so why hadn't she heard from Amelia? Was something going on with her? Was she too depressed to reach out? She should call her no, ***FaceTime*** her.

She FaceTimed Amelia and Amelia answered,

"Oh, good, you answered." Lily stated.

"She told you? Don't be mad at me. Grandma Katha promised she'd let me tell you and I was going to tell you, today."

"Tell me what?" Lily asked and then looked closely at the FaceTime image of Amelia. She looked gaunt and her hair something was different about her hair. It was a good imitation, but it was obviously a wig, how had she not noticed?

"Why are you wearing a wig?"

Amelia responded by removing the wig to show a shaved head.

"You have cancer?" Lily asked fearing the answer.

Amelia nodded, "I've been hiding it from you. I've been undergoing chemo and radiation." "

"Grandma Katha knew and she didn't tell me?"

"Don't be mad at her. The words wouldn't come to my lips. If I told you, it would make it that much more real Then when I did find that I had accepted I had cancer, frankly, I didn't know how to tell you with all you've gone through with Clover."

"I'm sorry I'm being selfish. Getting mad at Grandma Katha when you're the one with cancer. How are you doing?

"I didn't know how to tell you and then I felt really guilty for being selfish enough, for one moment to wish it was anyone else. but me; but the doctors say the cancer has advanced too far. I'm dying, Lil."

"We'll find you the best doctors. Someone who can help you beat this."

"It's not going to happen Lily. I wish it would, but I'm starting to come to terms with it and you need to as well. I want no tears in my last days of life. No one knows when their time is up. Anyone could go out get hit by a bus, have a brain seizure or heart attack and die at any moment so we have to live each moment as our last and enjoy them all."

Lily wiped at the tears running down her face pulled herself together there would be time for reflection later. Right now, she had to act like the grown-up Amelia needed.

"I'm sorry I'll try to honour your wishes. Does anyone else know?"

"No, but Carol will know when the sale goes through for Quirks Friday, but since she's starting university next week, she probably won't miss it as much."

"You sold Quirks?"

"Yes, I sold the inventory the store has been shuttered for a year, due to slow sales during COVID, but online sales have been wonderful. Carol has done a few of those orders for me."

"Who bought it?"

"I sold it to Susan Terrell."

"Susan must be happy; but it must be bitter sweet for her."

"She 's happy. She doesn't know, I'm dying."

Lily took another deep breath; she couldn't fall apart. She had to hold it together.

"Is there anything I can do for you?"

"No, just be there if I need you, and like I said, no crying over me. Now can we change the subject? Have you heard anything about Clover?"

"No,"

"I'm sorry that sucks. Hopefully you'll hear something soon. Have you talked to Grandma Katha then?"

"No, we haven't made up."

"And Emmett are you and he back together?"

"No!"

"Lily life is too short. We don't know what will happen tomorrow. Don't you think it's time to forgive and forget?"

Lily thought about it she missed Grandma Katha. Maybe it was time to forgive everyone; everyone, but the people who had caused all this heartache…Eileen who had cause her early labour and Lily's mother, Heather who had taken Clover, she could never forgive. Yes, it was time to forgive Emmett and Grandma Katha all this heartache was taken a toil on Lily and she needed some peace.

Lily checked the mail. Wonderful an envelope from the insurance company crossing her fingers she opened it. Thank goodness they approved her sick leave. She was covered, she didn't have to worry about money for a least a year. Then she'd either go back to work as Crown Attorney, or start out again as a defence attorney, something she'd been thinking about.

Lily's mind turned once again to Emmett. She loved him, still, she really should call him. Emmett still called frequently, despite her coldness and he still loved her… Lily knew he did. She didn't want to lose him. Lily did love him and maybe if she worked harder at it; she could forgive Emmett. They could move forward with their lives; but it would be so much easier if their daughter was in Lily's arms.

"Lily we'll talk again later. I have an appointment."

"How are you getting there?"

"Regan is driving me she's been a wonderful friend. Pitching in when grandma Katha couldn't."

"I'm sorry I haven't been there for you."

"It's okay. Lily we're like sisters we fight but we always make-up. I love you."

"Love you, too, Amelia."

"Bye talk to you later."

Lily was worried about Emmett. Emmett was hiding something from Lily. Was it something bad? Something he was afraid to share? Was it about Clover?

The phone rang and Lily jumped to answer it hoping it was good news about Clover.

"Lil?"

"Emmett? How nice to hear from you," Lily said softening.

"I'm so glad to speak with you too, Lily. I've missed you."

"Then come over. We've lots to talk about."

"We do, but I'm in London, Ontario. Dafydd drove me."

"Why did Dafydd drive are you okay? Why are you in London? Did you both go to see Caleb?"

"Lily…"

"What is it, Emmett? You're frightening me. Is this about Clover?"

"No, I haven't heard anything new about our daughter. I wish I had and it was good news, I'm sorry for terrifying you. I've got a lot going on and I need to tell you some things I've been keeping from you.

Lily gasped and Emmett continued reassuringly, “The things I haven’t told you have nothing to do with Clover. I promise.”

“You’re still worrying me. Tell me what’s bothering you, Emmett.”

“I told you I’ve been keeping something from you Lily. The reason I didn’t go flying to the UK to look for our daughter was I was restricted from travelling.”

“I don’t understand why would you be under restrictions? Is there’s something wrong with you?”

“It was the carbon monoxide poisoning; but I’m getting better from it. In fact, they believe I may be able to travel soon; but not for a few months.”

“Oh, Emmett and I’ve been holding that against you. You big dolt!! You should have told me, you idiot. Why didn’t you?

“I should have told you; but with Clover missing and all you’ve gone through I couldn’t.”

“You should have told me!! I can handle anything as long as I understand and I still love you despite the anger I've been showing you. I'm sorry."

"I'm sorry too. Sorrier than words can express the truth is I love you, Lily. All that matters now is that soon I can join my friends and find our daughter. That is, after I get some other stuff settled."

"Medical stuff, I assume. You can't enlighten me some more in person but for now tell me, how have you been working?"

"I've been doing a desk job with limited hour"

"A desk job? You must hate that."

"I do, but I also need the money and the benefits; however, I'm seeing a specialist in London Ontario today. Maybe I can get back to real policing, soon."

"There's more though, I hear it in your voice what's happened?"

"My brother-in law died."

"I'm so sorry. Was it COVID?"

"No, Jason had a heart attack and died; but my sister, Paula is devastated. She's had a mental health break and I've taken custody of my nephew Austin."

"Oh Emmett. I'm so sorry I know you didn't like him much, but I know how much you love Paula."

"We haven't talked much lately; but Terrence says the lawyer who was fighting the temporary order for custody of Deirdre and Rebecca will call today with the results from the court filing today."

"What about Joseph?

"This should cover the future custody of Joseph when he gets out of juvenile detention."

"There not going to delay it again are they because of all the COVID restrictions, are they?"

"I hope not, all these delays have made them spend so much more time with their grandmother, making her look like a more obvious choice."

"Wow I've really not been there for you, have I?" Lily asked.

"You've had your own trials."

"We should have faced this together."

"I have to stay in London for awhile; but I want to discuss this again."

"Rose can stay with Katha, or my dad. Rose is in a crucial part of her school year. I'm coming to you, if you still want me?"

"Still want you are you kidding? I told you I love you Lily now and forever. I fell for you the moment I met you even though you were a married woman and a suspect. I tried to hide it but it was hopeless. You were the one. You'll always be the one for me."

"I love you too. Will it be okay with Paula if I stay at her house?"

"Austin says she changed her mind about you and she can tolerate you now. His words not mine. He's been listening to me talk to and telling me I should go to you. Paula felt bad that Clover was gone. I think she thinks Clover's dead and we're delusional."

"Will she be mad when she finds out Clover's alive?"

“She’ll be overjoyed; but not as happy as we will be when Clover’s back with her parents.”

“That will happen, right?”

“It will; we have to believe it Lily.”

“It’s getting really hard to believe it Emmett.”

“I know I didn’t want to tell you this yet, but my buddies, Thomas Mancini, George Gagnon, Henri Cote think they’ve spotted Heather but they want to see her with Clover to be sure. Then they will move in on her with the police and get our child back safely.”

“Oh, Emmett I hope that’s her but they will be careful Heather is unhinged.”

“They promised me Clover comes first.”

“I’ll trust them; but soon you and I will go get our baby if they don’t.”

“Yes, we will that’s a promise. Don’t you worry.”

Lily heard a knock at her door with cell phone to her ear, she let Terrence and Grandma Katha in.

"Terrence is here Emmett. I'll make sure Katha can look after Rose and come to you."

"Are you sure? Rose needs you, too!"

"She's being spending a lot of time with Grandma Katha. I'm sure she'll be fine,"

Grandma Katha overheard and nodded in agreement. She then said, "I'm going to the kitchen to make tea do you want one?"

Lily nodded that she wanted a tea.

"Is that Emmett on the phone?"

Lily nodded.

"Can you put that on speaker phone? I have some news about Rebecca and Deirdre and Joseph."

"It's on speaker. Go ahead Terrence."

"I have terrible new the judge has ruled against us."

"But why?" Lily asked.

"They used all the murders that your family has discovered over the last few years against you. Then they said you had bad judgement and put forth the hiring of Laura/Eileen."

"She was vetted. I made sure of it, but obviously, she slipped through the cracks," Katha protested from the kitchen.

"I argued that the agency was at fault but they didn't care. They also use Clover's disappearance against you, Emmett." Terrence explained.

"How dare they?" Lily protested.

"Lawyers will use anything against you," Emmett commented

"I did get them to agree to temporary custody. The court will re-look at the custody agreement in a year's time."

"In which time the girls will have moved on with their lives and adapted. I won't be able to take them away from any stability they have gained," Emmett commented sadly.

"You have generous visitation. You get them two months in the summer and for two weeks at Christmas."

"She agreed to that?"

"Are you kidding? No, the judge did because the children cried when she won."

"Are the children going to be, okay?"

"She may send them to boarding school."

"Those poor girls." Lily blurted.

"We will be there for them even if it's twice a year. Right Lily?"

"Yes, we will. What's happened with Joseph?"

"Joseph has added time to his sentence. He'll in custody for two years more. He's gotten into several fights at the facility."

"Oh no, poor Joseph! Is he okay? Is he safe?" asked Lily.

"I objected to the facility they were keeping him in and they offered to transfer him to London but it won't happen for two months. I've accepted that. He's serving his two years in London, Ontario. He will be angrier and maybe a different boy, when he gets out. Do you still want him?"

"I want Joseph! He's my sister's boy and he needs to know we love him. You want him too, don't you, Lily? Can we visit him in the facility in London?''

"Yes, we'll give him what he needs and he'll prosper. He'll be able to find himself. In the meantime, like Emmett asked can we visit him in London? He has to know we support and love him."

"I've made sure of that. Visitation is once a week limited to the two of you and of course his lawyer, me."

"Goodbye, Terrence and thank-you, Now please let me speak with Lily privately."

"Sure. take it off speaker, Lily and I'll exit the room few minutes giving you time to talk to Emmett. I have to use the facilities anyway."

Terrence then left the room.

Emmett continued speaking, "I love you my beloved, Lily and we will weather all of this and find our little girl."

"When you say that I almost believe you."

"I have to go but I'll call you tonight."

"I love you too. We'll speak more tonight, when I arrive at Paula's in London, Emmett. We have a lot to talk about."

"We do. Bye honey."

~0~

Chapter 7 – Chomping at the bit

Heather was bored; there was only so much streaming you could watch and most of it had been children's programming for babies. Clover was growing up fast, from a baby into a toddler with lots of words. Her favourite word… No.!! Not that it got her anywhere, but she was her own personality now and oddly like her independent mother, Lily. Things were opening up again. The lockdowns had been advantageous at first, hiding out in their apartment meant no one saw them and Emmett and Gerhard had not been able to find Heather; but looking at four walls everyday hearing only the chatter of a baby was driving Heather up the wall.

Heather realized she was a people person and she needed to see another adult; but where was it safe, not only because she didn't want Emmett or Gerhard to find them but because of COVID. She couldn't afford either of them getting sick. Heather had a shot against COVID but Clover wasn't eligible yet and while they were ardently saying children wouldn't get the disease so easily, or so hard the research was not backing them up. Daycare wasn't an option because of that either. Clover needed some interaction with children she was going to become egotistical and unsociable. The park? Maybe interaction with one child wouldn't be such a big risk?

Heather decided then and there that she would take Clover to a park. Finsbury Circus Gardens was close and it had nature, old trees, no it probably would be busy with too many people and CTTV. CTTV just meant that Heather had to use her disguise but a park to play at was important it had to have playground equipment. Maybe she'd just take a hackney and go to Drury Park. It had some lovely equipment. She'd check it out and see how many people hung out there.

Heather packed up Clover and two masks sized appropriately and then placed Clover in her pram. Of course, she began crying automatically. Heather lost her temper and yelled at Clover, then regretted it immediately and apologized soothing Clover. She was a bad Grandma, babies always fussed when you put them in a seatbelt. She talked to Clover telling her they were going some place new where Clover would have fun.

The man watched as Heather left the building, finally and entered a cab. He'd been patient as he knew his contacts were savvy and that they'd seen her when they delivered some food but she'd been hold up ever since. The COVID lockdown had still been on when he had arrived but he'd gotten around the lockdown, no one kept him trapped. He hailed a cab and followed noting that the baby looked happy. He breathed a sigh of relief; Lily would be happy. He'd bring Clover back to her and then settle with Emmett Rogers. Emmett had let down Lily and he would pay for that.

He glanced at the woman…her name was Heather Kelly, he remembered but she was calling her self something else. What was it? Oh yes, his sources told him she'd started out as Sarah Crouse, but she was now in this apartment calling herself Amanda Lee. Did she know the London Bridge is Broken Down rhyme?

Tee-hee, she better hope she wouldn't become like Lady Lee that was embed in London Bridge as the Leigh family of Stoneleigh Park in Warwickshire claimed happened to one of their family members. He didn't know the exact story why they entombed her; but she must have deserved it… you don't kill family unless they are totally out of line and Heather was out of line kidnapping her grandchild bringing such great pain to her daughter and to her other granddaughter, Rose. Rose poor Rose. He met her biological mother now that woman was evil in his book. Cordelia was a basket case and a terrible mother. He thought that she had protected Rose but she had protected herself. Really in that woman's mind she had been a loving mother, but does a loving mother put her child in a pimp's hands? Maybe, being entombed in a London Bridge would be a fit punishment for how Lily had suffered at her hands? He'd have to think about it.

The original London Bridge where that lady was possibly entombed was not there anymore; some politicians had sold it to some Americans. The new bridge was probably to busy for entombment anyway, but he'd think of a just punishment for Heather the betraying mother. How could she run away, pretend she was dead and all that time only to take her granddaughter from her injured daughter?

First, he'd get her trust; it was easier to kill someone when you had their trust and as she was a former spy, she was a wary target and would be suspicious of everything, so he had to make it good. She had to accept him as innocuous, then he could move ahead with his plan which was in flux. It was better when he winged it anyway.

He glanced down at his outfit. Nerdy glasses check. Although he felt like he looked like someone famous. He toned down his good looks and if he acted less confident and shy that would work better than his gregarious self. He had two personalities or maybe more, not a lot people knew that but his shrink did. The confident man and the child in the body of a man who was too trusting were easily accessed. He thought the shrink was full of it when that damn shrink said there was others that hid with him. Absolute nonsense that would make him crazy and he wasn't, he just wasn't!! He read the psychology manuals when they had him locked up, he was just suffering from what his father did to him as a child. Maybe the shrink should be locked in closet for weeks? No, he could never do that to anyone. Only a monster would do that.

He'd hid that childlike persona for a long time after he took his better personality back. Everyone loved gregarious one better anyway. Did he dare let the child in him out? Even to catch a prey? He'd have to take this chance even though the child liked to be free and he struggled to get the one who should be in control back.

Drury Lane Park looked beautiful with Ticktacktoe, slides, swings and a roundabout (what we'd call a spinner, or merry-go - round in Canada), and old fashion water fountains (why would anyone drink out of those?) but he knew different it was a field for the dead.

Heather had taken Clover to Drury Lane Park was she crazy?

He needed to calm himself and project and image of a gregarious man. but did Heather know that Drury Lane Park was built over bodies? They claimed they moved the bodies, like he believed that!!That would have been too costly.

Did Heather have a fascination with bodies? No! Heather probably had no idea that St Martin- in- the- Fields had struggled to bury all those bodies from diseases and modern living (the prostitution and crime didn't help either) with the expanding population in London back in the early 1800's. Where, had they buried them? Right where this nice little park was now, bodies on top of one another possibly 60000 + people in a small plot of land. Of course, the bodies oozed grease and filmy. strange materials spreading disease; so, they decided to move the bodies (after some complaints from famous people like Charles Dickens). After all they had been burying bodies one on top of each other barely 2.5 metres down. So, where did they buried the others. the wealthy? Why down in the catacombs. they created below the church and the park like the other bodies didn't fall down there and add to it all. Those bodies in the catacombs in their nice, little coffins, were probably still there. If he weren't so claustrophobic, he might consider going into the catacombs to check them out; but that was him, he hadn't expected this of Heather. Heather was a grandmother and mother this was no place for a child she loved.

As he exited his cab, he could see the old red brick mortuary, lodge and the original gates were still there. He heard that some of the gravestones have been moved to the back and were still there today. Perhaps he'd come back another day and check those out himself; but today was all about Clover and Heather.

What the heck Heather looked like she was leaving already, she was a good grandmother! Still, he didn't want to be seen. Heather looked at the park shook her head and hailed another cab

Of course, Nelson Square Park was nearby here apartment and there was a playground and gardens, plus outdoor fitness equipment the small football pitch was not ideal, as he realized that Heather would avoid those people. Heather was practically chomping at the bit to see other people even without true interaction.

There she was the child was on the slide and she was holding her. The bench, nearby, was perfect for him to sit nonchalantly, that would get him near his target. Heather had placed the stroller near it, no they called it a pram in this London. Should he use a British accent? No, that would make her more suspicious, his Canadian accent would have to do.

This London was better anyway older, and more sophisticated. The other London was too nice those other Canadians (unlike himself) were really into getting to know your neighbour offering unsolicited things, like food and help. At least here in London, England though, the people were nice enough. COVID had made them mind their own business a bit more. He only hoped that would continue; he didn't need interference in his plans. It didn't hurt that there was a rich history of people (like himself) here in London, England who had gotten the business of dispatching villains out of the publics' hands and made life a little easier. He might be classified as a serial killer; but he wasn't Jack the Ripper after all. He didn't want to compete with London, England's gifted killers, (after all his duty was only to his adopted family the Kellys); so, he didn't want to be on the Kellys' radar. Jack had killed one a Kelly that made him his enemy.

But to the task at hand tamping down the so-called villain in himself, letting his inner child come out to play. He just had to make it clear to the boy that he must come out, if he explained the situation, that the child was kidnapped from her mother, that both were suffering, that this grandmother was bad, but the boy was arguing. The boy didn't trust his motives. The boy also said the child would grieve the loss of the grandmother.

He didn't want to harm Clover; maybe he should let Heather live? He would have to take on the subject himself. He could be charming; the boy could come out to play with the child and that was all. Showtime.

He sat down on the bench near Clover playing took out his I-pad and pretended to read the Daily Mail.

Heather looked alarmed and made like she was going to pack up. He worried that it wasn't working he had to make himself seem safe, then he got a break. Clover threw her ball and it landed at his feet. He smiled benignly at Clover and then threw back the ball. He then went back to his tablet. Glancing sideways under his eyelashes he saw that Heather was unfazed, she was buying it. Clover threw the ball at his feet again. He smiled again at her and threw back the soccer ball.

"I'm sorry, she seems to really wants to play with you."

"That's okay she reminds me of my niece back in Canada."

"You're from Canada?" Heather asked in a British accent.

"Yes, I live in London, Ontario. but my company is expanding and we are making some deals and contacts here in England."

"So, who did you bring with you?'

"I'm on my own. My company is small and I'm the CEO and do most of the scuttle work. My best friend (and partner in this business), Marcus is holding down the fort and keeping the factory running while I'm gone."

"What is your business?"

"Cups, we make lids and paper cups that dissolve, plates container for take-out and cutlery that are better for the environment. They dissolve after they are disposed of; so, it's not such a big deal that they are single use."

"Wow, that's a great product especially with how much take-out there has been during the lockdowns."

"That's part of the problem, with the restrictions, I haven't been able to conduct my business."

His phone buzzed with a message, which he quickly read.

Soldier leaving Afghanistan dies from heart attack.

Why was his contact sending him this? Then he read the name and he understood. Lily needed him and Emmett could be dealt with now. He could straighten him out but he needed to leave for the other London now. What about Heather? He was making progress. No, she was still a little wary heather would be more accepting with a little distance. Absence makes the heart grow fonder, after all.

"You'll excuse me. I have to leave now."

"It was nice to meet you, right Clover."

"Bye," Clover stated.

He smiled and said “Nice to meet you, too, little one, bye.”

He pointedly didn’t say goodbye to Heather to pique her interest. He knew it was working as he felt her eyes burn into his back, as he walked away and out of the park.

He went straight to the airport in a cab and caught the first plane to Toronto with a connecting flight to London. He’d be there soon. He’d sent an an agent to discretely watch Heather, because Lily and Clover came first. He'd scared away that cretin who was watching them, but better safe than sorry. I’m coming to fix you Emmett, he thought as the plane took off. You’ll pay, you jerk. He adjusted his mask in first class and fell asleep, smiling.

~0~

Chapter 8 – Meeting Old Friends

The doctor's appointment went smoothly. The doctor recommending one day, weekly oxygen treatments, for two hours for three weeks. The doctor seemed to think this would help and restore some of the lingering damage. Since Emmett was staying in London (at least that long) it would work out.

He's already spoke with the foster system, signed all the paperwork and they agreed to give him Austin. He would act as temporary guardian to him until Paula could take him back. After school Dafydd was driving Emmett to pick him up Austin. They would chill out at his home a little and then they would be dining on the patio with Caleb. He missed his son, but Caleb hadn't wanted to come home despite the restrictions of COVID and the online classes. He insisted he could stay in his apartment with his two roommates. But Emmett still worried, what if he contracted COVID who would look after him and would he get some medical assistance? Caleb had gotten very angry when Emmett had mentioned this a month ago and said he was an adult. Emmett needed to trust Caleb would do the right thing. Then Caleb had acted like the eighteen-year-old that he was, by asking for some cash, since he had gone over his budget ordering in food with the guys. Caleb would probably be happy that they were taking him out for a meal and Emmett would slip him a few more dollars discretely so Caleb would have a little additional cash. Lily called to say she'd be arriving late as she hired a car service who couldn't get her, (Lily) to London until after nine p.m.

Emmett called Dafydd who was waiting nearby, (Dafydd had been visiting some old colleagues at the hospital.) Dafydd said to meet him at the parking garage.

Walking to the parking garage Emmett received an usual feeling, kind of like someone was watching him. Emmett in turn became hypervigilant. His eyes searched from side to side, for the person who was sending out these waves of curiosity to him. Stopping and waiting at Dafydd's car, Emmett saw a man approaching two cars over.

The man was tall roughly Emmett's height of six feet one and weight. He was wearing a purple Western hoody and a surgical mask over his face, while his head was covered with a baseball cap under the hoody. Emmett tensed ready to fight.

"Lieutenant Emmett Rogers is that you?" asked the man through his mask.

Emmett looked at him for a moment perplexed then it hit him who this was.

"Felix Vitoria, is that you. you old dog?"

"Yes, and it's damn good to see you, Emmett."

Emmett relaxed, obviously, Felix had been watching him trying to figure out if it was Emmett he was seeing (through Emmett's mask.)

"What brings you to my hometown, Emmett?"

"Just an appointment. How have you been Felix?"

"Pretty good. You would hardly know I had a fake lower left leg, would you?"

"That's true, no cane, no crutches you've come a long way."

"So. what are you doing now Emmett? Still in the military?"

"No, I'm a cop in a small town called Happy Valley. It's about six to eight hours from here, depending on how fast you speed," Emmett joked.

"And you a cop, joking about breaking the law, "Felix chuckled.

"What are you doing these days Felix?"

"I work at the base, in the office."

"Never would imagine you'd do office work." Emmett said, then thought oh my goodness did I say that what a stupid thing to say, the man lost part of his leg.

"It pays the bills; but something else is going on with you. You look like you have the wait of the world on your shoulders, Emmett."

"My brother- in law, Jason Spriet died."

"Not that scumbag you used to rant about? The one you suspected of beating your sister. Did someone take the bastard out?"

"Yes. God did. He had a heart attack."

"Karma Baby! So why so glum?"

"My sister is pregnant and she's devastated and so is her youngest son."

"Don't they have another older kid?"

"Yes, Greg he's in the army."

"Greg Spriet? I met him. He had to learn not to be so mouthy. I guessed he learned too much from daddy. There were some rumours that he abused women."

"Oh no."

"Is the younger kid going to be, okay?"

"Yes, I'm going to take him for awhile."

"That will be good for him. He'll learn how a real man acts."

Dafydd appeared suddenly at Emmett's elbow and he realized his attention had been totally taken up with Felix.

Dafydd asked," Who is this, Emmett?"

Dafydd noticed that the man when he pulled down his purple hoodie and adjusted his ball cap that the man was oddly roughly Emmett's height of six feet one and weight and his hair was even the colour of Emmett's, dark and styled the same way, cut short and military style. He must be an army buddy of Emmett's, Dafydd concluded.

"This is an old friend, Lieutenant Felix Vitoria."

"Actually, it's Captain Vitoria, now."

"Good for you. coming up in the world," Emmett commented.

"Nice to meet you I'm Doctor Dafydd Jones."

"You need a doc, Emmett?"

"Dafydd is a coroner, so no," chuckled Emmett, "Besides Dafydd is family. He's my son's step-father."

"Only you would be friend with your kid's step-dad, but you seem like a nice enough guy, so nice to meet you., Dr. Jones."

"Dafydd, please."

"Sure, Dafydd."

"You have a kid, Emmett?'

"Actually, I have two children, while one is adult and going to Western. Caleb is 18 years old then there's Clover who is almost 15 months, and I'll soon have a step-daughter, Rose," Emmett explained.

"A really family man. I never had the chance I was too much love'm and leave'm when I was younger; now they love me and leave me when I wish they'd stick around," Felix commented then looked embarrassed.

"We have a reservation at *The House of Pasta* .at eight why don't you join us?" Emmett offered.

"Is that okay with you Dafydd?"

"I should have extended the offer first Please come Felix. You can meet our son."

"Then I'll except with pleasure,"

"You can bring a significant other or kids if you want," Emmett offered.

"I'm footloose and fancy free. Will I meet the mother of your kids?"

"No, my wife died," Dafydd commented.

"Lily Kelly, the mother of our daughter is on her way to me; but unfortunately. she won't arrive until after nine."

"Can I meet her, sometime?"

"Why not, but there is something I left out about our daughter so you won't speak of her to Lily."

Emmett then told Felix the whole story of Clover's birth and her kidnapping.

"Holy cow, Emmett. I hope the guys can find your soon to be crazy mother-in law and get your daughter back."

"That's the plan as soon as possible, Lily and are going to London England to find our daughter Clover."

"I'd be happy to help anyway I could," offered Felix.

"After dinner you can come to Paula's house and when Lily gets her you can meet her just don't mention Clover."

"Are you sure?" Sounds like you've got a lot on your plate."

"I insist."

"I won't I promise," Felix said, "See you at the restaurant then guys."

~0~

Chapter 9 – Surprises are not all bad

Emmett enjoyed the dinner with Caleb.

Dafydd, Austin and Felix. Austin seemed to settle down and actually enjoyed talking with Caleb and Felix. He was a little shy with Dafydd but he soon opened up. He talked about how he wanted to get into medicine. Not a coroner like Dafydd but maybe a cardiac surgeon or a neurologist Austin had commented.

It was nice to talk old times with Felix. Several times he felt like Felix wanted to say something to Emmett, but he seemed like he was holding it back.

Emmett was glad that he had invited Felix back to Paula's house to meet Lily. Maybe Felix would open up to Lily. People often did she just had the kind of vibes that offered people the opportunity to open up to her and have Lily truly listen,

It was time to pay the check. Emmett pulled out his credit card. Dafydd waved him off and said," You're both too late, I paid all ready when you both went to the bathrooms.

"That was kind of you but I pay my way, Doctor Jones, "Felix protested.

"I won't take your money. We invited you it's the least I can do for the fine company you've given my step-son, Emmett and Emmet's nephew, Austin."

"Thank you," Emmett commented and all the others also thanked Dayfdd.

"Here's my sister's address I'll meet you there in a half hour after we take Caleb home.:"

"See you soon," Felix said as he left.

Dafydd drove Caleb to his lodgings and then Emmett to the house where Emmett insisted, Dafydd stay the night. With a quick call to Doctor Claire Callister who was looking after Daniel. Dafydd was staying the night and driving back first thing tomorrow morning.

Emmett smiled Dafydd and Claire had been dating the last six months and she said she would happy to look after Daniel, when Dafydd called. Daniel was two now and he adored Claire. Emmett was sure it wouldn't be too long before the two of them tied the knot.

The doorbell rang and Emmett answered it but no one was there. Emmett was surprised but he guessed some of the kids in London played the old nicky-nicky-nine-door game. (Knocking on a door or ringing a doorbell and running away)

He closed the door and Felix arrived about fifteen minutes later.

~0~

Chapter 10 – Never A Lender Be

It was getting later by the minute and Lily hadn't arrived, Frankly, it was nearing ten pm. Emmett had called her cell phone, but she must be in a dead cell zone, or her phone was dead; because she didn't answer. Felix had made noises like he should go, but Emmett had enjoyed his company and the stories he told about them serving in Iraq. It had brought back some good memories and some good people now lost back to him. Even Dafydd enjoyed his company as well as Austin.

Felix talked about travels around the world and regaled them with stories of his life tailored to Austin's tender ears.

When Lily finally arrived in her rented car it was ten thirty and Felix enchanted her had her laughing and happy. Emmett appreciated

Felix's gregarious manner and how he put everyone at ease.

Lily got Felix to talk about his first wife, who had died in childbirth. Emmett felt bad that he hadn't known. Emmett had known about his second wife, Elena and their subsequent divorce; but he hadn't known how much Felix had loved and lost when his first wife, Angela had died.

"I'm sorry I'm bringing everyone down with this talk," Felix exclaimed sounding embarrassed, that he had shared something so intimate. "Time has gotten away from me, and it's nearly midnight, I should get going. I have to report at oh eight hundred hours."

"You've been a source of needed joy this evening. Thank- you Felix. It's been so nice to get to know you."

"Lil's right we'll have to get together soon."

Felix stepped out the door and shivered.

"The temperatures have dropped. I should have brought a coat. This Western hoody was fine earlier, but now…," Felix exclaimed.

"I'll drive you home," Dafydd exclaimed.

"No, no. I only live a few blocks away. I'll be fine, I'm not that cold. I'm a soldier, after all."

"Borrow my coat and hat. You can bring them back tomorrow," Emmett insisted.

"Are you sure?"

"Just take it Felix," Emmett demanded.

"Okay buddy. Nice to meet you, Lily."

"It was nice to meet you too. Felix."

"I'll return this tomorrow after work; Emmett. Say, 19 hundred hours?"

"Sure, see you then Felix."

Felix put on Emmett's coat and hat and Lily thought, how he looked like Emmett from the back. It must be the military bearing and height, she thought. She watched as Felix went down the block and disappeared into black, icy fog of the frosty night.

~0~

Chapter 11 – A New Start

It was a little cooler today, rather bitter

for an October day. Too early for snow, wasn't it? No worries, I loved the cold and the fog that was suppose to roll in tonight, it was magnificent and made him feel alive. I'd heard the theories that Jack had been here in this London, too. London Ontario was dull and he thought he'd move on, but I liked the Thames River and all the nature that it offered. Maybe I should act like Jack the Ripper and take out a homeless person by the Thames River tonight? I'd walked the trail seen the beautiful coloured leaves breathed in the peace that stilled the anger in me. The trail had carried me to very near the hospital. It had only been a skip and a hop before I had entered the hospital filched the prescription pad, that a foolish doctor had left his signature visible with a little pen scribbled on top of it. Writing out the prescription for the drugs, was easy then picking up the drugs at the pharmacy under my assumed name. I shook my head. I had to accept I was addicted. The doctor had forced the drugs on me and now it felt like my mental health depended on them. It was a month ago that I was so sure I could do without them; but that hadn't worked but without the smallest amount my clarity would weaken, however, I knew if I slowly weaned myself, I could get rid of the need. I'd seen and read about addiction this was definitely addiction; but it was not my fault and I could overcome it. Damn that doctor!! I wanted to strangle him, but the doctor might become useful at some point; so, I'd restrain himself from acting on that impulse. "See Doc, I have learned." Ha-ha.

I still felt that urge, though, that urge that had plagued me since I was a child, the anger that must be appeased or all hell would break out. Weren't those so-called mental health drugs supposed to control my urges? Maybe the quiet of the river, the simple sound of running water would help? Yes, the river was the answer. I must not act out, that would get me caught and caged again. I'd steal a car and drive downtown abandon the car and hangout by the river taking in the peace and tranquility. I just need to get my dependency and myself together; I could use some adjustment time, before I acted on my plan… just some time to get my head on straight.

Wait a minute, wasn't that Emmett Rogers in the parking garage? Height, and the look was correct. I snuck closer hiding behind a pillar.

Damn, it was him, what was Rogers doing here? Was Lily and family, okay? Emmett wasn't supposed to be here in a hospital parking lot.! I'm trying to have a new start!!Rogers wasn't supposed to see me. That man would ruin everything!! You'd think he be grateful for the life I gave him; but no, he'd capture and cage me if he got the chance.

I wasn't ready for Rogers, yet. My plans were still formulating.

Emmett would pay for his wicked ways!! Emmett acted all nicety, nice; like butter wouldn't melt in his mouth; but Emmett hadn't looked after my family. The Kellys were my chosen family and I had trusted him, made him one of my family, allowed him to get close to Lily, charging him with the most basic of tasks and Emmett failed. I hadn't wanted to leave my family; but Emmett knew, that, I'd lost my way and needed a vacation. So, I had allowed myself to rest and recharge, but Emmett had let me down. Hell, Rogers had let down the entire family.

I had trusted that bastard, Emmett Rogers to look after my dear ones and they had many disasters since then. Poor little Rose had found body, after body and had been tortured and kidnapped and even her family friend, Carol hadn't gone unscathed. Granted a teacher should be a teacher and not a lothario; but finding his body must have been devastating for a young girl like Rose. Then of course the killer targeted her. Did Emmett protect her? Not really, she tended to save herself time after time when she found these bodies. She was plucky just like the rest of the women in our family; but she shouldn't have to be someone needed to protect them from themselves. That would have to be me again. I had managed to take less of the medicines the doctor gave me, so my brain wouldn't be quite as foggy. I could formulate how to help them.

Damn that, Emmett! Emmett was a cop, why wasn't he protecting Rose and her beautiful mother, Lily? I'd moved on from Amelia, after I realized in therapy that she had feet of clay. At least I'd tried hard to!! I could move on and would! Somehow though Amelia still had a small piece of my heart, maybe she always would.

Lily however, now, she was a heroine worthy of my worship. If only I could be with her, he thought. No, those thoughts get me into trouble I must discard them, he thought. She loves that nitwit. Emmett. Also, Lily was a Crown attorney; being involved with Lily would be treacherous, she'd have to turn me in to save her own job.

Now back to Emmett, he in fact was an idol with feet of clay. Lily on the other hand was a mother goddess. Lily would fight tooth and nail for her family. I admired her so much. Stupid Emmett! He practically laid down and let that stupid nursemaid almost kill Lily and her family. Then he idly stands by and isn't there, when Lily's presumed dead mom comes back and takes Clover!

I needed to give Emmett Rogers, a talking to. The kind of talking to I'd given Eileen, was probably not the solution. They'd probably find her next week after the deed and they'd start looking for me; but my alibi was ready. The inmate I had used to poison her was ready and willing with the incentive of a little cash to do the act. The man admired Lily; it seemed she had treated him like a human being when he had been so broken. Everyone who was sensible loved Lily. She had a heart of gold and treated everyone even those who didn't deserve it as she would family. So. he'd had to pick through carefully the inmate that would put an end to the problem of Eileen.

The plan had been full proof. I was protected from being sought out as the culprit behind her demise. I still I had to be on guard and not let my temper get the best of me again, though. I didn't want to go back to that living arrangement again, for I was enjoying my freedom. The place reeked of censorship and oppression.

Emmett mustn't see me. Emmett was astute and he might surmise that Eileen was one of my victims after the fact and that wouldn't do. I needed to get in touch with Emmett.

I'd seen the obituary for his brother-in law, but I also knew his hate for him, so, I really hadn't expected to see him here. No matter, I'd catch up with him, perhaps later this evening. It's not like I didn't know where his sister lived. I'd pay him a visit. We could have words and everything would be settled. Then I'd disappear, for I wasn't going back, not even for my love of the Kellys.

Time to 'borrow' a car preferably an older one that would be easier to hack, then again, my dear friend Alberto had shown me how to hack a keyless entry. I always wanted to drive an expensive car; perhaps a flashy Mercedes-Benz vehicle? It wasn't like they'd miss the car for awhile, I'd seen this car before it belonged to a doctor who worked 12-hour shifts and by my calculation he had another eight hours to go.

I deserved this and more, so, I'd borrow the vehicle, drive carefully to not attract notice and go have a nature encounter for my mental health needs.

~0~

The time had gone quickly. as I slept away the hours in my motel room. The room was cheap and it looked it; but it served my purpose and I didn't think anyone would find me here.

I glanced at the clock, damn, it was after ten thirty at night with my luck that stupid Emmett Rogers would have gone to bed. I should take my medicine. No, I was going cold turkey tonight, my way of taking less I decided so, I could survey Emmett's sister's house.

One oxy wouldn't hurt. I'd picked them up from the guy I'd rolled in the park. He didn't need them, but I did I reasoned. I needed to stay calm, I justified, as I swallowed. I wouldn't become addicted to them, too. I would start slowing down all medications even more tomorrow.

Emmett's sister Paula's house was lit up like a Roman candle. I watched for some time and saw Dafydd leave with Caleb (Roger's son.) I guess I could mark that in Emmett's plus column he cared enough about his son to get along with his son's step-father. Dafydd looked stressed though like something bad had happened. He had been looking better since he started dating that doctor. What could be wrong with Dafydd, was it, Daniel? Who was watching Daniel anyway, the doctor?

Eileen had done one thing right, by getting rid of that trouble making Sherry- Anne; she saved Lily from Sherry-Anne's constant bad behaviour.

I was so deep in thought that I almost missed Lily at the door speaking with someone. Lily was there? She was supposed to be resting and getting better, and that idiot Rogers had her up at near midnight?

Emmett had his back to me and was dressed in his long black wool coat and watch cap; but I'd still recognize his military bearing anywhere. Lily shut the door and I watched Emmett take a walk down the street. So, the jerk was leaving her alone to take a walk, was he?

Emmett continued walking and proceeded to cross over Victoria Bridge's pedestrian part of the bridge, a red rage came over me. I felt a need, which I recognized from many times before. Pulling the knife from my shin, I quietly advanced on him. Before I knew it, I had stabbed him three times in the back and then a frenzied seven more times. I then picked him up and heaved him from the bridge. Scurrying into the night I stripped my clothes, as I walked throwing them into a nearby garbage bin. I entered a motel room and went directly to the shower when I was done, I put on mask and I poured bleach and ammonia down the drain, opening the windows to let the fumes out. Hoping the fumes wouldn't attract the fire department. I then took the rest of my clothes and threw them into a garbage bin, several blocks away.

Returning to my own room, I was satisfied they'd never find the blood in my shower. Emmett Rogers was dead and Lily would grieve, if only in the short term. I would make her happy again for I would find her mother, Heather and get Clover back to her family.

~0~

Chapter 12 – Death Escapes No One

The morning of the funeral arrived the sun quickly warming up the frosty of air of last night. Emmett couldn't believe how nice the weather had turned out; it should be raining, but then only Austin and Paula were mourning the bastard, Jason Spriet. Emmett was having trouble feeling bad about Jason's demise. Obviously though, Paula and Austin were suffering, he could be sorry about that. Austin had arranged the services to begin at two with some of his father's army buddies carrying the coffin in. Emmett was glad he hadn't included Emmett as a pallbearer. Emmett really wasn't up to the physical task of carrying a heavy casket but he wouldn't have wanted to explain why he couldn't lift his brother-in law.

Austin however took part and hoisted the casket like a full-grown man. He obviously took after the Rogers side…a lean, mean, machine. Yet, he had the softness and generosity of his grandmother Emmett's beloved mother, Matilda.

Looking around the church with Lily, on one side and Paula on the other (on a day pass),. Emmett was proud to note that Austin took his mother's hand in his and comforted her as he sat on the other side of her.

"They don't expect me to speak do they I can't I just can't," Paula blurted looking around.

"No, honey. Austin wants to do that for both of you. you just sit beside me and if you feel the need to leave you let me know and I will take you back to the hospital."

"Do I have to go back Emmett?"

"Just for a little while Paula," Emmett answered.

A few minutes later her mind seem to unclouded for a minute and she said," But what about my sons?"

"Greg isn't here, Paula and Austin will stay with me," Emmett answered patting her hand.

"But Greggie's right her she said touching Austin. "But where's my baby. Austin. You didn't let your mother take him did you Lily?"

Lily felt searing pain in her heart at this remark. She knew Paula wasn't in her right mind, but Heather had Clover. Was Clover all right? Emmett put his left arm around Lily and with his right hand he comforted Paula.

"Paula, Austin is beside you. Greg wanted to come but he's in the army and he couldn't get leave," Emmett lied.

Paula didn't seem to take this in and continued to address Austin as his brother.

Finally, Austin got up spoke of his father and the service was over. Time to advance to the grave site.

At St. Peter's Cemetery the weather had turned on a dime and rain started to come down filled with sleet. As they gathered by the grave site Emmett noticed Lily pulled out several umbrellas out of the car. Lily was always prepared he thought smiling. She smiled back at him and then hid her smile as she reached the grave. This sordid business was almost over, Emmett thought as he looked and saw someone he hadn't ever expected to see again. Cameron Grenor. Even after all these years he hated the man for taking advantage of Emmett's marital situation and sleeping with Emmett's now dead wife, Jenna.

Cameron was coming over he thought. Great he didn't want to have to explain to Lily why he hated the man, He tried to rearrange the hate that was showing on his face without Emmett's approval.

"Emmett Rogers? Constable 1st Class Grenor," Cameron said showing his badge.

"Can't this wait this is his brother-in law's funeral," Lily asked.

"I don't know who you are; but I waited long enough out of courtesy for Paula. Emmett couldn't give damn about his brother-in law."

"What can I do for you Cameron?"

"We're looking into the disappearance of one, Captain Felix Vitoria."

"Felix is missing? Shouldn't the military police be looking into this?"

"Since he was off base and presumably in your company (according to someone he spoke to last night) the city police are in charge. Now when did you last see Captain Vitoria?"

"We last saw him about midnight, or just before last night, "Lily answered before Emmett could.

"And you are?" Grenor asked.

"I am Lily Kelly, Emmett's fiancée."

"Where were you both after Captain Vitoria left?"

"We watched him leave up the street into the icy fog last night, and then we all went up to bed," Emmett answered.

"We?"

"Despite what you're implying Grenor. Lily and I went to our bedroom. Austin went to his room. Our good friend Dafydd Jones, the coroner for Happy Valley went up to bed in the other spare room, tired after driving my son (his step-son) home."

"I'll need to speak to with Doctor Jones can I have his phone number, please? And did Emmett leave your room, Ms. Kelly?"

"You're extremely hostile Maybe you should recuse yourself from this case. Constable 1st Class Grenor," Lily exclaimed.

Just then they heard a squawk come over the radio Grenor had on his shoulder.

"Grenor here,' he answered.

"Constable Grenor we've found a someone underneath the Victoria Bridge."

"But, I thought that bridge was closed for repairs?"

"No, the footpath is open and the person likely fell from there."

"Fell, or was pushed?"

"That's for the investigation to decide."

"Does the body fit the description of the missing man?"

"About the right height, but the coat and hat doesn't match."

"Was he wearing a long black wool coat and a black watch cap?" Emmett asked, afraid to hear the answer.

Grenor asked and the answer came back affirmative.

"Was it your coat and hat, Emmett? So, who did you piss off now? Are you into something nefarious?" asked Grenor.

"I'm a cop, the same as you Cameron. Just like when we met before. We cops meet lots of disgruntled citizens, you know that and I know that!"

"You think someone tried to kill Emmett? Oh. God it can't be my mother, can it?"

"Your mother? You made your mother-in law mad, Emmett?"

"It's a complicated story; can we discuss this some more after the wake. Cameron? After the wake. Lily and I will come down to the station. It might take about three hours though, as I also have to take Paula back to the hospital and get Austin settled."

Grenor looked pissed like he would refuse but he suddenly said, “Fine see you in three hours at the Police Station it’s on Adelaide Street and Dundas Street. You can’t miss it; but if you do; don’t worry I’ll come find you with these,”

Cameron then put handcuffs in his hand and shook them out.

“Good lord Uncle Emmett, someone wants you dead,” Austin said sounding impressed.

“It’s not impressive. Nothing better happen to my son, or my brother, because of you, Lily Kelly.” Paula cried menacingly.

“Over my dead body,” Lily cried.

“If either of them has anything happen to them, it better be!” Paula answered.

“Lay off Paula!” Emmett stated angrily.

“I’m just warning her. My boys and you are all I have left.”

“You have Suzy., too.”

“Suzy doesn’t give a damn. She’s not here, is she?”

“That’s not fair Suzy was on a work assignment out of town, and she was unreachable.”

“Unreachable? Nonsense! She’s a mom; she has to be available. You are always on Suzy’s side.”

“I’m sorry your hurting Paula; but if Suzy knew she’d be here. We do love you,” Emmett said quietly.

“I should go jump off that bridge and end it all.”

“Please don’t mom, I need you and so does Uncle Emmett.”

“I won’t for now, I think I need to go back to the hospital. Will you take care of my boy Lily? You and Emmett? Please, you owe me that.”

“I’ll gladly look after Austin. He’s a fine young man,” Lily agreed.

“I’m sorry for before I know I can be difficult.”

“You’re entitled, your husband just died. I’m so sorry Paula,” Lily exclaimed.

"Everyone's so sorry, but it doesn't bring him back. Let's just go to the wake they Austin arranged in the patio at the restaurant"

"It will get better," Emmett said.

"Maybe but it doesn't feel like it will ever," Paula replied.

"Come, we're your family we will support you, Paula," Emmett insisted.

"Thanks, I need that support today of all days."

"We all need a little help sometimes. I'm here, mom."

"You are a boy you shouldn't have to act so old. I'm sorry."

"It's okay. I'm your son strong and resilient just like you. It's a select group at the wake so you won't be too overwhelmed."

"Okay, I'm ready. Let's go," Paula cried.

~0~

Chapter 13 – Guilt

I slipped up and I didn't have my

cousin, or anyone to help me fix this. I liked Emmett and had admired him in the past. I should have just talked to him and then just disappeared like I'd planned to. Why had I so foolish? It was the damn pills I should never have refilled the prescription. I had worried because it said you shouldn't stop them suddenly, but this was worse. At least when I'd killed before I had a good reason and the victim wasn't family. Emmett was almost family. he had almost married my beloved Lily.

Okay, that was a lie I'd killed family before but they deserved it!! I was just angry with Emmett and I had allowed that anger to get away from me. Oh god, why had I done this?

Lily and Amelia would be devastated and that poor little girl, Rose who looked up to him as a father figure would cry her eyes out. What had I done? Okay, calm down, I told myself. Just don't get caught, or my family would hate me.

I had gotten rid of the clothes, safely. They'd never find them and the blood was gone. I checked the motel room, (making sure no one saw me), the fumes had dissipated and the clerk had told me yesterday that it was being rented out this afternoon to a family, I was safe.

Now I could relax and yet a heaviness weighed on me. I recognized the feeling finally it was grief. I had liked Emmett thought of him as a friend and now he was gone, I couldn't bring him back.

For a moment, tears slipped from my eyes and I decided to find a distraction. I turned on the radio and found them talking about a body that had been found in the Thames down river, from Victoria Bridge. I'd go down to the river and watch as the police found the body.

The phone rang it was my contact. Eileen Jones had been found dead last night, that idiot had killed her too soon or maybe under someone else's orders?

So, that's why Dafydd looked so upset. He was torn. This woman had harmed all the women in his life. She'd killed his wife endangered his baby, tried to kill Lily and endangered Clover. Yet she was his beloved little sister, someone he loved. Eileen just caused pain despite the fact that she had been killed too early, it was okay. I'd be in the clear they'd never be able to prove I'd counseled the inmate. The man would probably kill himself now sure that his deeds would assure his place in heaven, or such drivel. They'd never trace Eileen back to me only the inmate.

I needed to concentrate on this new killing I must not be found out. I'd go down to the river and get intelligence. I could look shocked that someone had been killed. They'd correct me, of course. No, I'd better wear a disguise, they'd probably recognize me from before. A COVID mask, cutting off all my hair, and buzzing it until I was bald; leaving a scraggly beard, that was a good disguise. No, vanity made me only want to give myself a buzz cut. I'd wear some pants and a jacket with the name ***Derek,*** I'd stolen a uniform from a delivery service and if spoken to I would change my voice.

No, uniforms made them suspicious and antsy; besides would a delivery person be near the river? It wouldn't work. I had to rethink all of this.

A homeless person would be better choice. There were a lot of them camped all over the city. It wasn't getting worse all the time, a lot of them were medicating their mental illness with street drugs and it wasn't working, except if you wanted to get rid of people who were killing themselves, slowly. I'd relieved one of their burdens, a few years ago. Maybe, I should assist a few of them, and help them get into safety and love? No, that would draw more attention to me and I needed to do something…something that would benefit my family, I had to be free to do that. I had to find out how far they were along in finding out who killed Emmett.

Would I see my beloved Lily there? I'd hate to see her grieving, maybe I could find someone else for her? No, what she really wanted was her daughter. I needed to get on a plane and get to England and find Heather. But I was waiting on my passport. One that would pass through all the airport checks. My guy assured me it would; but that he needed time to make any background check pass.

I should hate Heather, but she was Lily's mother so I couldn't. Mothers were irreplaceable even misguided ones. I would find her and convince her to bring Clover back gently and if that didn't work stronger methods would have to be taken. Clover needed to be with Lily. I'd be Lily's hero which would make her feel better and then she wouldn't miss that ass, Emmett Rogers at all. I might even put my hand in at matchmaking, so, my dearest, Lily wouldn't be lonely. Lily deserved some happiness and I would make a very good step-daddy.

~0~

Chapter 14 – One of them

I wandered to the river's edge a little further down stream, looking disheveled and like I'd been on the street awhile. The others there accepted me so the cops would. A cop was asking some people outside the yellow tape if they'd seen anything. I heard them muttering no. None of them had seen anything, I was safe.

The cops pulled own some tents that were nearer the crime scene. I hope the people would get them back.

The sun had been shining earlier and it hadn't looked like rain; but here (at the riverbed) it was still cold and the sky filled with sleet, was coming down in sheets.

I heard them say the cops say they were investigating and I crept a little closer skillfully hiding behind some homeless that resided in the nearby tents and a tree.

"Seems the victim was wearing a borrowed coat and hat," the man who wore a long black trench coat and seemed to be the one on charge.

Son of a bitch! The victim wasn't Emmett. Who the hell was that? Who had I killed? At least I hadn't killed Emmett. That was good thing, wasn't it? I still had to warn him to be better; but he'd escaped against my better judgement I would let him go this time. But he'd better realize how lucky he was. I was sure he would; after all *that guy* had left Emmett's temporary abode. He must know the dead guy.

I needed to find out who the guy was and if they could tie him back to me. I wonder if there was anyone, I could bribe without revealing who I was? I should leave town now; but I needed to keep on an eye on this situation but how? My contacts had dried up while I was away, maybe I could find an old con a little under pressure who could use some cash? That would be no problem, as I was flush thanks to my bio mom.

She wanted to get close to me and had set up a trust fund in my chosen identity. She wanted to believe me. when I told her I was being railroaded scapegoated by the Happy Valley police because of my adopted cousin. I had convinced her I was innocent, that I had killed no one. Part of me had told her those lies; because I wanted her to still love me like my mother should have all a long; the other part of me knew I'd need her help behind the scenes to escape my shackles.

Besides her story had broken my heart. They had ripped me from her arms when she was fourteen years old all because my father was a criminal. She loved my father still and hated her parents. She had insinuated that she had something to do with the 'accident' that had taken their lives and left her a wealthy eighteen-year-old, I then had admitted that I killed my adoptive father, but only because he abused me. She had cried for me then and said she would never let anyone hurt me again. I was amazed and full of love for her; until I investigated her story. She'd lied she had slept with every Tom, Dick, and Harry. The woman hadn't wanted me!! She had convinced her parents she had been raped and then she couldn't look at the child. She was a victim and I was the villain's spawn in her womb. Women had the right to their own bodies. I believed in that strongly, but she'd had me, didn't she love me?

Her friends now, or should I call them hangers on? They said she bragged about having a serial killer son and how she was going to find him and study him for some paper she wanted to write and now she could do just that now.

I pretended I was confused and that if she really loved me, she would set up bank accounts and drafted a will leaving all to me if she passed away. I lied and told her I loved her, that I'd always wanted my mother. That I understood how hard it had been for a young girl and maybe that would have been true; if I hadn't heard those truths.

That woman (my biological mother) thought she was tricking me; but it was really the other way around, for after I escaped last month and went to her house, I drugged her (I had some conscience after all). I then staged an accident of her going over a cliff, making sure she'd be found only after the drug had left her system.

She had finally done her duty as my mother. I was rich and free, for now but I had to stay on top of this mistaken identity accident. Okay, so, it was simply murder… semantics, on my part. I knew that deep down my shrink would insist murder, was murder, even if the stupid guy deserved it; but it was hard to figure out what was so wrong with this.! Frankly, the only thing to worry about was getting caught. The point though, I needed to find out who this unfortunate was and if it could be traced to me; before I saved my family in England, because I it had to be me that was this family's hero who rescued Clover. At least it wasn't my soon to be son-in law, Emmett.

Heather was family, so, I take it easy on her; I'd make her my wife that would control her. but she had to give back that baby. Clover needed to be with her mother and even that idiot Emmett. Emmett wasn't a totally useless father; Caleb had straightened out and was attending Western University, I reconsidered. So, it was probably a good thing that I'd mistaken him for this unfortunate man. It wasn't my fault, but definitely this man's; that he was dead.

It was fate of course and you can't argue with Fate. You are at the wrong place at the wrong time, and this kind of thing happened. The main lesson to be learned? Be sure of who you are killing, and why. If the stupid fool hadn't borrowed Emmett's coat and hat, he wouldn't have perished. Yet, he had done me a favour; he'd spared me the pain and the recriminations, I felt about killing Emmett. Emmett had shown me contempt when I had acted the playboy and I respected that he treated women with the respect they were due. He'd shown me kindness when I broke down despite my transgressions; maybe I should do the same and just talk to him by phone or message? Yes, that was better than in person at least until I returned his daughter to Lily.

Back to my real problem, I needed to find out if this fated murder could lead back to me. Maybe, one of these unfortunates by the river would like to make a buck, or two, and inform me of anything the cops could have? I had a guy, or was it a girl? They could possibly hack the lead detective, Cameron Grenor's computer. It was worth a try. What a minute, why did that name seem so familiar? I searched my memories. When I had investigated Emmett Rogers, I had come across his name. That rat bastard was a cuckolder, He'd slept with Emmett's wife while he was in Afghanistan. Emmett had taken back his wife and she'd died. Emmett was a good guy, I realized, he had supported his wife despite her flaws, seeing her into her eternity happy and forgiven.

Grenor had better not treat either Lily, or yes even Emmett badly or he'd find out pretty quickly how I treated people I disliked.

Then I heard words that both calmed and alarmed me at the same time.

"So, do we know who the dead guy is?"

"The guy is not dead, he's in the ICU at the hospital. You must have seen the missing flyer this morning. We think he is Captain Felix Vitoria, but we need proper identification."

"So., we need to go to old the barracks?"

"No, Grenor has it in hand. He's interrogating a suspect and if he checks out; then he'll take the guy to make a definite identification of Captain Vitoria."

I was elated that Emmett wasn't dead; but knowing how much Emmett hated Grenor this was not good. Emmett wouldn't be happy, that I'd tried to kill him. Lily would hate me too. Emmett would move heaven and earth to find me for hurting his friend, maybe it was good that I was leaving town. Enough of these thoughts, it was time to move on with my plans; I was off to my informant and my computer expert. I'd be better used somewhere else, perhaps the other London? Yes, that could be a real solution. What was an attempted murder after all? If I was a hero, they'd forgive me, wouldn't they? They were my true family, the ones I'd chosen and real family forgives family,. even when they are a little naughty.

~0~

~0~

Chapter 15 – Inquisition

Three hours after the wake Emmett and Lily nervously entered the police station. They waited and then were directed to an interview room.

"Is this normal, Emmett? I thought we were only going to give statement. Why does this cop seem to hate you?"

"Do you remember how I told you I neglect Jenna and she found someone else while she was in Afghanistan?"

"I think you're too hard on yourself. Wait a minute he was the one that she left you for temporarily. That doesn't say a lot about him he knew she was married."

"I was innocent in all of this, but I have to admit I don't like him either."

"He doesn't seem to just dislike you; he treats you with anger."

"Jenna didn't want to see him when she was dying. I think he blames me. He certainly blames me for her getting breast cancer and then dying."

"Does he think you kept her a prisoner? She made her choice and it was you."

"You can't reason with someone who wants someone to blame, other than themselves"

"Telling your sweetie lies, Emmett?"

"Grenor, can we just get this over with?" Emmett asked, "Where do we write our account of the evening."

"I just have a few more questions."

Four hours later they walked out of the interrogation room, exhausted, they had answered all the questions including any of those involving Lily's mother, Heather and their supposition that Heather had kidnapped Clover. Grenor had tried to argue that Clover was dead that he had seen the paperwork, but Emmett and Lily had strongly objected and had told him to checkout all the evidence and Heather's records.

Lily couldn't believe how arrogant and controlling that cop, Grenor was. When he finally let them go after signing their statements, she was relieved. She thought the was going to keep them for even more hours; but Emmett's hand squeezing hers and had gotten her through this inquisition.

"One more thing I need you to identify Captain Felix Vitoria."

"I can go to the morgue with you. You need not involve Lily."

"We're not going to go to the morgue. We're going to the ICU at the hospital."

"You bastard, you let us think he was dead!" Emmett yelled angrily.

"That was your supposition. I never said he was dead," Cameron Grenor answered.

"You are despicable and a disgrace to the uniform Officer Grenor."

"Maybe I should be detaining you, Lily Kelly. You've been involved in a lot of mayhem and murder."

Lily thought for a moment that Emmett was going to strike Grenor; but he closed his eyes took a breath and said, "Don't pull any more stuff like this, Grenor. You know that Lily and I are innocent. Your bullshit won't play anymore. I have friends too and I won't hesitated to let the brass know how you are behaving. Just so you know, your boss is actually my godfather, so watch your step. He's a by the book man and he won't appreciate you colouring outside the lines."

Grenor smirked, not appearing worried.

"I still have a few questions for you, Emmett but you can answer them on the way to the hospital. As for you Ms. Kelly, I'll be in touch if I have anymore questions."

"I'll be happy to come with you; but first I have to see Lily to her ride," Emmett insisted.

"Fine, when you're done meet me in the driveway on the King Street side."

On the sidewalk in front of the police station, Lily called a car service then she whispered in Emmett's ear. "I'll see you back at your sister's; but watch your step, Grenor has it in for you."

As Lily got in the car service. she hoped she never see Cameron Grenor again, but somehow, she thought that wouldn't happen Constable 1st Class Grenor had it in for Emmett and as long as he could, he'd be in Emmett's face.

~0~

Chapter 16 – Midnight Move

The man was back and he brought friends. They thought Heather didn't know they were watching her? They weren't from Gerhard; unless he was suddenly hiring ex-military types.

Emmett!! Of course. Emmett was searching for his daughter, maybe he wasn't such a bad father; never the less she wasn't going to give Clover back to him. She would shake things up a little, she'd no longer be Sarah Crouse. Sarah Crouse was moving to Canada. Amanda Lee and Clover would have to be Clare for while or perhaps C. C.?

They'd move into their upscale London Bridge apartment. It was ready. Heather believed in being prepared she had detailed plans. She instructed Henry the doorman to donate all her apartment things to charity and sell the apartment. People were desperate for housing; it would go quickly and the money would be forwarded to her lawyer, who would then deposit in her Cayman account. No one would trace Heather and Clover… they were safe Heather reassured herself.

Heather took the packed bags and the stroller and placed Clover in it.

“Damn,” she thought, she had forgotten Clover’s favourite doll and her teddy, not to mention some chewys and Clover’s favourite Giraffe one. Did Heather have everything else? It would have to do; if she forgot something then she would have to purchase it. She’d already left a note for Henry on the front desk so that was taken care of. She’d told him she was leaving tomorrow; but that was a lie they were leaving now, tonight.

Heather snuck down the back way and out the service door. She lifted the key off Henry weeks ago and he since replaced it; but hadn’t changed the lock. Heather had arranged for an Uber to pick them up three streets over. Heather and Clover had met said Uber by going through backyards and back alleys where the men wouldn't see them leave the apartment but Heather kept and eye out and listened for any sudden sounds but the only sounds, she heard, were some traffic noises and a barking dog.

Soon they were home. Heather entered her London Bridge apartment took Clover out of the stroller and let her toddler loose into her new home. All was well they hadn't been followed and Clover seemed happy, she liked the light flowing in through the large windows. Clover was chasing balls of light glinting off the mirror on the wall and onto the floor. So, why was Heather on edge? She shook it off, Heather would remain vigilant. no one would find then, not Emmett and his friends, and certainly not Gerhard.

~0~

Chapter 17 – Escape

I d seen all the information; this idiot, Captain Felix Vitoria, who had borrowed Emmett's coat and hat had brought this all on himself. He had a bit of a concussion some contusions and broken bones and they were keeping him in a coma to get the swelling down on his brain. You'd think an army man would know to protect his head in a fall. It really wasn't my fault that I had mistaken him for Emmett; Grenor should have been happy that someone tried to take out his rival/ enemy but I was sure the jerk wouldn't look at it that way.

I wonder if Lily was on to me yet? Did she know I escaped?? Would she be mad that I hadn't done anything before now? Those damn doctors and staff had kept all the news from me if I hadn't found that Happy Valley paper that told of Eileen's misdeeds and how she had tried to harm my 'sister' Lily. How dare that woman I'd tried to get her first, but someone had beaten me too it.

Eileen was dead. Today! Huh it was my man, but not on the day I picked. Maybe Heather did love Lily? Maybe Heather had paid him to do the deed? Or was it Lily's father or new step-father. This was a real turn of events the breaking news that I had been privy to. Imagine Lily having no idea her father was gay, until he married his butler. I always suspected something was up with that guy, that he was hiding something. Some people thought being gay was sin what nonsense it was just nature...the way he'd been born. He was still Peter, so, that was okay with me.

When I heard about Lily's injuries and Clover's kidnapping, I obviously had to help my beloved Lily, my adopted sister and my adopted niece. I had to see her to decide what to be done to help my family; but this stupid Felix had gotten in my way when I had tried to punish Emmett. It had worked to Emmett's advantage and possibly to mine. I would have regretted harming Emmett, or killing him; because that would have devastated my Lily and she was a shadow of herself as it was. Emmett's demise would have killed her. Fate had decreed that he not be harmed; so, who was I to argue with fate?

I'd see the moron Felix was being well cared for, then I'd leave and go find a way to save Clover.

My passport was ready and my ticket was bought I'd soon be winging it back to London, England and Clover.

Lily would soon have her bay girl back after almost two years it was time this huge mistake was rectified and I was the man to do it.

~0~

Chapter 18 – The Surprises Keep Coming

Emmett peered down at his old friend.

"Is Felix going to recover?"

"I shouldn't be telling you this because you're not family; but he's doing much better we may be able to bring him out of the coma in the next day or two, "the nurse whispered.

"Thank-you," Emmett replied.

"You've positively identified him as Lieutenant Felix Vitoria?"

"Yes, Grenor, it's Felix," Emmett replied wiping a tear from his eye.

"You are a lucky hotshot, that whoever did this didn't kill you!!"

"Can we take this into the hall Grenor? I don't want to disturb Felix."

“He’s in a freakin’ coma; he can’t hear us!”

“That’s where you’re wrong. People in comas can hear,” the nurse said overhearing.

Emmett ushered Grenor into the hall.

“Please Grenor, I know you don’ t like me and the feeling is mutual, but Felix is a good guy he didn’t deserve this. Find who ever did this!”

Grenor smirked and looked like he was going to say something, when his cell phone loudly rang Westminster Chimes.

“Do you know you’re supposed to turn off your phone in hospital. This is an I. C. U. you could kill someone!” Emmett complained.

Grenor ignored Emmett and answered his phone.

“Yes, sir, I am with Emmett Rogers. Yes, I’ll give him my phone,” then turning to Emmett he said,” My boss wants to talk to you.”

Emmett went further stepping into a stairway and then took the phone followed closely by his nemesis. Emmett soon found godfather, Chief Alexi Roman on the phone.

"Emmett. I got a phone call from a source that fills me in on escaped prisoners, I think you should know about this one. It's not good news, apparently, two months ago Brad Owens escaped from Pinecrest."

"What? Why weren't Lily Kelly and I notified sooner?"

"They were trying to cover their own butts and they hoped to recover Owens, before others found out; but he has not been seen since his escape."

"It's possible he tried to kill me, but instead harmed Felix, though, isn't it?"

"We certainly have to put him on the list as a viable suspect. But you're a cop. You know that a lot of people are not happy with you."

"I have to let Lily and her family know. The hell he caused Lily and her family was unbelievable. He killed people close to them as well."

"That's why I'm letting you know son. Your Lily spoke to me about my officer, Grenor and his vendetta against you. I could take him off this case. Do you want me to do that?"

Grenor overheard the conversation and looked both angry and upset at the same time.

"No, Grenor is just doing his job and doing it sufficiently. Lily misunderstood, as she's not a cop. Thank-you for telling me Uncle Alexi."

"Give the phone back to Grenor. I have a few things to discuss with him."

At this Grenor still looked angry and then motioned for his phone to be given back which Emmett complied with.

"Grenor here. Yes. Sir. Yes, Sir, I will let him leave now and go back to the scene. What? Fine!!" Grenor said then hung up.

"Of course, my boss is Your Uncle or something. Do you have horseshoes up your butt?"

Emmett said nothing not wanting to start a fight.

Grenor looked confused as he pondered the conversation," You didn't have to defend me to him, why did you?"

"I'm willing to give you a little slack, because I know you loved Jenna; but I expect you to act professionally and investigate what happened to Felix like the cop you must be to have achieved your rank."

"Don't expect me to do any favours for you."

"I won't!!"

"The boss says if you'd like to come back to the scene with me and help me investigate as a guest investigator, I am to allow it."

"I wouldn't want to step on your toes and of course I can't participate as a friend of the victim. Besides my sister, my fiancée and my nephew need me right now."

"Tell my boss if he asks that I invited you, will you?"

"I will that is if you let me know if this points to Brad as the perpetrator."

"Who is this, Brad Owens?"

"He's a serial killer. A crazy stalker who stalked the Kellys and killed people close to them. For years as police officer, he had even greater access to them and was able to easily commit his crimes with his cousin helping him cover his tracks."

"Where's the cousin?"

"He's dead. Brad killed him because he threatened the Kellys. Brad considers them his family and if you threaten them, you're on his radar."

"Is he totally off his rocker, or was he faking a psychiatric break to avoid jail?"

"Brad has mental issues from childhood trauma, sometimes he's crazy like a fox and sometimes he's just slipped a cog, or two."

"Great then he is a dangerous viable suspect. You better watch your step, Rogers. Would you like me to assign an officer to watch your sister's home?"

"Thank-you I'll take you up on the offer for Lily, Paula and my nephews' sake. Now I'm going to my sister's home to tell Lily.

"I'll drive you. Come with me." Grenor said.

“Your positively scary when your nice, Grenor,” Emmett commented.

“Don’t get used to it. My boss says play nice or I’ll be written up so, this is me playing the game because I like my rank and my job.”

“Just be civil and we’ll get along.”

~0~

Chapter 19 – Back to every day life

Heather knew it would be tough being a grandmother acting as a mom; but this was ridiculous. She'd had help when she was raising Lily. Her mother had helped as well as Peter, when he was busy working but raising a child was ten times as hard when you felt the sting of old age creeping in.

She should take Clover to the park. They'd been a few times since she'd met that Canadian business man in the park; but they hadn't seen him again. If he'd been a plant, she would have seen him over the last six weeks but he hadn't been back. She almost regrated that, because he was so nice and everything else seemed so insane.

Her eyes scanned the park of their own accord. She didn't see him and she was disappointed; it would have been nice to talk to an adult. Then she spotted him. He was on the bench, near the swings dressed in a business suit, Saville Row, if she wasn't mistaken. This man was doing well, or just had a lot of money. It might be nice to cultivate his friendship but was it safe? She looked him up and down again he was kind to Clover and he didn't show any over interest. She'd talk to him that wouldn't hurt.

"Hello stranger," Heather said.

"I am a stranger, but maybe we could change that?"

He was flirting with her and he was younger than her was he a plant? No, her first instinct was correct; he was just lonely like her. She smiled at him.

"I'm Derek Archer," he lied introducing himself.

"I'm Amanda Lee."

"Nice to meet you. So, what do you do?"

"I'm on leave," Heather explained.

"Of course, probably one of the best times to be on maternity leave during COVID. "

Heather frowned. He had assumed she was Clover's mom; what would he do if he found out she wasn't. Was he working for them is that why he said that? Just to test her?

"Sorry, a poor joke."

Clover threw the ball to Derek who threw it back. Clover kicked it to him like he was the goal post.

"Wow, you're good at soccer, little one."

"Soccer?" Clover repeated, confused.

"Sorry, you call it footie here."

Clover grinned a toothy grin at him and he found himself genuinely smiling back. Clover looked so much like her mother and grandmother.

"I want the swing, man" Clover demanded.

"Clover! Ask nicely. We don't demand things, use please and thank-you."

"Come with me sweetheart," Derek said.

"You don't have to take her," Heather exclaimed.

"I don't mind. I miss my niece and nephew this will be good practice."

As the man pushed Clover back and forth on the baby swing Heather asked, "What was your business, again?"

"Cups, we make lids and paper cups that dissolve, plates container for take-out and cutlery that are better for the environment."

"Wow, I think I said this before, but that's a great product, especially with how much take-out there has been during the lockdowns," Heather replied honestly impressed.

"Like I said before, that's been part of the problem, with the restrictions, I haven't been able to conduct my business and then I had to fly back to Canada and fix a worker shortage."

"But that's all fixed now?"

"Yes, COVID restrictions were a bitch; but I've got my workers making the product again and it's all good again. My partner can handle it until I return."

"How much longer will you be here, if I may be as bold to ask?"

"Long enough to ask you out for a coffee."

"You know that's not. what I was asking."

The man raised his eyebrows and smiled.

"I don't know," Heather answered wavering but looking then at Clover.

"Don't worry I know a coffee place, that has a patio we can sit outside and I've had my first two COVID shots."

"Okay, just coffee though. How about now?"

"Sounds good," he answered, "Will the little one be ready to leave, or should we wait a little longer?"

"Can we go Nana?" Clover asked.

"Would you and Nana like some ice cream?"

"Cream!" Clover shouted excited/

"Sorry, I should have asked you first. I should know better, my sister would have my head," Brad said seeing Heather's frown.

"How did you know I was her nana? You were joking about me taking maternity leave."

"She called you nana. I really did think you were her mom at first for you look too young to be her grandmother. Now, do you have to take her home to her mom?"

"No, her mother is dead. She died in childbirth."

The man thought for a minute, maybe she really believed Lily had died. Is that why she took Clover? It would make more sense. She loved her daughter, Lily; she wouldn't hurt her. She was grieving and she wanted to protect Clover the way he had wanted to protect Lily from Emmett. he could forgive her and maybe admire her a little. He'd gently let her know Lily was alive. This might take a little time; he didn't want to spook her. He'd already chased away the man who was tracking her and they called her a spy? The woman hadn't noticed him.

"I am so sorry for your great loss that has to be tough. I can't imagine losing my child and then having to swallow my grief and raise my grandchild."

"It's been hard."

"I'm sure it has why don't you let me take you and the little one out for dinner on the patio."

"I don't know."

"You could come back to my hotel room it's a suite; but I didn't want to make you both uncomfortable."

"Let's go eat on a patio, but don't we need a reservation?"

"I'll call in a favour with a friend who runs a restaurant."

He made the call.

"All set, let's go," the man requested.

Heather bundled up Clover and asked, "Are you hungry, baby? Would you like to go to get something to eat with the man?"

"Derek." Clover corrected.

"Yes, Derek."

"We eat, let's go. I want cream!!" Clover demanded.

Soon they were eating on the patio. Heather was soon enjoying herself and so was Clover. as Derek fussed over her. Clover demanded ice cream, but Derek got her to settle for a cheeseburger and fries with chocolate milk first.

Heather found herself agreeing to meet up with Derek in a couple of days for lunch. That led to more and more dates and fun with Clover. Soon, Heather was happier than she'd been in a long time but that made her worried. She always had a long fall when she became happy should she doubt this? No, she was ready for some good luck it was her time and he seemed nice, she didn't have to worry sooner or later he'd leave and go back to Canada. She'd be okay, no matter what, she vowed.

~0~

Chapter 20 – It doesn't rain, that it pours tears

Lily dialed Amelia's cell phone again and there was no answer. Lily hadn't wanted to believe that Brad Owens had escaped; but everything pointed to it. Had he killed trying to kill Emmett? Emmett had assured her they were safe, but what about the rest of Lily's family? Emmett had said that Chief Stewart had his best guys on it; but she was still scared. He had terrorized her family before, including Rose. Rose… she had to try Grandma Katha again. No, no answer.

Where was everyone? She tried her father, Peter Kelly and his husband, Charles they were answering either. Should she be worried. No, the sun was shining and it was a warm summer day; they were probably just enjoying the weather.

Lily decided she better alert Amelia. Brad could be stalking her again and Amelia didn't need that when she was already suffering from the ravages of cancer.

"Hello, Lily. How's Emmett?"

"He's part of the reason I'm calling. Someone tried to kill Emmett."

"What is he okay?"

"Emmett's fine but he's friend who was mistaken for him was injured."

"Will his friend, be, okay?"

"It's still touch and go. They have him in an induced coma."

"Does he have an idea who could have tried to kill him?"

"I've got more bad news, Amelia. Brad Owens escaped and he may be the person who tried to kill Emmett and injured Emmett's friend."

"Are you kidding me? No, of course you're not! I always worried this would happen, but they assured me that place was inescapable. Oh, God, what if he comes after me, or Grandma Katha, or Rose?"

"I think he thinks of us as his family, so, hopefully he won't hurt us. Step-Uncle Neddy assured Emmett that he has assigned police officers to protect us all; until Brad is apprehended; but remember anyone around us in danger, so, please use caution."

"You're calling our Chief of police, Edward Stewart, Neddy? I mean I know Terrence calls his son that; but I don't think he likes anyone else calling him that," Amelia giggled.

As Lily had planned it had made Amelia laugh. Lily wanted to scream and cry, every time she spoke with Amelia, but she had to be strong that's what Amelia needed. Lily could make this all about herself that was selfish.

"Aunt Regan would laugh too," Amelia continued filling in the silence.

"You've been spending a lot of time with her/"

"Like I said Regan has been taking me to my appointments, when Grandam Katha couldn't."

Lily had to admit she was a little hurt. that Amelia had leaned on her before now; but when she thought about it, she really hadn't been able to physically, or mentally to help so she should be glad Aunt Regan had helped. She had neglected people over the last year what with her recovery and her depression over her missing daughter. Something was going on with Rose. She knew it Rose said she'd failed her year because she too was depressed over her missing sister, but Lily suspected it was that and more. Maybe Lily should go home to Happy Valley. Emmett would understand. They'd made up and things were much better between them. Emmett needed to stay in London for a little while but Lily could go home and help her cousin and Rose. Emmett had his friends looking for Clover and Heather so she could focus on Amelia and Rose, couldn't she? Except a little nagging voice was telling her that heather was unstable so how safe was Clover?

"Are you mad at me for not relying on you more?" Amelia guessed.

"No, I have a lot on my mind and I'm just glad someone could be there for you, especially when I couldn't … when you needed them most."

"I love you, Lily."

"Love you, too. You've always been like my sister. You know that."

"I'm glad; because I feel the same way."

"I'll be home as soon as I can. I promise Amelia. Maybe even tomorrow; but I need to talk to Emmett first. I'm the only one here."

"Where's Emmett and his nephew? At the hospital?"

"Emmett is at the London Police Station talking to the officer in charge of the investigation, Paula is at the hospital at her doctors, getting her regular baby/ pregnancy check and Austin insisted on going to school."

"I'm sorry I wasn't here How is Paula?"

"She's doing much better. She's coming to terms with her husband's death, we both know how awful that is. Paula and I were talking this morning and Paula was actually nice to me."

"Paula was nice to you?"

"I know shocking! Paula told me she feels bad about how she's behaved to me and wants to be friendlier."

"Are you sure you were speaking with Paula and not a robot? Did they give her mood medicines?"

"Maybe but they have to be careful what she takes because of the baby."

"Wow, I'm glad things are finally getting better between you. Don't worry about rushing home. I know you will be home soon."

"Oh, drat there's someone ringing Paula's door and I'm the only one here."

"Be cautious, check through the peep hole and make sure you know who's at the door."

"Paula has a door camera" Lily said looking at the camera screen. "Oh, it's Suzy. Just a minute."

"Call me back later. I know you have to tell her about Paula's husband's death."

"Are you sure?"

"Yes, now call me back later. I need a nap anyway."

"Love you. Amelia."

"Love you more." Amelia said hanging up.

Lily opened the door and Suzy came in with a man. The man was five feet ten inches tall, with a slim build. but muscular arms. His hair was blonde, curly and cut tight to his head. His eyes were blue and searching.

"Lily what are you doing here? Where's Paula?"

"I'm sorry Suzy, we tried to reach you."

"What's happened?"

"Jason had a heart attack and died in Afghanistan."

"What? Where's Paula? Greg? Austin?"

"Paula is at the doctor's getting a check-up for her unborn baby. Greg is serving in Germany and Austin is at high school."

"Paula's pregnant?"

"Yes!'

“Poor Paula, a dead husband, and a baby on the way, that’s too much stress. How’s she handling that? “

“At first not so well; Paula is also under psychiatric care. She broke down and they had to hospitalize her at first when her husband died.”

“I’m sorry I wasn’t her for her but I am now. Where’s Emmett then?’

“Emmett’s friend was harmed. He’s in a coma”

“What? But who would do that and why? Is Emmett, okay?”

“Emmett is okay for now it could be much worse; the man, was wearing Emmett’s coat and hat when he was attacked.”

“Who would harm Emmett?”

“It may have been Brad Owens.”

“But he’s in a mental hospital for the criminally insane! He can’t have don this, could he?”

“We found out yesterday that he escaped four weeks ago.”

"Did Emmett know that?"

Lily shook her head.

"Oh no, Trent, Brad Owen is so dangerous! He's killer," Suzy exclaimed turning to the man beside her.

"Why would he be interested in any of you?" Trent enquired.

"Brad Owens terrorized Lily and her family, stalking her and her cousin Amelia for years. He killed his adoptive father, Amelia's husband her son, Lily's first and second husband (who was the mayor of Happy Valley).

"Why isn't he still locked up?"

"He was sent to a forensic mental facility but he escaped. I'm terrified Trent. Lily is my family too. Like I said, Brad killed their husbands and he killed Amelia's son. He also killed Lily's former mother-in law and his own cousin. Those are only the ones I remember. They think he may have killed more people, but nothing was ever proved."

"A serial killer? Do you have a picture of this guy? I'd like to protect my wife." Trent demanded.

"Trent, I was going to tell everyone we got married, now you've spoiled it," Suzy whined.

Then turning to Lily Suzy begged, "I wasn't on a training course at all. You won't tell Emmett, will you? Lily We've just come back from Vegas and our wedding."

"Sorry, honey," Trent stated.

"Married? You got married? Does Emmett know your husband?" Lily asked.

"No, but I'm sure once he meets him, he'll love him, like I do."

"I'm sorry that we haven't met before. I'm Staff Inspector Trent Buhr of the Ontario Provincial Police"

Lily didn't quite know why; but she didn't like Trent at all. Suzy had picked another winner and this time she'd married him, she thought. No, she was being judgemental. She needed to get to know hm better. How bad could he be? The man was a cop. Then she remembered Brad had also been a cop. Was she judging him harshly simply because of Brad reappearance? She had to tried to be fair, Suzy was happy, Lily must accept him for Suzy's sake.

"Trent this is my family; you don't have to introduce yourself as a cop."

"I just wanted her to understand why I need this stalker's picture."

Lily thought about it and remembered that she taken a picture several years ago on her phone of Emmett, with Brad in the background. She scrolled through her numerous pictures mostly of Rose, Caleb and Emmett until she found it. Thank goodness she hadn't erased it.

"Brad's the guy in the background; but you can probably make this bigger and get a better image of him."

Lily held the phone out to Trent who took the picture and fixed it so it only showed Brad. then sent it to his own phone.

"Thank-you," Lily."

The doorbell ran again. Lily checked the camera and the opened the door to Grandma Katha and Terrence.

"Who is this?" Grandma Katha asked.

There were introductions all around and congratulations said. Grandma Katha excused herself as her *FaceTime* tones on her phone chimed.

Grandma Katha was gone for a few minutes and then held out her cellphone to Lily a ***FaceTime*** call from Rose. Lily left the room followed by Grandma Katha.

Lily took the call.

"Rose? Oh, hi sweetie. Where are you?"

"I've been keeping secrets from you and I'm sorry after how hard I've been on you and Grandma Katha for keeping secrets from me," Rose admitted. "

"Secrets?"

"I'm in London, Ontario seeing a doctor."

"Why didn't you tell me?" Lily asked," Have I been so out of touch, that no one could tell me anything?"

"Oh, so you know about Amelia's cancer," Rose declared.

"Amelia told me in secrecy. a few months ago. She wasn't ready to tell you yet, how did you know?" Katha asked.

"I skulked around in corners listening; since you people are good at keeping secrets. This world, sucks! I can't believe there isn't a cure for Aunt Amelia. How can she die of cancer, she's only thirty-one."

"Amelia's dying? Why didn't anyone tell me?" Suzy asked coming up behind Lily.

"She hasn't told a lot of people. Please keep this to yourself until she tells you," Grandma Katha commented.

"I'm sorry I shouldn't be listening in on your conversation; but Trent is in the bathroom and after that we're going to lunch… we wanted to know if you wanted to join us?"

"Maybe later, Suzy," both Grandma Katha and Lily replied.

"I know it may seem presumptuous, but we'd like to throw you a wedding reception next month," Terrence offered.

"Yes, we would," Grandma Katha agreed.

“But I’m not even family.” protested Suzy.

“You feel like family and you are our friend.”

“You two are the best, thank-you. Trent and I were going to continue our honeymoon for the weekend, but all of this is awful. I don’t know if I want to.”

“Be happy Suzy, you just got married. Enjoy your honeymoon,” Lily insisted.

“I guess we could still take the weekend, I’ll call Emmett and let him know about our wedding.”

“Congratulation Aunt Suzy, please tell your groom, I said welcome to the family,” Rose commented.

“I’ll let you get back to your conversation. I’ll just be in the kitchen.”

“Bye Suzy.” they all said. And then Lily listened while Rose explained herself.

“The secret I’ve been keeping is a doozy, but I’ve taken the right steps though, (the adult steps) I’ve checked myself into the hospital; because my eating disorder has gotten out of hand. It’s part of the reason, I flunked my year and then had to repeat my grade eleven year while Carol got to finish school this year, but they say I maybe able to catch up and finish with her."

"I'm sorry Rose. That must have been so hard for you. No wonder you're having such a difficult time. You and your mother almost get killed by a homicidal maniac, and then your baby sister is kidnapped by your grandmother, your mother has a stroke and almost dies and then your aunt gets untreatable cancer, it all sounds like a soap opera; but it's not it's real life… ours." Lily exclaimed gulping back tears.

"It's okay, mom."

"No, it's not, but it will be baby. We're going to get Clover back."

"Yes, *you are* Lily. I've hired bodyguards to protect you all; but Katha and I have to go, we have a solid lead on your mother. She's living under an assumed name; but your Grandma Katha and are going to London England in just under four hours. We will get Heather to give back Clover but I'm sorry if we want to make that flight we have to leave now," Grandpa Terrence said interrupting.

"Is that a good idea? She hates you, Grandma Katha," Lily stated.

"She loves me, she just so hurt. I can fix this," Grandma Katha exclaimed, "That is if you promise to get better, young lady."

"I will I'll gain back the weight and take the required classes I promise," Rose declared.

"We have to leave now but you continue to talking to your mom. I love you."

"Love you too Grandma Katha, tell Grandpa Terrence, I love him, too and have a safe flight."

Grandma Katha then left out the door complaining loudly, "I have nothing packed."

"We'll get everything there; I promise, and we're flying first class."

"Frist class? Ooh that sounds nice; but you're sure it's booked for London England?"

"You make one mistake and they hold it against you forever!"

Rose laughed as she overheard the conversation and Lily was glad Rose could laugh about anything, as she felt terribly guilty.

"You should go too, mom. Emmett could go with you. Suzy is there maybe she could look after Austin and Paula?" Rose insisted.

Suzy came back in the room.

"You're sure about lunch? We're leaving now." Suzy commented, but Lily didn't hear and continued speaking.

"I would like to go, Rose but I'm torn; but you need me," Lily indicated.

"I've got this handled and I'll feel much better if you are on your way to get my sister. Maybe she thinks your dead, like I did. Maybe Heather will see you and realize she made a mistake."

"I hope you're correct, Rose. That would mean, she didn't really want to hurt me…that she's still somewhat the mother, I remember."

"Listen Lily, I can look after Paula and Austin. You need to get your daughter. You won't mind will you, Trent? We can finish our honeymoon later." Suzy interjected.

"We were only going for the weekend anyway and I can pick up shift this weekend then. You know I have to work some night shifts for the next month to make up for my time off, so this will be better anyway. You'll be safe from that serial killer with the cop guarding your sister."

"There's no cop guarding Paula; but Grandpa Terence has already promised to send bodyguards to protect us," Lily explained.

"As long as we're together Suze, and you're safe," Trent agreed grabbing Suzy's arms and hugging her possessively.

"We're leaving now for lunch, but we'll be back at 3 p. m. We can formalize all the details then," Suzy promised.

Suzy and Trent then went out the front door and Lily locked it.

Lily wasn't sure what she thought of that. Trent seemed a little possessive; but they were on their honeymoon and a serial killer had tried to kill Emmett, so, no wonder Trent was acting this way. She was reading things into it that just weren't there. Suzy seemed happy; she should be happy for her. Suzy and her sister Paula seemed to pick their partners wrongly.

"Oh no, I can't go! Who will be there for Amelia?" Lily cried, then she remembered how Regan, had become a good friend to Amelia and knew if she called Regan, she'd look after Amelia until they made it home.

"Just get the okay from your doctor and tell Emmett you're going mom, so he can join you." Rose insisted

"Thank -you, baby, if you're really, really sure that you'll be okay then I'll bring your sister safely back to us but I'm going to miss you and feel bad the whole time I'm gone. I still feel guilty leaving you and Amelia."

"I know you will mom, but I really will be fine; now sorry mom; but I have to go my doctor's calling me."

"Are you absolutely sure?"

“Mom, I’ve got this now just go! I want to see my little sister and teach her a hundred and one things.”

“If my doctor says I can go to England, I’ll fly there and bring Clover home.”

“Bye mom.”

“Bye baby, get well. I love you.”

“Love you too. Call me when you get to London and if I don’t answer leave message. Bye, now!”

Lily hung up the cell phone. Then she quickly dialed Emmett to tell him what she planned to do with or without him.

~0~

Chapter 21 – Reunion

Heather left the apartment building cautiously, as she would have said to her colleagues, her Spidey sense was tingling. She saw no one, but felt eyes on her. Where were they hiding? Should she worry that Emmett had found her?

She walked quickly pushing Clover's stroller. Clover chatted on about the trees and their leaves turning colour.

Heather looked over at the London Bridge could the eyes be there? The bridge was rising to allow a boat through and the bridge. Tomorrow something was being fixed on the bridge and that would disrupt traffic.

A man came into her peripheral view, striding at the end of the bridge near her; she noticed. had a long black trench coat and a hat obscuring his face and body. Heather really couldn't get a look at them. Were they just walking down the street, her way?

Heather quickened her pace. The man seemed to quicken his. Heather threw all cautioned to the wind and began to run. That is when the man shouted, "Heather? Oh my God is that you, Heather."

Heather's blood ran cold and then her heart began to beat wildly could this truly be?

"Heather it's me, "he cried.

Heather looked at him closely, his hair was now gray; but still had red streaked through it. It was still worn in as short and military cut and his stature was still straight and proud despite his age. Seventy-three years old wasn't that the old she thought, not really, but he had betrayed her and that she couldn't forgive.

"What do you want?" she shouted angrily.

"I thought you were dead, until I saw you today."

"Bull. I don't believe a word of it."

"Is that why you didn't meet me in Prague?"

"Like you expected me to be there! The word could only have come from you."

"Word what word? What are you talking about? I can't believe you are in front of me, here, alive!!"

"Liar!" Heather answered, not quite ready to speak to him. Why hadn't he searched harder for her. She had been taken to Siberia. Worked in a work camp, then she had finally escaped with the agency's help. When she'd searched for him, she hadn't found him anywhere, where had he been? Was his name really Jacob MacKay? Should Heather trust him at all?"

"Where have you been, Jacob?"

"Where have you been? I went to the Prague Astronomical Clock as we had planned. You didn't come!! I was so sure that you had you changed your mind. You broke my heart."

"You're trying to make me believe, that you had nothing to do with me being taken a prisoner?"

"You don't have to make up a lie; obviously you didn't want to come."

"A lie? I wish it was a lie! Jacob then I could believe you gave a damn about me."

"You really were grabbed, by who?" Jacob asked narrowing his eyes in a way which Heather was beginning to believe him.

"I wanted to be with you. I wanted a life with you and our Lily, but after Lily was traumatized, I was going to return home get our daughter and join you. Unfortunately, the gang grabbed me on the way to the clock to tell you we would be delayed for few weeks while the doctor's treated Lily."

"What gang?"

"It was someone I met through my work. They wanted me to die in a work camp in Siberia."

"Siberia? But you were a low-level spy, why would they snatch you?"

"It was Gerhard Brandt."

"Who?" Jacob said narrowing his eyes, like he knew the name.

"You know him?"

"I know of him. He's a nasty man. How did you get mixed up with the likes of him?"

"He still wants me dead."

"After all these years? Why?"

"Some information I gave the agency was used to plant the bomb that killed his wife and child."

"But you didn't plant the bomb?"

"No, but I might as well have. The guilt I have for them killing the poor woman and her child…"

"You aren't guilty. Information is traded. The man brought this on himself; as I understand it, he was about to bomb and embassy when his wife and child were killed."

"That's true. How do you know so much?"

"I tried to find you though my resources at the embassy and at MI5, but I came up dry. People were all whispers and conspiracy theories when talking about the embassy bombing, but I didn't know it had anything to do with you."

"Nana who is this?" Clover asked.

"Nana? I thought perhaps you were babysitting. but you're a grandmother. Is she Lily's child?"

"Yes, this is our granddaughter, Clover."

"Clover, this is your grandfather."

"Come watch my movie at our apartment, grandfather," Clover invited.

"He probably has other things to do."

"No, I don't and I'd love to watch a movie with both of you."

Heather was still a little leery, but she decided that watching a movie wouldn't hurt and she had missed him. He said he'd looked for her. She looked over at him and he smiled begging her with his eyes to agree. So, Heather did. Jacob followed her into their apartment. Jacob sat down and Heather was amazed how Clover took instantly took to him. Heather told him how she had let down Lily and Eileen had contributed to Lily's death. Jacob was shocked and grieved but he took it well.

The afternoon went quickly. The fell into the easy friendship and the love they had once had was breaking through. Heather felt happy and alive, more alive than she had in years. Was this real?

Jacob ordered supper. Foods they had eaten years ago. Clover asked for stories and Jacob told her how they had met during a class at the college.

Before Heather knew it; it was Clover's bedtime. After Clover went to bed they talked into the night and then before Heather knew it, they fell into bed. She had missed his touch, his lips on hers. The taste ambrosia. Their arms encircled one anther and they tasted each other lips joining, skin and flesh becoming one.

After their lovemaking Jacob declared his love again and begged for another chance to spend time with Heather and Clover. Heather really wasn't ready for all this; but she had lost her happiness all those years ago she wasn't about to throw it all away again. She would set aside any fears it was time to love again. Before Heather even had time to think of the answer again, she found herself agreeing to marry him and raise Clover together.

Heather told him about Derek and how she had to let the man down easily, but Jacob wanted to be there, when she did. Heather knew that was something she couldn't do so the next morning she left Jacob sleeping while she and Clover went to the park and then on to meet Derek and let him down easily.

~0~

Chapter 22 – London's Calling

Heather saw the man again; it wasn't just a coincidence. He was carrying a newspaper and he was following her. The man was French Canadian she'd heard his accent, as he'd bought a paper, yesterday. As if she didn't have enough problems breaking up with Derek and now another man she had to deal with, someone who could harm her. Who bought papers anymore? You read them online with your subscriptions. Was ***he*** from the agency, or Gerhard?

She heard his name; it was Doctor Pierre Rétrécir. Why had they sent a doctor was he sent to torture her? He had other men with him. What did they want? Had the agency sent them were they a kill squad, or was it

Gerhard? She had to get to Derek with Clover without being seen.

She should have been more prepared but she'd become complacent since the COVID lockdown began that's why she'd let the Derek into her life? She grabbed her go bag out of her locker in the basement storage area and quickly donned a gray wig she would take it off before she entered the building, this wig would get her safely to the restaurant

She passed one of the men in her disguise and heard them mention Lily and Katha. Had Grandma Katha sent them? But why had the man mentioned Lily? She was going to call Grandma Katha, when it was safe. She had decided that Clover needed to be raise by her father. Jacob was wonderful but they were too old to continue raising a child. She'd call Grandma Katha tonight. Grandma Katha filled her with fear and dread she feared her punishment, for taking Clover, wouldn't even Grandma Katha understand why she thought that was necessary? Grandma Katha loved Lily, too. She must know Heather would never have taken Clover if thought she'd be safe with her father. She must know the blame had to be placed with Emmett Rogers, for not defending Lily and of course the now dead Eileen Jones. She spared Emmett's life surely that should make Grandma Katha happy. She'd give Clover back and Emmett could raise Clover. Heather could be forgiven, couldn't she? Grandma Katha would come and act as a go between Heather and Emmett and she wouldn't bring the police. No matter what Heather had done she knew deep down that Grandma Katha loved her and would protect her. But first Heather needed to handle Derek, carefully and gently.

Praying the wig would hold and they wouldn't recognize Clover, Lily took a step outside. Heather thought about Eileen and the problem there. She wouldn't be found out it was full proof, wasn't it? She could have her life with Jacob, if he didn't find out about Eileen. Heather was so sure he would forgive her solution,

Eileen had died as she had lived in a mental institution. Poor Eileen had hoarded her pills so she could kill herself, not what really happened; but it was what the authorities believed and it couldn't be traced back to Heather. Good help was hard to find Heather had thought the dark web and money brought assassins to do what was necessary; but she'd had to find someone a little closer and one inmate was really irate that Eileen had harmed Lily whom he loved like a sister. Lily had treated him with respect when she had prosecuted him and for the first time he'd felt like human being.

He didn't know who Heather was; but he agreed, readily. He had gleefully agreed to the transaction. Heather heard about Eileen's death by suicide shortly after she contacted him. He was dead now he couldn't be traced back to her so Heather would keep her counsel and tell no one.

Heather rejoiced that Lily's murderess was now burning in hell, but now she had to feel guilt that she had killed Eileen, didn't she? Hate burned in Heather for the woman who had tried to kill killed her daughter; Jacob's reappearance couldn't dampen that hate. Damn the consequences!! Surely, Jacob would also hate Eileen; for what Eileen had done?

~0~

Chapter 23 – Happenstance, Serendipity, or Madness

The man who called himself Derek was confused how had this happened he was the player, not the playee. How had he fallen so hard for Heather? She taken Lily's daughter he still didn't know why; but she must have a good reason, right? His plan had been to lull her into complacency and dispatch her rescuing Clover, then deliver Clover into Lily's grateful hands. Plans evolve however, he'd learn that over the two years he'd been at Pinecrest. He managed to survive there and actually learn more about himself and the Kellys, His family had never been far from his mind. Heather was family too. She was Lily's mother, so, if he followed through on his new plans…life would be wonderful. Was it happenstance, or serendipity, that he had fallen hard for Heather? It didn't matter he was happier than he'd ever been in his entire life. Heather completed him like no other women had. She was twenty-five years older; but what was a few years?

He wanted to stay with her forever; but first he needed to convince her to marry him in his real name and her real name. She had to know the real him and love the real him. He even change his last name to Kelly, to match hers. He'd get her to give Clover back to Lily. She also gift Lily, her long lost mother and be a new step-dad to Lily. He'd be the hero of the story; like he was always meant to be.

The best part of this? He'd really be a Kelly and no one could take that away from him. He'd finally have the family he truly deserved…the family, he'd worked for, killed for secretly, all these years before they'd locked him up. But none of this would be possible if she didn't say yes and admit to him her real name.

He was excited, but everything must be perfect. None of this would be possible without a perfect proposal. He'd planned the proposal carefully, ordering roses for the restaurant. and picking up two heart hearts, one a heart shaped toy for Clover, the other a facsimile for his heart, that Heather would have forever. He almost hesitated they could keep Clover (she was acute enough kid), but that was the problem she was a child and he didn't want the responsibility. Lily would get her daughter back and they'd visit occasionally he'd play grandfather; wouldn't that be fun?

The restaurant, The Garden Café, Lambeth, was perfect. It had a small enclosed garden that Clover could play. near the reserved table he'd booked. The restaurant itself was close to the houses of Parliament and The London Eye, quite frankly it was and ideal location. Perfect for a Valentine's Day proposal.

The menu was astounding as well. Clover could have pizza, while they could have more sophisticate adult palate items like, gnocchi with wild garlic, and Parmesan, or plates of freshly baked focaccia. Sticky toffee was his favourite and they made it like ambrosia here. He hoped Heather would like that for desert too.

He'd instructed the chef to put the 14k ***Petite Cathedral Solitaire Canadian Diamond*** engagement ring in the pudding. He worried that he maybe, he hadn't spent enough as the ring only cost $1600; but he hadn't a lot of immediate selection. He could always purchase a more expensive one later to join it. After all they'd be married for a long time. There would be years to spoil Heather. Clover, the little sweetie, was going to receive a bracelet with her name spelled out in diamonds. A girl should always have diamonds they said and he wanted to buy her affections as her new grandfather.

There she was, Heather, the woman of his dreams. If he had only known years ago this would have been oh, so, easier. The Kellys would have been his family, a lot sooner. They had felt like his real family for years; but this was going to be the icing on the cake. When he became a real Kelly…like he thought before maybe he'd even change his last name to Kelly.

Heather walked over to the table and he watched as she fussed over Clover and then she turned to him and smiled. He smiled back his special smile, the one he had perfected by looking at the mirror and imitating the men he had seen in love. The deceptive smile that he knew got his way time and time again.

Heather was beautiful. She did not look in her sixties, if he hadn't seen her birth certificate, he would have thought it a lie. She looked at the most forty. Lily and Amelia were beautiful; but his woman shone from the inside out. He wanted to bathe in that sunshine and goodness forever. He was sure she could make him a better person even if she had made an error and taken Clover. Everyone was entitled to one mistake after all then he saw things that made him realize why this had happened. He was sure that was all a lapse in judgement brought on by her forgetfulness. He noticed how she forgot things; it must be the fault of those doctors she'd seen and the medicines have prescribed that she took. He forgot things, when he took all his medicines. He was sure if he told her that Lily was suffering and that she needed Clover; then Heather would return the little girl. In fact, he had arranged for that soon.

"Derek, this is too much. Look at this place."

“Nothing is too good for you and Clover. Let me spoil you.”

“Thank you, dearest.”

Derek loved it when she called him dear, and dearest, His mother had done that when he was little before she died and he’d missed it.

“There’s a place for Clover to play. See there’s a garden,” Derek pointed out.

“It’s lovely but…”

“No, buts, just enjoy.”

Derek pulled out Heather’s chair and then handed Clover a heart toy. He then gave Heather roses and the heart. Getting down on one knee and producing the ring he said, “I love you. Will you marry me?

Heather looked shocked and extremely surprised. She said nothing and Derek grew angry. Would she refuse him then he remembered what she was hiding of course she just need assurance.

Clover jumped up from her chair and shouted,” I have to go potty now Nana.”

"Sorry, Derek. I 'll answer you in a few minutes, but right now I have to take Clover to the loo."

"I understand," Derek said but he really didn't why she couldn't answer now. He could explain all and she'd say yes. It was all very simple.

Heather was relieved, for a few more minutes she could think up an easy way to let Derek down. She had enjoyed their time (hers and Derek's) together, but a few kisses and some walks in the park, didn't not compare with the love of her life. The love of her life had walked back into it and she was going to grab happiness with both hands. Derek was acting odd though, had he sensed what she had decided to tell him?

"NANA!!" Clover shouted as they got to the doors of the loo.

"Clover, we don't shout."

"Sorry. I gots to tell you sumpin'"

"Go ahead darling, tell me, but in a normal voice, please."

"I'm scared." Clover whispered.

"Why are you scared?" Heather asked alarmed.

"Derek is Hans!"

"I don't understand."

"You know like in the movie, the man who tries to marry the princess, but he's a big liar. He wants to be da King, but he hurt her and her sister."

Heather thought about what Clover was saying '***out of the mouths of babes***' came to mind. Could this man who had romanced her be up to something? Heather was trying to let him down carefully and he had his own agenda?

She knew in that moment, that Clover was right. She seen his face when she hadn't answered Henri right away. He looked angry. Good grief she was a former spy; she was supposed to have the best of instincts about people. How could not have seen through him? Had she been so lonely that she had let down all her intuition go by the wayside? Or was that doctor she had visited correct and she was losing her mind, slowly and irrevocably? In the meantime, she had to get Clover and herself out of this situation.

The love of her life was waiting she could finally be happy after all these years.

Why had Derek asked her to marry him? What was his game plan? Was he working for Emmett? The two didn't seem to corelate, but something nagged at her and deep in her heart and she knew they did. They had to leave the restaurant now and take on new identities. Time for plan C they could hide in Canada, in some big city, like Toronto, or Calgary, or Vancouver, no one would notice them there. She had a Canadian back-up passport in the name Susan Bell and Mae Clover Bell. They could do it, but they had to sneak away now, before Derek knew they had gone and her true love could meet them there.

"I think you're right darling so, were going to play a game."

"What kind of game?"

We're going to sneak out of here, but we don't want Derek to see us."

"Okay, nana, but I don't like Hans."

Heather looked out the door and did nor see Derek he must be in the loo as well, she thought. They crept silently to the door and as they turned the corner of the building there was Derek.

“Oh hello, darling. Don’t look so scared. It’s perfectly okay, you don’t have to run, I know your real name, Heather.”

Heather blanched he knew her real name, he had to be working for Emmett, it couldn’t be Gerhard’s man, he wasn’t skillful enough.

“You know?” Heather said faking trembling but planning to run at the first chance she got. She would hear him out find out his angle and if all else failed she would charm him.

“Yes, I know darling girl and it doesn’t matter I still want to marry you.”

“You do? But I took Clover,” she admitted surprised.

“Darling, I’m sure you had a good reason.”

“Lily is dead! Don’t take her back to her father, he failed my Lily, you know that, don’t you?”

"Emmett did Lily wrong; but Heather Lily's alive."

"Don't lie to me, my daughter's been dead almost two years."

"Heather, Lily is alive. Would you like to her voice?'

Derek then dialled a number Heather knew so well, she could have dialled it by memory, a voice come on the line.

"Hello?"

"Sorry wrong number, "Derek said and then he hung up.

"She's alive but…" Heather fumbled.

"Did you take my mummy?" Clover asked her green eyes glinting just like her mother. when she was angry.

If Brad hadn't been so disturbed by the kid's reaction, he would have been impressed by the genes that cause her to react this way. This is why he loved the Kelly women; they were strong and they stood up for each other.

"No sweetheart; we're going to take you to your mummy, Clover," Derek said in the sickly-sweet voice, he hated, but knew others loved.

"Are we going to see, mummy, Nana?"

Heather thought a moment and then she looked shrewdly at Derek. This man was dangerous. Was Derek even his real name? He'd fooled her and she didn't fool easily. She must have hesitated a little too long to answer, for he grabbed her wrist forcefully and said," I knew you'd agree. Let's go, Grandma Katha is waiting."

"Grandma Kaffa?" Clover asked but was ignore.

"But she hates me." Heather protested.

"She loves you. Family forgives and that's forever."

"Do you really think so?"

"Yes, I do! I've spoken to her; she's waiting for you. on London bridge."

Heather was surprised.

"Where is she?"

"We'll get to that; now before you tell me you'll marry me. I have one more thing to confide to you."

Heather became fearful. What more was this man holding back, was she going to be arrested?

"Heather, darling, my name isn't Derek."

Heather heard the darling and relaxed a little, someone who called you darling, wasn't going to turn you over to the police; but if he knew that you were dumping him then that might make things a little different. She needed to continue to play him,

"So, what is your name?" Heather asked.

"Before I tell you, remember, I'm not judging you for any of your past mistakes and although mine are many, I have atoned for them."

"You're stalling. It won't matter darling you've accepted me now let me accept you. Tell me," Heather pleaded.

"My real name is Brad Owens."

Heather tried to keep a straight face; but she knew who Brad was and none of it was good. She had been a fool of the worst kind; Heather had lost any of the skills she once had. This man was a serial killer and she'd let him into their lives, willingly. Maybe, she really was losing her mind. Was he a danger to Clover, or just her?

"Oh, you've heard of me? Yes, I'm pretty famous; but remember (in case you find me scary now) that I never killed a Kelly. You're my family and I love you. Remember I love you most of all; that's why I want you to marry me. Whenever I'm with you I'm a better person. The closeness to the Kelly blood makes me a stronger, better person. If you marry me, then you will truly be my family, once and for all. So, you will marry me, right?"

"Of course, my darling. I love you, too, Brad, this changes nothing, my love," Heather lied

Heather had to do whatever she had to, anything to protect Clover. Once Clover was safe with her Great -Great-Grandma Katha, then Lily would take care of Brad. He would never harm Lily and her family again, she vowed. Then she could be with the love of her life, maybe even be forgiven by Lily and live out her life in Canada near her grandchild with him. He should be able to get to know his grandchild too.

"Oh good, then that makes it easier. If you're not too hungry; maybe we should order to go, then leave and meet Grandma Katha. I can call her, again and tell her we are coming."

"Actually, we are hungry; aren't we baby and this day is just for us."

"I'm hungry," Clover chimed understanding the need to agree.

Heather marvelled at Clover, almost two years old and she was smart enough to pacify a villain, maybe those movies Heather had let her watch on repeat during lockdown hadn't been a waste of time. The child had the wisdom of an adult at times.

"I like how you think. Grandma Katha can wait. I'm sure she'll be happy for us. Lily can wait one more day for her daughter. Let's go eat."

Heather went back to the table. They had to get away. but how? Clover looked a little scared, but Brad didn't notice. He had believed Heather. Heather knew his psychiatric type. They believed what they wanted, what they needed came above anything else. Brad's fixation on Heather's family was his whole world; but what he didn't know is that Heather had more Grandma Katha in her, then he knew. He would kill to keep her family; but so, would Heather and she knew some people that could help get rid of him if she could get to a phone.

Jacob would help her; but should she involve him? She couldn't bear to be parted from him again, Maybe, she should handle this herself. She'd play along for awhile keep Clover safe and then they flee to Lily's side. As long as this madman was alive, he was a danger to Lily and that Heather wouldn't allow. Heather also had to warn Grandma Katha, for Brad could harm her if his psyche was threatened by Heather running away.

She pretended to be happy, ate some of her food and then excused herself taking Clover to the bathroom once again. Without a word being spoken, Clover had somehow known the plan and had picked up her coat.

"You don't need your coat to go to the bathroom Clover," Brad scolded.

"I'm cold," Clover lied.

""' Fine then, be quick you two; for I'll miss you," Brad claimed.

Heather scurried away while she could. She went quickly by the loos and into the street. The brisk wind was cold without her coat but at least she had her purse. She whistled for a cab and they got into it quickly, out of the back window she saw Brad staring at the cab with anger. Would he go after Grandma Katha now? She picked up her phone.

"Grandma?"

"Heather?"

"You've spoken to Brad?"

"That was Brad that called me, who promised to reunite us?? Oh my god! You've sunken so low that you're with Brad?"

"Are you out of your mind? I had no idea that was Brad, thee Brad, that one who stalked my Lily. He disguised himself."

"You are selfish. How could you have harmed Lily this way; of course, you're with Brad!"

"You're not listening as usual Grandma Katha. It's not fair that you judge me this way I'm not your daughter, why do you judge me by her?!!! I tired to tell you if you had listened, this man told me his name was Derek. I'd never met Brad and it was a very good disguise. I also didn't know that my Lily was alive. Do you think for one minute, I'd take Clover, if I knew Lily was alive?"

"Are you in danger?"

"Yes, Brad actually thinks I'll marry him, at least he did; until we escaped him at the restaurant. I shouldn't have called. We'll manage."

"I'm not saying all is forgiven, but we are family. Please, Heather come to me. We can move to forgiveness. We can protect you and Clover."

"How can you and Terrence protect Clover and I, you're old and decrepit."

"If that was you trying to hurt me and push me away, it won't work. I still love you, Heather. I'll always love you and Terrence is your Grandfather Terrence now!! Grandpa Terrence loves you too."

"Terrence doesn't even know me."

"Grandpa Terrence is all about family and he took on all my family when he married me. Terence cares about you, too. We have some other protection here as well."

"Other protection?"

"Some former soldier friends of Emmett's."

"Then they'll want to harm me. You think I don't know that George Gagnon, Henri Cote, Tommy Harrow, are waiting for me? Please explain to them the truth. I thought Lily as dead and I only wanted to protect Clover."

"I'll explain it to them they'll understand. They won't they only want you to return Clover, I promise they won't harm you."

"Are you sure?"

"I'm listening too, Heather. Come in from the cold. We love you and will support you. Lily will forgive you. eventually especially if she has Clover in her arms," Terrence insisted.

"Do you really think there's a chance Grandma Katha?

"Yes, I'll meet you anywhere any time."

"Come to the St Magnus the Marytr's Church, on Lower Thames Street in an hour. We'll meet you there."

"Will be there," Katha promised.

Heather heard Terrence explain excitedly, "The archway under the tower itself is from the original London Bridge."

"I must go now, see you soon." Heather exclaimed sitting back into the cab.

Clover asked in an angry tone, "I heard that man say she was alive, but you said my mother was dead, Grandmother!!"

"I know I thought she as dead pumpkin and you know I never lie."

"Then the bad man told the truth, she's not dead?"

"No, a bad lady made me think so, but you'll see her soon," Heather promised.

"Okay, but first, we're seeing your grandma?"

"She's my grandmother, but your great great-grandma baby."

"Another grandmother, I'm so lucky Will she like me?"

"She already loves you," Heather answered.

"Then I'll probabee love her too."

Glancing behind the carriage still worried that Brad was following Heather glanced behind them. She should get another cab to meet Grandma Katha to foil Brad. Heather spotted a cab idling by the curb ahead instructed the cab to pull over and tipped him heavily, instructing him not to give information freely. Heather showed the cabbie a picture of Brad; commanding him to tell Brad (if he asked) that they had gone to the train station spinning a story about an abusive ex. The carriage driver was ready to do anything she asked; even without the generous bribe. Heather then got into the second cab with Clover to meet Katha and Terrence, breathing a sigh of relief when no cabs followed.

~0~

Chapter 24 – London Bridge is Broken Down

Heather arrived at the St Magnus the Marytr's Church, on Lower Thames Street. She'd called Jacob a few minutes ago, and he said meet him there, too. What a busy place this was going to be. There were tourists back again now wearing masks as well to deal with; Heather had to keep on her toes and see who showed up. If Gerhard, or Brad showed up, she was prepared to run.

She needed to find a good place to see all but where? Could the answer be the walkway from London Bridge, the one that was over top of where part of the old church used to be?

"Hello, darling," Jacob said creeping up on them, as they stood now on the walkway.

"You scared me."

"You've lost some of your abilities, darling; but I'm here now and I'll keep watch. You pass Clover to them and then we'll leave."

"Do we have to?"

"Darling, they make promises, but you know you'll be arrested. So, we follow the plan."

"Grandpa, do you and grandma have to leave?"

"Yes, darling, but we'll see you someday," Heather promised.

"I'll miss you," Clover said solemnly.

"We'll miss you too, but you've only to look at your necklace I gave you and it says…"

"Lobe, you till da moon and back."

Heather smiled and nodded.

"That goes for me, too. You are our little pumpkin; never forget that," Jacob exclaimed.

Clover looked upset, but there was nothing else Heather could do. Clover needed for safeties sake and for Lily's sake to be reunited with her mother. Surely, Emmett would protect her? She would have to trust that, because Heather had run out of options.

Jacob's cell phone pined and he glanced at it, A look (that anyone else would have missed) passed over his face, like it was bad news but he quickly hid it.

"What?"

"Huh, London Bridge is broken down, that's why this walkway is here, but now the real bridge…it's temporarily closed. There's been some traffic accident or something."

"But that's where we were going."

"I always have a back-up plan. It will be fine besides you know the rhyme?

"I thought the rhyme was London Bridge is falling down?"

"That was how they changed because the original had too many bad connotations. They built that original bridge with bodies, real body pieces, some claim, but the original bridge was sold to some

Americans…. if you can believe it. They sold our history away! The new London Bridge, however was erected in the 70s in a slightly different place."

"Bodies? Gross!!"

"Yes, that's probably why they talk about building up with iron and steel to make it stronger and not so, distasteful. Do you know it mentions a Lady Lee, as you are now claiming to be?"

"Really? Here I was living in London Bridge apartments, ha-ha."

"The London Bridge is Broken Down rhyme goes at the end, *Dance over my Lady Lee and company. Then we'll set, a man to watch, Dance over my Lady Lee. Then we'll set, a man to watch.* Lady Lee was the poor Anne Boleyn, they believe."

"The poor thing, held a prisoner."

"As you were darling, by circumstance, but now will fix that. I'm your company and were going to dance over to your freedom, you can bet on it."

I'm not Anne Boleyn, I'm not trapped."

"No, you're not, because I have a plan."

"I trust you. Let's do this. I'll call Grandma Katha to meet us somewhere else, but where do I tell her to come?

"The Tower Bridge is not too far and we can meet her there and still carry out our plans. This might even work out better," Jacob said and then whispered an exact place.

"Can't you give me a hint?"

"When the time is right. Let's just say we have to hurry high tide, today is somewhere between 8 p.m. and 8:20 p.m."

"The Thames? Yuck the water is gross."

"So, is a Canadian jail, if the extradite you."

"I get the point, so, I'll follow your lead."

"You make your calls and I'll make mine. We'll be prepared."

"Don't worry I won't tell them about the tides. I don't want the policeman to get mad at you, grandma," Clover stated.

Jacob looked worried, but Heather decided to explain.

"I didn't know your mommy, was alive; darling, I promise you that. I loved your mother, I still love her, but the policeman won't believe me."

"Why?"

"They'll refuse to understand. They'll put your grandmother in jail. It's really important you understand this. You can't tell mommy, or Grandma Katha."

"I won't! I promise."

"Or even daddy. any of our plans."

"Daddy? I have a daddy?"

"Yes, sweetheart and your daddy will be waiting for you in Canada. Daddy is a policeman. A very good policeman, but he would have to arrest grandma."

"I won't tell daddy anyting or mommy, or that other grandma."

"You promise?" Heather asked.

"I pinkie swear, grandma."

"I love you sweetie."

"Lobe you too."

"Stay with Grandma and help her make her call. I'll be back soon."

"Don't worry Grandpa I'll protect my grandma from the bad man. I did before, I told her he was like Hans and we ran."

"So, you did, now if you see that man who called himself, Derek; don't wait for me, run with grandma, where ever she says."

"I will, I don't like him," Clover agreed.

"Good girl!"

"Now here is a present from grandma and I."

"What is it?"

"This is the picture of your mother, Lily."

Clover took the picture and said, "She's beautiful and looks like grandma. I can keep this?"

"Yes, sweetie," Jacob said and Clover smiled back.

~0~

Chapter 25 – The Best Laid Plans

Brad was upset, Heather had taken

Clover and ran. Why didn't she trust him? She was scared, obviously. She had said she loved him so it wasn't that. Grandma Katha! Of course, he had mentioned her and Heather had bolted. She was scared that Grandma Katha would punish her. Had Katha acted like his father? Had Heather been abused and that's why she hid from Katha. Had Katha regretted her behaviour, her abusive ways over the years and changed into this woman he'd met? He had to be patient with Heather and loving that would sooth her fear. He'd help Heather see, that he would not allow Katha to harm her ever again.

He wished someone had stepped in for him then he remembered his dead cousin, Silas and for a moment, he felt guilty. Then he remembered the reason Silas was gone. Silas had made a mistake that no one should cross. Silas shouldn't have threatened Brad's chosen family, then Brad wouldn't have had to take his life. No, he wouldn't think about that anymore the guilt was too hard on him. Silas had brought his demise on himself. There that made him feel better.

Now to find Heather. She'd probably have fled her apartment, but where would she go? He was being silly, he'd placed a tracker inside the lining of her purse, unbeknownst to Heather just for this reason. He went to his room and checked the equipment. Brad noted with relief, that Heather was at St Magnus the Marytr's Church. He'd find her there and all would be well. St Magnus the Marytr's Church, was a church, not Catholic like he preferred; but maybe he could convince the Anglican priest to marry them today it was a wonderful plan. They could always be remarried in a Catholic church, in Canada, in front of all the family later. He'd be a Kelly today, maybe he should change his last name to Kelly? Why not! He hated being an Owens!!!

~0~

Heather stepped into Jacob's car. She had kissed Clover on the forehead, (a precursor to saying goodbye for the final goodbye to her) then buckled her in the car seat. How was Heather going to do this? This was going to kill Heather. She had to remember that she was Clover's mother. but her grandmother and this would protect Clover. Clover needed to come first. After all Lily was her mother and Clover needed to be safe and loved Lily would keep her that way. She'd be in too much danger if she stayed with Heather and Lily had already missed too much time because of Heather's mistake.

Jacob reached over with his right hand and took hers.

"It will be okay, my love. Clover will be safe with Lily. Once Brad finds out, he's never going to marry you the psycho will turn on you."

"I know but Brad will never harm Clover. He loved Lily… loves Lily and Amelia and therefore Clover.

"But he wouldn't hesitate to harm you if you don't marry him. If we do this, Brad won't find you and Gerhard's men won't find out about Clover either."

"I know we have to do this, but my heart is breaking," Heather said as she looked at a now sleeping Clover, in the back seat. Clover gripped the picture of Lily tightly, so, she didn't drop it in her sleep.

"Put this on under your clothes, Heather."

"Is this really necessary?"

"You know it is now, get ready; we'll be at the Tower Bridge soon. You'll send Clover ahead to Katha when she's sighted and then the plan will start."

Heather quickly squirmed into the outfit and then put her clothes over top.

"That's my girl." Jacob said and smiled lovingly at her.

Heather took a deep breath and then thought, at least I'll have Jacob. I won't be alone again, but somehow, she wasn't comforted and she didn't quite now why.

~0~

Chapter 26 – The Tower Bridge Affair

Jacob looked over at the glass Clover and Heather was standing on in the Tower Bridge walkway. Clover had awakened and thought it was so much fun to look down at the river below. He had slipped an employee extra they could be here after hours and they could return Clover to Katha. He himself was hiding in the corner and had planned a way out for them. There was an employee door he planned to use and he told Heather where it was, before he'd hidden in plain sight.

Jacob had found a tracker in Heather's handbag, that Heather knew nothing about; which meant that Brad would also show up everything had to go according to plan. There was no margin for error.

Jacob turned as he heard people approaching. It was Katha and her husband Terrence. They were followed by those military friends, George Gagnon, Henri Cote, Tommy Harrow. Jacob pulled the balaclava over his face and then touched the taser on his left side and the handgun, strapped to his right. They would be under pressure, but Heather had a gun and a taser too, if she needed to use it, they'd be okay. They could get away.

"Clover this is your Grandma Katha and your Grandpa Terrence," Heather introduced.

Clover hid behind Heather.

"Darling, girl. We talked about this you need to go with your Grandma Katha and she'll take you to your mother."

"I don't want to. I want to stay with you."

Jacob was worried if Clover delayed too long, this plan could go south.

Jacob heard the sound of footsteps and he pulled up his balaclava, removed his gun and advanced. Brad must be early.

He turned to the noise and saw to his surprise, Lily , his Lily and Emmett Rogers.

"Lily, is that you really you?" Heather asked.

"Mommy?" Clover asked looking stunned.

"Yes, Clover, I'm your mother," Lily answered smiling with tears in her eyes.

Clover ran to Lily, the picture she held still clutched in her hands and she folded her self into Lily's arms.

Heather whispered.," I'm sorry, Lil. Goodbye, Clover, I love you both," as she took advantage of the moment to slip into the shadows and leave with Jacob while all were distracted.

The soldiers were the first to notice her disappearance and the man in the balaclava with a gun at Heather's side. They ran after Heather and Jacob, but the door h he had pulled Heather through was now locked. Jacob and Heather ran to the exit (with Jacob pulling her) to follow and find out where Heather had disappeared to. They exited the building followed by Terrence and Emmett to see Heather being ushered into a car. The man in the balaclava then took the wheel. The man in the balaclava gunned the car. Emmett found it hard see the black car as it sped away from the curb, it was getting darker outside and nearing 10 p. m…

Suddenly, another car sped up behind Heather and the gunman. Emmett realized in surprise that it was Brad Owens following Heather than who was the gunman; who had grabbed Heather?

Brad was attempting to overcome them and make them pull over to the side of the bridge.it all seemed like minutes but it was only seconds later that the bridge's lift suddenly went up. Emmett watched in horror as the car, (the car which held Heather) accelerated and sailed off the end of the bridge, just as the lift went up spiralling into the Thames below.

Brad got out of his car and looked down over the edge as the car was now moving down the Thames after crashing into the river. Minutes later Brad peered over the edge looking into the Thames below and then fell to his knees crying," No."

Emmett ran to look hoping, against hope that Brad was wrong and that Heather had hopefully survived despite the fast-moving water. He'd called for emergency services but it wasn't looking good. He noted the high tide had come in, it looked higher than he'd seen even in pictures. He pulled out his cell phone and accessed the search engine. This was high tide and low tide wouldn't come in until 2 minutes before midnight. The high tide was estimated to be 4.32 metres or over 14 feet high at 8:20 p.m. It was now almost 10:15 p.m. Heather's chances of survival were slipping away; but maybe she'd got washed to shore?

What would he say to Lily, if the worst happened? How could he comfort her? Lily was conflicted, but she still loved her mother. Who was this masked gunman? Was he an agent of another government, who wanted Heather dead?

Emmett pulled the zip ties he'd placed in his pockets before meeting with Heather. Running to Brad expecting a fight, Emmett was shocked when Brad turned to him and cried, "I've killed her. I was trying to protect her, but somehow, they found her."

Emmett easily took Brad's wrists placing them in zip ties, he then pulled them behind his back.

"Tell Lily, I'm sorry, Emmett. I loved Heather. I was going to marry her. I was going to be her father. We were finally going to be family."

"Save it Brad. You tried to kill me!" Emmett stated.

"But I didn't and that idiot that borrowed your coat is going to live. I couldn't kill you; Lily loves you. We're family."

Lily had come out with Clover and Katha and looked stunned. Emmett shook his head; he had to take this situation in hand. Brad was spiralling again, he could have harmed someone maybe even Lily. The sooner he was extradited and back on Canadian soil, in a mental facility, the better. He had to give him to a Bobby; that's what they called the cops, here right? Where was a cop when you need one? Then he saw the police car and he walked Brad over to it explaining the situation and why Brad was now zip tied to the police officer with George Gagnon, Henri Cote, Tommy Harrow.in toe. The four of them explained all to the cop, who then radioed in a half hour later. It was nearing eleven p. m. when they took Brad away and they were no closer to finding Heather.

The emergency services had arrived on scene and were scouring the shoreline to find out how to reach where the car had gone down, or to see if anyone was floating in the water, but neither the car, or anyone swimming was seen.

“Is she dead, Emmett?” Lily asked.

“Mostly likely,” George Gagnon, Henri Cote, Tommy Harrow all answered at once.

“There’s no chance?”

“I’m sorry Lily. there's little chance of no loss of life. It’s high tide and while it may wash the car to shore, the impact of the car hitting the water, probably killed them both. The tide will soon be going out and when it does any chance will go with them..”

Emmett had his arm around Lily who held a sleeping Clover in her arms.

“The police insist Clover be seen by a doctor, because she was kidnapped. I’ve got them to agree to her seeing one at the hotel,

Terrence has a doctor coming there in a half an hour. I'll take Clover back to the hotel, so she can be seen by the doctor, and you can stay here," volunteered Katha.

"Yes, do that, I'll stay here, too," Terrence insisted.

"No, I stay with my mommy and my daddy, Clover said opening her eyes.

"Baby, you can go with Grandma Katha," Lily said.

"No, I don't like her!! She was mean to my gramma. My gramma said there were other bad guys, some of them policeman. My daddy is a good policeman and he will protect me from Hans," Clover insisted.

"Who?" Lily asked.

"Da bad man who is like Hans. That guy who daddy tied up and gave to the police."

"I thought you were sleeping," Emmett exclaimed.

"Who is this, Hans?" Lily wondered aloud.

"She's talking about Brad, Lil. Hans is fictional baddie/ character in a children's movie." Emmett explained.

"See daddy knows."

"Oh. I'll come back with you baby then," Lily volunteered.

"Okay, but can daddy come too?"

Emmett wanted to stay, but Clover needed him more; so, he nodded and then asked George Gagnon, Henri Cote, Tommy Harrow to stay and keep him updated.

Katha, Terrence, Lily Clover and Emmett then took a taxi back to their hotel.

At 2 a.m. Emmett received a call. He looked over at Lily and Clover peacefully sleeping in the bed and took the call into the sitting room.

"Emmett? I'm sorry buddy, we've been kicked off site."

. Emmett asked," By who, Tommy?"

"They wouldn't say, but my guess is they're MI5, or some spy agency."

"Head back to the hotel and get some rest, Tommy. We'll reach out to them in the morning. Lily is her daughter and under Canadian Law, I'm technically I'm Lily's husband already and I'm Clover's dad. They have to give us information."

"They'll only give you ***some*** information Emmett. I've worked with people who know these people, they're not only ruthless with people, they're ruthless with information."

"Terrence has some ties to some people in the industry. He found out about Heather before, he should be able to again."

"I'm sorry I let you down, after everything you did for me, Emmett."

"I have my daughter, safe with me! You did that!! "

'Thanks Emmett see you at 0800 then."

"See you then, Tommy."

Emmett was startled to looked up to see that Terrence had been sitting in a char in the dark the entire time.

"You heard them?"

"Either they were trying to get Heather and failed, or Heather is alive and has faked her death," Terrence stated.

"Could Heather have done that? That kidnapping looked real and I think Brad was the one thing they had counted on."

"I don't think anyone could have survived that plunge. I'm sorry to say they failed, or maybe they consider it a success as Heather's dead."

"Will you speak with them?"

"I will and I'll find out what they know."

"That's all I ask. Lily deserves to know the truth. Somehow, we'll have to tell Clover, too."

"I know but we'll get through this. We'll take Clover home and she'll get to meet her sister and live the life she should have been living in Canada. Now go get some sleep tomorrow will be a busy day."

Emmett went to bed and tried to sleep thoughts were racing through his mind of how he could tell Lily and Clover. His next thought was maybe they really needed to leave England as soon as possible, before someone found out their closeness to Heather and they found themselves a target of one of Heather's enemies.

Emmett took out his cell phone again and booked them all on an afternoon flight, leaving in the afternoon flying to Toronto, Ontario Canada and then to London, Ontario, He then booked a car to drive them from London, Ontario, to Happy Valley. Hopefully, by then, they'd know one way, or the other what had happened to Heather; but either way they had to be safe and they'd be safer in Happy Valley. Edward was the police chief and he; Emmett, and all the other Happy Valley cops would help keep Clover and Lily safe. As lovely as London England was, it wasn't the most secure place for them.

~0~

Jacob threw himself across the front seat and into Heather's space. With quick action he threw open the passenger door. Jacob quickly fixed a belt that connected the two of them. Then he clipped a small device to it, Heather had already prepared putting on the gloves, Jacob had given her. Jacob then opened Heather's door hurling them out. The two of them dangled from a small steel like rope attached to the door, as the car dropped. Jacob shot off a gun-like object which spun a piece of metal rope into the bridge struts and they then swung over to that rope. Jacob did it again and they swung over to another strut, like great apes, or monkeys. They scaled down the rope into a space by the water, which appeared to be under the Tower Bridge. This all happened in a matter of minutes, and Heather was amazed that Jacob was able to maneuver them that fast.

The alcove they landed in, though old was beautiful, with glossy, white tiles looked old and well -used and Heather became worried that they'd be discovered.

This is the dead man's hole; it used to be the spot were people washed up from the River Thames for years. There is a walkway here. Those steps there go down to a mooring. There are actually 12 old moorings for boats near here. We'll have to be careful of boats as well." Jacob commented.

"This is risky," Heather commented.

"Life is risky," Jacob answered.

"Who is that?"

Out of the shadows came two people, also dressed in wetsuits like Jacob and Heather.

They carried a lot of equipment. One of them handed Heather and Jacob two water propulsion water propeller submersible devices. The other a woman passed two personal air tanks to Jacob and Heather and then they took their own equipment out of the same things. One of them handed Jacob what looked to be a boat that could be instantly be thrown to full size.

"Expected company."

"We'll leave after you do. We are even now Joseph," the woman said addressing Jacob.

Heather then realized all of what they were going to do and how dangerous it truly was; but it was better than be apprehended by Brad, or Emmett Rogers or the agency so, she was game if Jacob was. They would have a life together this way; she had to do it.

She took a huge breath placed the air into her mouth and dove into the Thames with her water propulsion water propeller submersible devices turned on. Heather tried not to think of the sludge she was swimming through.

With Jacob's help she swam, against the tide and they were soon almost out to sea. There

Jacob constructed the dingy they climbed in connecting their devices for outboard motors, the motors quit and Jacob cursed.

"I'm sorry Heather they call this the death route for a reason."

"We'll make it," Heather declared, "Or die trying."

They fought the winds. the choppy sea and six hours later, at 6 a.m., they thanked their lucky stars for delivering them onto the coast of France. Pulling their dingy up they disembarked, buried the dingy deep in the sand, striped of their wetsuits and walked into the nearest town. There Jacob got into a waiting a car and they drove to the next town where they took yet another waiting car which Jacob then drove to Paris. They were safe.

~0~

Chapter 27 - Aftermath

At 8: 00 a.m. Emmett was up and

dressed. He'd told Lily that he thought they should leave for safety reasons and that he'd booked them all on a flight this afternoon. Lily reluctantly agreed to leave, despite not knowing where her mother was alive, or dead. Lily was acting so strong; but he knew that she was suffering and he felt devastated for her. He would do his best to make sure that their life going forward would be happier, and it already was... for they had Clover back. Emmett was sure that Clover would awaken, as soon as she heard all the voices out here. Emmett had checked on her several times, just to make sure Clover was real last night and he knew Lily had done the same.

Clover had been up so, late last night, Emmett hoped that Clover had enough sleep. He had ordered breakfast for everyone. He wondered what to order for Clover and Kelloggs had come through, a breakfast variety pack 8 pack surely, she would like one of those. He ordered some continental breakfasts for everyone else and coffee… lots of coffee, they all needed that.

A few minutes later answering his hotel room door Emmett ushered in all the food trays. Katha and Terrence came out of their room and sat down at the table in the suite.

"Daddy, you are here. I did not dream you. I have a daddy!!" Clover said bounding out of the bedroom door, followed by a bedraggled, limping Lily.

Clover than crawled up into his lap put her arms around his neck and said," Good morning, ***my*** daddy."

"Good morning, pumpkin."

"Why do you have tears in your eyes, daddy?"

"Daddy has waited a long time to say good morning to you, I'm just so happy."

"Like you said you were happy, too, Right mommy."

"That's right, pumpkin."

In the next second Clover pouted.

"What's wrong, pumpkin? Daddy will be back soon," Lily comforted.

"I don't have Elsa and Anna. I want my babies, "Clover cried dissolving into wails.

"Maybe Grandma sent them to our house, but if she didn't, we can buy some new ones when we get to Canada."

Clover continued to pout and Lily continued, "You'll love your new house; we have a big yard to play in and daddy is going to put a swing set in the yard in the spring. I'll make it just as you like Clover."

Clover did not look convinced, but in the next second she stopped crying, long enough to say, "Grandma said we were going to fly on a big plane; but I want my baby to fly."

"I brought something special for you," Lily said.

"What?" asked Clover her eyes getting bigger.

"I brought my baby doll, from when I was little. Your Grandma bought it for me, when I was little."

"It must be very old; can I see it?" Clover said seriously, as everyone else hid a chuckle.

Lily pulled a doll out from behind her back. It was a soft-bodied doll with hard arms and hard legs, but it looked like a tiny baby. It was dressed in a white bonnet and a long white nightgown, slightly yellowed from age.

"Oh. she's bootiful," Clover cried, "What's her name?"

"Her name is Jenny. If I trust you with my baby and if you take very good care of her, you can keep her."

"Really, you'd give me her, mommy?"

"Of course, I don't need a dolly. I have you to love.," Lily said picking up a giggling Clover and kissing her on her cheek.

"I love you mommy."

"I love you too, darling."

Clover had a little of each cereal, as Emmett spoiled her and they all had a wonderful breakfast. Lily did not know how she could leave Clover, now she had her little girl back, she never wanted to let her go. How was she going to go to work ever again? She might have to start over and make a new business plan. One that she could take Clover to work most of the time, but she'd take a little time off, so, Clover could get to know Lily first.

After breakfast Emmett gave Clover the gift, he'd bought her and brought from Canada in his luggage. There were three barbie size dolls, there was Kristoff, Anna, Elsa and of course the reindeer, Sven and the sleigh. Clover was ecstatic and took it into the bedroom to play. Lily smiled at him and said, "So, that's what that package in your luggage was."

Lily put Clover's favourite movie, that she had rented on the screen, and left the door open, so they could discuss what happened to Heather without Clover hearing they spoke softly.

Terrence had been in touch with the authorities and they were ready to declare Heather dead. They had located the car, but they thought the current must have swept her body and her kidnapper's body out to sea.

“How can they decide that so quick?” Lily asked.

“Most likely, the agency is putting pressure on the authorities to close it and are continuing their investigations only if they choose,” Terrence suggested.

“So, is there a chance that Heather is alive?

“I think not granddaughter. If I thought there was any chance, I would have told you”

“Thank- you, Grandpa Terrence for all your help. I do appreciate it.”

“Katha and I love you all, honey. We would do anything for you. That is what family is for but I will keep my ear to the ground to hear if anything should change.”

“I love you both two. I don’t know what I would do without you.”

Lily listened as Terrence explained how Brad would be extradited to Canada. Taken by a UK officer and transferred to a Canadian official who would escort him to a secure mental facility, until he could be brought before a judge. As for the Kelly’s the government was asking them to leave.

The government felt given Heather's kidnapping and subsequent death, that they were all at risk, (as Emmett had insisted to Lily) and they advised the Kelly's to leave on the next available flight. In fact, Terrence claimed they were happy that Emmett had booked them all a flight.

"You booked us a flight without consulting us?" Katha exclaimed angrily.

"I did it at three this morning, when I started thinking of us in danger, of Clover in danger."

"I'm sorry, you're right. I should have thought of that. My granddaughter has put us all in danger," Katha apologized.

"It's my mother.

"It's not your granddaughter's/ mother's, or your fault. It is not something we need to assess blame on. We just need to be safe," Emmett stated.

"We'll all be safer in Canada in Happy Valley, right Emmett? I bet you thought I never say that and agree so, easily?" Lily exclaimed.

"We 'd better pack then, Terrence," Katha conceded.

"Thanks for understanding. I booked us all on a seven-p.m. flight to Toronto."

"Then we better all get packing. Right Lily?" Katha said.

"We'll need to get Clover some clothes," Lily protested.

"I'm way ahead of you. I paid extra and they will deliver some things for Clover in the next hour. I ordered a suitcase, so, she could take her things home and a car seat for the plane so she'll be safe," Katha exclaimed.

"Thank-you, Grandma Katha. You think of everything," Lily cried.

"Mere gifts for my grandchild. I'm going to win her love; you wait and see."

"She'll get to know you and love you as Amelia and I do."

They packed up all their things. Lily knew that Clover loved the child size, Elsa suitcase and Elsa clothes that arrived soon, for Clover gave Grandma Katha a shy smile. Clover also loved the ***I-pad*** which Grandma

Katha had bought for the plane. Lily wasn't reassured, however, until Grandma Katha told her there were safeguards to limit time and lots of parental guards.

They quickly go ready as you needed to be at the airport hours before your flight. Then Katha produced COVID tests. Screaming ensued as Clover protested the nose swabbing but the promise of a chocolate bar from Grandpa Terrence was enough to complete the tests. Still when Clover finished, she ran (with chocolate bar in hand) to Emmett and said, "They're mean to me, daddy."

Emmett explained that it was test to go on the airplane and Clover and then allowed him to help her pack her suitcase. Soon they made it through security and were waiting to board the plane.

Clover ran circles around them at the airport and they had to chase her, but Emmett didn't mind, he had his daughter back, and with the papers that Terrence had gotten from the embassy Emmett, could not take his little girl home.

Seated on the plane in first class (because Terrence secretly purchased an upgrade for them all) Emmett thought how lucky he was to have found his little girl again. He and Lily could be happy again. They would be landing soon, he had to turn on his phone. He had, had it off for hours, since he forgot about it. Clover was sleeping in her car seat and had her hand in Lily's. that made him smile, she loved her mother, obviously, Heather had shown her pictures and told her how much Lily loved her. They'd be happy together and once Clover was happy again, they could plan a wedding, finally, Clover and Rose could be Lily's flower girls. Although the honeymoon would have to be postponed unless they took both girls, Clover and Rose with them. Neither of them wanted to be parted from the girls again, if they could help it.

Emmett glanced at his phone and the 40 text messages he received. Most of them just said congratulations. He thought they were speaking of his daughter and finding her until he scrolled through and found out what they were talking about. Going to his email he found the news. He gotten the job he applied for; in six months. He'd be the Chief of Police to replace the retiring Edward Stewart. They were announcing it tomorrow in the press, and on television. He had to tell Lily, before she read it somewhere else. He shook Lily gently.

"We're going to land soon, but I also have something to tell you. I' going to be the Chief of Police of Happy Valley in six months."

"A desk job; are you sure?"

"Yes. it will be better for me and our family. I'll have more time with you. Rose, Caleb, and Clover."

"Good then. I've got news too. I've quit being Crown attorney. I'm thinking about setting up my own defence practice. I've been looking at an office near the courthouse. I will make my own hours and take the cases I want while my partner will take the rest."

"Who will be your partner?"

"I have an old friend from law school who has been practicing in Toronto and he's very unhappy since his wife passed away in Toronto. He has three children and his been thinking about living somewhere more rural."

"He?"

"Are you jealous?"

"No, I just wanted to know his name."

"His name is Justin MacBain, and his oldest daughter, is Brooke, Brooke has just turned eighteen and is going to Western next year as she's repeating grade 12. His other daughter is Mia, she's nine and he also has a daughter almost Clover's age, her name is Isabella. They have the same last name as their father. He has agreed yet but I think I can get him too. It's going to take some convincing and possibly another full-time lawyer, to pick up the slack. The firm is probably not going to exist for another six months, as I want to spend time with my daughters and you, so it's a good thing one of us have a job."

"I'll be working again as a cop, until then now that I'm better, but I'll that will give us drug and dental insurance," Emmett quipped.

"Just stay safe until then, no acting like a cowboy."

"I'll stay safe, because I have my family to come home to. Lily. I know you said yes before but, I love you; will you marry me?"

"I love you too, but when would we get married?"

"June! Doesn't the song go that the June bride is always a bride?"

"June. That sounds wonderful, but what about your new job?

"I'll take a month off, before the job and we'll enjoy ourselves. Clover can be our flower girl and Rose, our other one."

"What more could a bride want. I'll start planning a small wedding with Clover and Rose when I get home."

Grandma Katha who had overheard the exchange across the aisle said, "In lieu of your parents, Terrence and I want to give you the wedding of your dreams. You plan it and will pay for whatever you want."

'Within reason," Terrence added, "no rock stars performing at your wedding, or anything."

"Better cancel ***Laurel*** then Lily," Emmett laughed as Lily broke out into barrels of laughter that woke Clover up.

"Are we dere?" Clover asked,

"Yes. We 're just landing and then when the captain says we can take off our seatbelts and get off the plane."

As they got off the plane Lily couldn't believe who was waiting in the lounge for their flight to London, Ontario.

"Rose?"

"I couldn't wait mom. I had to see her."

"Are you feeling better?"

"Yes, mom. I'm much better I gained 15 pounds since I went to the program and they agreed I could do outpatient therapy from Happy Valley by ***Zoom***."

"Mom, who is this?" asked Clover interrupted.

"This is your big sister. Rose," Lily explained

"I have a sister? Then I'm Anna, not Elsa?"

"I hope, I'm your Elsa, Clover, because I love you more than any sister in the whole world."

"You are like Elsa your hair is yellow like hers, mine is yellow and brown like Anna's. I always wanted a sister."

Squatting down Rose then hugged Clover.

"I am so glad to be your big sister," Rose stated, "but your hair has beautiful red streaks in it, not brown.

"Ooh I like red. It's my favourite colour, tank you. I can't believe it I have a daddy, a mommy and a sister, Rose. Your name is like that story. grandma told me; I don't remember the name, but it had Rose in it.

"Was it Snow White and Rose Red?"

"Yes, can you tell me the story?"

Rose then told her the story

When she finished the story Clover asked, "Will you watch my movie on my I-pad?"

"I'd love to Clover."

"You have to sit beside me on the plane!"

"I don't think I can," Rose said sadly.

"I changed your ticket. So, Emmett can sit beside us and you can sit with Clover," Grandpa Terence interrupted.

"Oh, Grandpa Terrence, thank -you," Rose cried.

"Thank-you, Grandpa Terrence, "Clover parroted which brought a smile to Grandpa Terrence's face.

"So, when are we going to become a family?" Rose asked.

"We are a family," Clover answered.

"That's right Clover. We're all moving in together today, but your daddy and I are also going to get married,"

"You're finally getting married?" Rose screamed, excited.

"I gets to go to a wedding?"

"You both do. You'll be our flower girls, but it is a little way away. It's in June and it takes time to plan a wedding."

"I'm going to be in a wedding," Clover told everyone at the airport to big smiles.

Home in Happy Valley, Lily felt happy and then felt guilty, as her happiness had come at the cost of her mother's life. Heather had been kidnapped and murdered again it seemed to Lily, because that is what she thought had happened to Heather years ago, so, why was she grieving? The authorities had explained it to Lily that Heather had form of dementia and she had still managed to see danger for Lily and her grandchild and try to protect them despite he way Heather had done it. How could Lily hate her despite her pain? She couldn't she was slowly learning to forgive Heather so she could go on with her life. Captain Vitoria was on the mend and would be going on with his life. He might even visit soon, now that his attacker, Brad Owens was back in a secure mental facility. This was good, the guilt had been weighing on both Emmett and Lily. Lily felt they had enough to deal with as Amelia was dying. Amelia thought she had perhaps a year; but who knew except the grim reaper? Lily only hoped they could enjoy each other's company as long as possible. Amelia wanted to be her matron of honour and Lily hoped Amelia would be strong enough to stand or even attend. Just in case, Lily sadly made plans for a wheelchair, to allow Amelia to attend but silently mourned the moment she knew would come when she would have to say goodbye to Amelia. She put it in the back of her mind. Today was for happiness not sadness.

~0~

At a post box in Paris on February 15, two days ago, Jacob picked up their new identities and passports and then headed to the airport.

At the Paris Charles de Gaulle Airport they took their seats in first class in a plane going to Montreal. Jacob said he'd bought a home there. A home base where they could live, but still drive across the Quebec/ Ontario border to see Clover and Lily if they wanted to. Heather was happy they would be a family, one of these days again; but until then she'd have Jacob to live out her life with. She would settle for momentary glimpses of her daughter and granddaughters knowing that one day there would be, more.

Gerhard, the second watched, as his brother Jacob triumphed again,, stunned, He'd almost been able to get Heather; but she gotten away in

London England changing house and then when he found her that man had threatened him and Gerhard had seen those kind of eyes only in serial killers. He'd backed off to make his plans and then Jacob had shown up. Like a hero and taken her away again.

That bastard always kept wandering back in daddy's good books. Erhard had thought he could be the good brother and make Jacob relevant again, but here Jacob was breaking Gerhard and his father's trust. His love/ hate relationship with his brother always swung to protecting Jacob; why was that? What would dad say when he found out Jacob was shacking up with her? Heather Kelly would pay for turning his brother. Heather was responsible for his mother's death. Jacob didn't care about his half-sister, or his step-mother deaths at that woman's hands; but father did and so did Gerhard. The traitor would pay, but first he'd let them think her think they safe before he pounced. He might let Jacob live just to see Heather die and because he was after ll his flesh but her? Heather deserved torture and worse. Gerhard could wait a year, or even a year or two, if it took that long to plan her demise. Heather Kelly would pay for killing his sister and mother, or his name was Gerhard Brandt, the second.

~0~

Excerpt From~ The Butcher, the Baker, the Candlestick Maker

Preface:

In this story three evil men, are not what they seem but which three? Here is the traditional nursery rhyme I based it on about three men, you should avoid, they seem nice, but they not to be trusted, but as I said before who are the three?

Rub-a-dub-dub

Three men in a tub,

And who do you think they be?

The butcher, the baker,

The candlestick maker,

They all jumped out of a rotten potato!

Turn 'em out knaves all three.

Belinda Allen the owner of Allen's Cleaning on Wheels was a hard boss. She had begrudgingly given Sarita Acharya the week off and Sarita had spent time with her two daughters enjoying the wonderful August sunshine.

Sarita was about to have her vacation interrupted, however, by an urgent phone call from Belinda.

"I said I would call if I needed you and I need you to work," Belinda stated, The Bailer's cabin needs cleaning. They rented it out and they would like their cabin ready for their return tomorrow."

"That will take more than an hour I want time and half, and a raise of two dollars," Sarita bargained.

"You just have to add some chlorine to the hot tub turn it on and disinfect approximately five minutes or more so there are no germs COVID or anything else. Then clean the filter. Wipe down the pillows, the control panel and skirt with decontaminates and then wipe the hot tub cover off with a cleaner that won't scrape and ruin the cover, but disinfect it. All and all it should take about seventeen or eight minutes and unless the tenants were animals it shouldn't take that long to clean the cabin."

"Time and half, and two more dollars an hour, Belinda."

"Okay since I'm in a jam."

Sarita called her sister Meera and asked her to met her there so they could complete the work quicker giving her the codes for the place. Taking out her supplies to her car Sarita drove to the edge of Happy Valley where the Bailer cabin stood.

Entering through the gate in which she keyed in the code, she went straight to the hot tub cleaned the top of the cover and removed it to clean out the tub. She was about to put the chlorine in when she noticed fabric in the hot tub and cursed the careless people who had left it there. She looked around and finding a mop handle she poked it with it trying to remove it only to meet flesh. There was a dead woman in the tub. The long brown hair spilled across the cloth. Sarita Acharya looked on in horror as the body turned over. It looked like someone she knew, but that could be, could it? Her brain screamed, yes, and all she could do was scream, "Meera. Meera!!"

~0

Chapter 1 – Where's Brooke?

Emmett Rogers was settling into his job as Police Chief of Happy Valley, when the call came in about a suspicious death in a hot tub at the Bailer's place. The poor maid, or did they call them sanitation engineers nowadays? Anyway, one, Sarita Acharya had thought at first the victim was her younger eighteen-year sister, Meera. Meera arrived as the body was being removed, having got a flat tire and changing the tire herself. It was not so that made it imperative, that they found out who this person was. People drowned from time to time getting drunk and passing out, but the cop that had responded to this told the dispatcher that it was a young girl, possibly a teenager. They would no more after the autopsy, but there had not been any reports of a missing girl. He hoped to hell they catch the culprit soon, but it was going to be harder since the Bailer's had rented out their cabin. The Bailers were expected home at 9 a. m. according to the cleaning company, maybe there be some information from them then.

Frankly Emmett was itching to work on the case; but he was the Chief it wasn't his job but someone else's. so, he did the next best thing he sent Kendall Evans his former partner and the best cop he knew.

His thoughts were interrupted by his phone ringing,

"Chief Rogers. How can I help you?"

"Emmett Rogers?"

"Yes, who is this?

"It's Lily's law partner, Justin MacBain. Listen, I've got a huge problem it may be nothing but…"

"What's the problem, Mr. MacBain?"

"Justin, please. My daughter, Brooke is missing."

"Brooke's missing?"

"Yes! I called around and the friend she went out late last night."

"You've heard nothing since?"

No, she hasn't called and she's always called before, even if she's five minutes late."

"I see do you have any other information about where she planned on going last night?"

"She was invited to a party with some girl she met. I asked her to call me if she felt unsafe, or she didn't want to stay. I know since she's eighteen, and the police will think she ran away; but I'm telling you Brooke had plans with her sister, Mia today she wouldn't have just run away anywhere," pleaded Justin MacBain.

"Give me a description of your daughter?"

"Brooke is five eight, one hundred and twenty pounds with long dark hair and was I think wearing a knee length blue jean skirt and pink tee shirt."

Emmett did not know what to tell him should he tell him a teenage girl matching his daughter's description was found dead but that her features had been obscured by hot water?

"Can you meet me at the station Justin?"

"I'll get the next-door neighbour to watch the girls and I'll be down to fill out the paperwork in fifteen minutes," Justin answered before Emmett could explain why.

Emmett prayed that it wasn't Justin MacBain's daughter since Lily knew the child, but this poor girl was someone's daughter and that grieved him. If she was murdered then they had to find the murderer and bring him or her to justice.

~0~

Excerpt from Dead Center

Preface:

The thing I learned about Driftwood.

Colorado (since I'd moved here from Chicago), just wait and the weather would change (after all a thunderstorm could plunge the temperature 30 degrees in just 15 minutes). The great thing though was that it also was sunnier. The old folks told me they didn't need to look at a forecast; look to the mountains and you can see the weather coming long before it reached Driftwood.

That said the last two days had been horrendous; nothing but a deluge of rain. Somehow, I hadn't expected the rain. A river of water ran through downtown causing flooding and hazardous conditions for the citizens of Driftwood. I that wasn't bad enough I'd received a report a half hour ago that Fair Creek had overflowed its banks and was now creeping towards the homesteads of a number of Driftwood citizens.

I was just past Turner's Corner when I noticed something lying in the middle of the road about 800 yards up. As I got closer, I noticed some clothing and realized it was a person lying dead center of the road.

I drove a little close and got out of my patrol car to approach the body and I heard the woman moan. I then ran closer calling on my cell for an ambulance. This woman looked so familiar… but that was impossible. The woman she looked like was my ex-wife and she was still serving part of her fifteen years for trying to kill me.

My cell phone rang and I answered it to Gordon Chum who had left the F. B. I.to become one of my deputies.

"Gee? Oh, good I finally got you. She's escaped."

"Who has escaped?"

"Gina has escaped not only that they but my sources think she's headed to Driftwood. She heard about Stella-Marie's death."

"Oh crap, she might already be here."

"Why do you say that, Gee?"

"I found a woman who looks like Gina and she's dead on the road," I stated.

"Where?"

I told Gordon and he said he'd be here soon. I hung up and my cell phone rang again.so I answered it, "Gordon?"

"Oh, is my other quarry in town too? Fantastic. Do you like my present?" the voice I recognized as Luis Cervantes.

"Fair warning then let the games begin, I'm back," he continued then suddenly I had dead air on my cell phone.

~0~

Look for Book 3 of the Sheriff Bullet Mysteries~ Dead Center at your local book retailer.

If you have enjoyed London Bridge is Broken Down~ A Tale of two Londons, please consider leaving me a few words in a review where you purchased this e-book.

Sincerely S. G. Lee

Excerpt from ~ Penny Saved A Murder Earned- *Chapter 1 – Bloody Shoes*

The book that started the Kelly Murder Mysteries~

"A penny saved is a penny earned" ~ Benjamin Franklin

The blood streaked across the floor, but he had carefully sidestepped it. Stupid bitch! She got what she deserved. How dare she defile his Angel's property? He hadn't left a trace...had he? No, he was too clever by half.

A voice he didn't recognize interrupted his thoughts, "I didn't spot you entering.

Working late, dear? Of course, I forgot; you have an early opening tomorrow."

The man strode closer to the killer and the body lying on the floor, "Wait a minute, you aren't the lady. Who are you? You shouldn't be here," the man continued clearly alarmed.

"You shouldn't be here either," the murderer insisted.

"You, you killed Megan. I'm telling."

"Really? You know this was something you shouldn't be allowed to see."

"I'm leaving. I didn't notice anything," the man lied, witnessing the blood.

"I'm sorry pal. Wrong place, wrong time!" the killer answered.

The homeless man ran dodging racks, finally deciding to hide behind some shelving. The killer ran after him, puzzled for a moment because he could see no trace of the homeless person. The murderer then laughed, as he realized how foolish the vagrant was being, his stench gave him away. He subdued the man with a Taser gun. Waiting seconds, he then pulled the man from his hiding place. Taking ties from within his pocket; he fastened the man's arms and feet. Satisfied that the homeless person was now trussed up like a turkey, he smiled.

"P...P....P...Please! I don't want to die!" the man cried, visibly sweating and starting to shake.

The man tried to kick out his legs and arms but failed.

"You've heard about fate? Well sorry but this is your fate, buddy!" the murderer explained.

"P...P...P... Please, I'm begging you! Couldn't you let me go? I won't tell! I'll move to another city. Besides who would listen to a homeless man?"

"Someone would. My Angel would."

The homeless man then smiled as if to gain trust from this killer, "You won't hurt the lady who owns the store, will you?" he asked.

"I would never harm my Angel. How dare you?" the killer responded outraged.

"S...S...S... Sorry! I didn't mean to insult you! Please just let me go. I'm harmless ask anyone...."

"What is your name?"

"Why do you need my name?" He asked looking puzzled then reconsidering he answered, "My name is Al."

The killer put his gloves back on and smoothed them and then turned his back on his victim.

"You're going to kill me now. Aren't you? Just don't harm the sweet lady who owns this store. Will it hurt?" the man asked resigned.

"I would never hurt my Angel. She is sweet, isn't she? Unfortunately, that also makes unscrupulous people take advantage of her."

"I promise I would never take advantage of her kindness. I wouldn't!!! She's the best part of my day and this city, Happy Valley, Ontario. She picked me up from the gutter and helped me."

"I know you wouldn't and it hurts me to do this. Tell you what though, I'll make your death painless because I like you, Al," the killer offered, feeling suddenly sorry for the man. Then he checked himself. Living on the streets was hell; maybe he was doing the guy a favour? Yes, of course he was.

Taking a pill bottle out of his pocket and opening the dispenser, he placed some in a coffee cup he took from the sideboard. He filled the cup with the tepid coffee from the coffee pot, stirring the pills in rapidly.

"C...c...c... couldn't you let me go? I won't tell and I'll watch over her when you're not here."

"Sorry, times up, Al. Here now, drink this coffee," the assassin commanded placing the mug at Al's lips.

Al tried not to drink and spit some of the coffee out, but the assassin plugged his nose and the cup was soon empty.

"Admit it Al, you had a crappy life. Just give in and go to the light. I hear good things wait there for people like you," the killer stated.

Al tried to fight some more, but he soon found it was losing battle. Al's breathing slowed as he slipped into a deep sleep and stopped breathing altogether. His age and living on the streets made the pills work fast.

Now what to do with the body? The killer thought. His Angel must not find this man's remains here, bad enough he left Megan's body here for his Angel to find. He couldn't hide Megan though she needed to be found. Every needed to know she suffered for her crime. Maybe even his Angel would see Megan's evil and protect herself from people like that. This man, Al however knew his Angel and she cared about him. It was so like her to look after the homeless. He could let her cry over Al. Where could he put the man so he wouldn't be found?

The dumpster of course...the perfect place for Al! The day after tomorrow was garbage day. Covered in garbage no one would find Al.

~0~

The next day

Lily

Ominous clouds replaced the morning's sunlight, turning the skies to shades of deep purple and navy blue, streaked with gray. Lily Kelly stared at the sky for moment, and then departed the courthouse doors in Happy Valley, Ontario, Canada, skipping down the steps. The city looked its age of over a hundred, as the buildings downtown looked old and decrepit. If only the town could find some money to fix downtown Lily thought.

Then her mind turned to Amelia, her cousin and best friend. Amelia needed Lily to support her in her grief. Lily had a fight with her husband Horace, again, this morning about how much time he was spending at the office, and how much time she spent supporting Amelia.

Lily was always working, and so was Horace, so how much time was Rose their fourteen-year-old daughter really getting?

Lily had won in court, but all she could think about was her family. Everyone needed her and she felt like she was being pulled in three different directions. Something had to give and it looked like it was her job. She would have to cut back on some of her work. Her family had to come first.

Lily stumbled some more over the steps, only stopping from hurrying across the courtyard to her office, when her heel broke on her shoe. Today was supposed to be about her victory after her win in court; but it appeared with her expensive shoe's heel breaking, she was mistaken. They ought to get the ruts in the paving stones fixed; that was her reflection as she cursed her bad break. What did they say about omens? Maybe she should have taken a hint from the heavens' darkening? She noted as her bad luck had seemed to get worse with the arrival of some reporters.

"Ms. Kelly, give us a statement about the Rockwood case?" yelled one reporter.

"Ms. Kelly, how does the Sulimani family feel about your victory?" yelled another.

One bold reporter stepped forward, "Crown Attorney Kelly, congratulations on your win. Was it hard to try a case which involved a council member?" asked Paul Knight from the local television station, thrusting a microphone in Lily's face.

"Anyone who commits a crime in Happy Valley will be tried by the Crown with the full force of the law, despite their office. So no, I did not find it difficult to do my job," Lily replied testily.

"Thank you, Ms. Kelly. What does the Sulimani family think about the judgment?"

"Amani Sulimani was five years old, when Zebadiah Rockwood's truck went through a red light. His truck struck the back of the Sulimani's SUV killing her. He then left the scene pursued by good Samaritans, who wished to stop Mr. Rockwood from continuing driving drunk: a pursuit caused by Mr. Rockwood's actions, which put a number of lives in danger."

"Will the family be comforted with this conviction?" queried another reporter.

"Amani Sulimani existed as their only child. Mr. Rockwood's conviction will not bring her back, but hopefully will bring some peace of mind to her family knowing he will be behind bars." Lily answered.

"Do you sense, given your own personal tragedies that you'll be able to get a sentence fitting the crime?"

"My family's history does not come into my trial cases, only the person's guilt."

"And when will sentencing take place?" asked another reporter.

"Sentencing will take place next month."

"Thank you, Ms. Kelly. This is Paul Knight reporting, with an update on the Zebadiah Rockwood's drunken driving case. Zebadiah Rockwood was a long-time council member here in Happy Valley. He took a leave of absence to deal with his legal issues. Mr. Rockwood was charged with impaired driving causing death, two counts of failing to remain at the scene of an accident and dangerous driving last December. When asked about the conviction today Mr. Rockwood and his lawyer issued a no comment. We will have the complete story for you at six pm. Paul Knight reporting for CHPV-TV."

Lily hated speaking on camera, even though it was part of her job as the Crown attorney, so she was glad the scrum had been completed.

She hated sounding tough and unyielding; but it was all in the description of her job title. She had fought difficult challenges to get this job and she had to work hard and fight hard to keep it. After all there were aspects of her job her, she loved like putting the bad people that would harm others away. The press was gone and she was now free to go to her office to file her reports and leave early. She crossed the street, entered her building and went straight up to her office.

"Victory is mine!" Lily Kelly cried triumphantly as she walked into her office.

"So, you won?" asked Colleen Finn, her administrative assistant.

"Yes, I bested that idiot, Michael Taylor. He thought he would beat me in court. He actually believed his client would win."

"Good for you, boss, I knew you would nail his lily-white ass to the wall. He's such a scumbag lawyer all his clients seem to be as guilty as hell."

"Colleen! Language! But thank-you," Lily answered, showing pearly white teeth.

Colleen looked expectantly at Lily and she felt stupid did she miss something? Oh, the joke! Lily hadn't laughed at Colleen's wit.

"Funny, I got it. Zebadiah Rockwood's sentencing takes place next month, but he will be held until then; no bail, no goodbyes to his favourite watering hole. As the Crown, I'll recommend the longest sentence I can get that he can serve. It's victories like these which make my job worthwhile. I don't know how much satisfaction this will give that little girl's family, but at least they'll know her killer remains in jail. He can't take another life again, because he will be incarcerated."

Lily went over to her desk and sat down.

"Can you imagine Michael Taylor, tried to use the defence that Rockwood was not drunk. Just tired? He claimed Rockwood drank only after the accident, while driving his company's truck; therefore, the company couldn't possibly be responsible,"

"I believe you told me that before," Colleen commented, "However I'm glad you proved he'd drank so much before getting in the truck. That proved he was legally under the influence when the accident occurred. I hope I was some help in that aspect."

"Yes, you were invaluable."

"Thanks, Lily."

"It's still early; only nine forty-five, and my day's clear until what, two-thirty?"

"That's correct." Colleen replied.

Colleen checked a day planner, frowning, "Is everything okay, Lily? You seem a little down."

"Everything is fine. Amelia's grand opening starts at noon, but I promised to be there sooner if possible. If I go right now, I'll surprise her," Lily grabbed her coat to leave.

"I'm glad she's doing so well. Although after what happened, Amelia needs the encouragement. Please tell her, I'll try to get to her store another day. I hope her store has great success."

"Thank-you, I will tell Amelia. Hold all my calls Colleen. Unless it's urgent then call my cell."

"I'll do that. What time should I say you'll be back?" Colleen responded to a departing Lily.

"Tell whoever asks that I'll be back after two p.m..."

"And if they ask where you are?" Colleen questioned.

"Tell them I'm meeting with a witness," Lily replied with a wink.

"If there's cake bring me back a piece. Please, boss?" Colleen begged.

"I ordered a cake, but it is not supposed to arrive until one thirty so we'll see. I'm leaving now. Remember only urgent calls to my cell phone." Lily cautioned, leaving through the front door.

She twisted her shimmering, brown hair, back up into its traditional bun. Pulling out her cell phone, she dialled Amelia's store. There was no answer. How odd! Amelia must be busy putting out last minute stock.

~0~

A few minutes ago

A lone male walked into the store. His left hand held a gun while his right hand steadied it. He strode in with caution. His dark brown eyes dart from corner to corner, searching for an assailant. His well over six-foot tall frame slouched. Ruggedly handsome, with dark brown hair clipped short to his head; he was dressed in a dark blue jacket and dress pants; a badge is also clipped to his belt buckle. Finding the scene secure he putting his gun away and pulled a pair of gloves out of his suit coat pocket and a pair of booties, which he slipped on his shoes.

He checked the victim. No pulse. Advancing forward, he bent down to check the second woman; her phone still in her hand, her head bloody. He noted the second victim was still breathing, though unconscious. He looked around, as if waiting for someone. Deciding they weren't coming yet; he took out a mini recorder. He started scanning the scene and speaking aloud.

"This is Sergeant Detective Emmett Rogers. I am at the scene of a homicide, at Quirks, one forty-five Maple Street. A woman lays sprawled out across the floor. The woman's arms are positioned underneath her, as if to break her fall.

The back of her head and her long blonde hair are streaked in rusty-brown blood, as well as her clothing below the hair. Blood pools across the floor spiralling out in two long streams. Footprints are noticeable, as if someone stepped through the drying blood. The weapon appears to be a pair of scissors, found beneath the victim. I have marked both of these."

The man spoke aloud as he walked around, carefully avoiding contaminating the evidence, by stepping over a paper cup.

"A coffee cup... possibly one of those lattes is overturned. I'm sure the forensics team can determine this if necessary. Its contents are also spilled on the floor and countertop. Coffee is spilled at the front door and possibly on the shoes. The second victim's shoes are not on the bruised victim, but on the floor. The shoes can be found near an overturned ladder, at the front door. It appears the woman, who appears unconscious, may have been carrying a ladder and toy stock to place on the shelves, when she slipped in the blood.

The man paused to think.

"This might be a setup by the second victim to cover the actual crime. The woman, however, seems to have the victim's blood all over her clothes and hands like she crawled through the blood. I believe there are two possible scenarios here. One the owner of the shop, one Amelia Kelly (the unconscious person), murdered her employee or unknown victim and set this up to appear a perpetrator broke in and killed her accidentally hurting herself in the process. Or two... it is at it now seems that she stumbled on the crime scene and harmed herself."

He pulled out a notebook again and examined the room taking some more taking notes.

"Is it a robbery gone wrong? It is too soon to tell. The store owner will be en-route to hospital as soon as the EMTs have arrived.

Interview to follow. The time is now ten twenty a.m.," he concluded turning off his recorder.

He examined the room scribbling on his notepad.

~0~

Now

Lily and Detective Emmett Rogers

The man's eyes turn and his vision focused completely. A woman entered the store. His eyes took in her tall and slender form and her long shimmering brown hair, pulled into a tight roll. He noted she was closely followed by the Emergency technicians and gave a sigh of relief. The woman entering the store had brilliant blue eyes. He had a feeling she often turned heads, even dressed as she was, in her business attire. But he noted something about the way she walked screamed money and upper class.

"Oh no, Amelia!" she screamed and tried to rush to Amelia, but was stopped by the man's arm.

"This is a crime scene ma'am. We don't want you disrupting our evidence. Let the EMTs and detectives do their job. Then you can go to ...you're er...friend?" Sergeant Detective Rogers commanded.

"Crime scene? What has happened?" Lily asked politely, wanting to be cooperative.

"Ma'am, I'll know better after I assess the scene. Until then, please remain near the front door." ordered Detective Rogers briskly.

"I promise I'll stay out of the way; but at least can I get her Adrienne Changs?"

"What or who, are Adrienne Changs?" said Detective Rogers looking totally perplexed.

"Shoes, those shoes right there!" Lily pointed to a pair of heels lying behind the yellow tape.

"You're worried about shoes? Woman! Do you have any idea of what's going on here?" Detective Rogers snapped, shaking his head.

"You sexist pig!" countered Lily under her breath, "Men!" Losing her temper now and louder she continued, "Those shoes are worth five hundred dollars! And she probably wore them for what a half an hour? And you want me to walk away and leave them to be destroyed in some kind of liquid!"

"Liquid that's blood! And five hundred dollars for shoes? Is she crazy?" Detective Rogers asked dumfounded.

"No! She's not crazy. How dare you?" Lily asked suddenly outraged.

He was smug, wasn't he? Handsome yes, but oh so smug, she questioned herself. That wasn't important! Amelia was injured on the floor and he questioned her? Instead of letting her go to her cousin! What was wrong with Lily? Why was she so worried and focused on the shoes? They were only shoes. Amelia was injured; who cared about footwear?

"Sorry, ma'am, the shoes are evidence now. Name? Occupation? Address?" Detective Rogers barked, ignoring her statement.

"I want to see your identification first, and then you'll get the information," insisted Lily.

"I am Sergeant Detective Emmett Rogers," the man revealed, showing his police badge.

"Oh, that's funny," Lily uttered laughing, "If you and Amelia were introduced it would be Aem and Em."

Lily followed this up by hysterically laughing and then alternatively crying. What was wrong with her? She never lost it like this. She always appeared a professional. She had seen crime scenes. She could handle this. Couldn't she? Amelia would be okay. Wouldn't she?!

"Get a hold of yourself Lily. You have embarrassed yourself," Lily heard this voice in her head, she recognized as her father's. Odd how her dad's voice, came back to her now, she rarely saw him, since he lived in Prague and he only called about twice a year.

"Ma'am, what you are saying is not remotely funny. Are you all, right? Put your head between your knees if you feel lightheaded. I think your friend's relatively fine. She might have a head injury and possibly a broken leg, but she'll be okay." Sergeant Detective Rogers then turned to the Emergency technicians (EMTs) to seek confirmation demanded, "Right?"

"Should be. But head injuries can be serious," the one EMT replied.

Sergeant Detective Rogers shot him a disapproving look.

"Yes, the Sergeant Detective is right. She'll be fine. She'll be taken to the hospital for treatment," the Emergency Technician agreed, finally.

"See...what did I tell you? Now that we have that out of the way; I need to see some identification and then get some answers to my questions. Name? Address? Occupation? The reason you are here?" Detective Rogers barked at Lily.

"Amelia's my best friend and more. This should have been the greatest day of her life, her opening of her new store; a one of kind toy and collectibles retailer. A grand opening and now it's ruined. Who did this to her?" Lily asked, uncharacteristically wringing her hands and still trying to regain her calm, as thoughts of Amelia's demise threatened to enter her mind.

"Ma'am, she slipped in blood. She hit her head on the floor and on the ladder. No one harmed her. She did this to herself," explained Sergeant Detective Rogers.

"I realize she's clumsy, but she didn't put blood there to trip in," defended Lily angrily.

"No, the blood was spilled by whoever killed the woman behind the counter."

"Someone is dead behind the counter?" Lily responded shocked and surprised.

"No comment; as I explained Ma'am this is an active crime scene. Now as I asked before what is your name?" Detective Rogers insisted forcefully again.

"Lily Kelly-Brooksfield. My husband is Horace Brooksfield, the mayor. We live down the street on Beaconfield. Do you want the number? It's nine hundred and sixty-two." she replied condescendingly.

"If you're Mayor Brooksfield's wife… then you're the Crown Attorney." Coming to this realization, Sergeant Detective Rogers hid a sigh.

"Please update me on this active crime scene, now," commanded Lily pulling back her shoulders.

Emmett Rogers put on his professional face and smiled. The smile was just so warm and inviting that Lily felt warm all over. Lily frowned back at him; she was just felt so angry. This cop who grinned back at her was the biggest reason. She was a married woman. She shouldn't be attracted to a cop who apparently existed to give her grief and solve a murder. She threw back her shoulders again. It was okay to look at someone attractive, she excused herself. Everyone looks, and most of the time it meant nothing. It's only if you acted on any attraction, it became wrong. She would never act on the temptation. Besides he appeared to be the most annoying man she'd ever met.

"Ma'am, you know I can't fill you in on any of this case. You'll have to recuse yourself from this case, as you're familiar with the crime scene." Detective Rogers emphasized, once again interrupting Lily's thoughts.

“Why don't you just come out and say what you think. You consider me a suspect,” Lily uttered.

“A lot of people are suspects in my book. I have to make a case for them committing the crime or I have to eliminate them as suspects. And don’t attempt to solve this yourself; amateurs just get in the way.” Detective Rogers explained, his eyes wandering.

Lily was slightly amused. Detective Rogers thought she wanted to insinuate herself into this murder investigation? She might not have before that comment, but she did now. He seemed to be focusing on Amelia or Lily as his prime suspect. Lily knew neither of them had committed this murder, so that meant she had no choice but to find out for herself who had committed this crime. She would pretend she wanted nothing to do with this situation, even as far as passing it off to her underling Barbara. After all she could always investigate behind the scenes.

Spotting the emergency technicians Detective Rogers exclaimed “Oh good, the ambulance has arrived to take the victim to the hospital. Now can we can get down to brass tacks; you can fill me in on these people and anything else you know or have held back from me."

"I want to go with her," Lily protested.

Lily pulled herself back taking several steps back putting distance between herself and this cop. It was odd, how alive she felt when she jousted with him. He was a cop investigating a murder and she was married.

"Stop this now Lily!" She told herself.

"Ma'am, I realize you want to go see your friend. Before I could release you from the scene, I need something from you. We need you to identify the other victim. Maybe you'll recognize her when I turn over the body." Detective Rogers explained, softening a little, as he slipped on another pair of gloves.

"Only if you'll stop calling me Ma'am. Call me Lily or Crown Attorney Kelly, but not Ma'am. It makes me feel eighty years old."

"If it will get you to identify the victim...thank-you Crown Attorney Kelly."

"Let's look, shall we?" Lily agreed.

Lily took a breath as she gathered herself to observe who lay there dead. She gasped as she stared over the counter to see the back of the woman's head. She covered her mouth in horror.

"Good grief! I never realized they appear so alike from the back," replied Lily shocked.

"Who do you think she looks like ma'am?" demanded Detective Rogers.

"What did I say about ma'am? Don't they give you sensitivity training at Police College? You want to know who this is? This is Megan, Megan Fowler. She's an employee of Amelia's. But she works evenings she's...is.... was a college student. I can't believe this is Megan. Megan is such a sweet girl and worked part-time to be able to go to school and support her mother. Why would someone kill her? Do you think it's possible someone mistook her for Amelia?" Lily rambled, tears slipping from her eyes.

"That's a possibility, ma'am. We will explore all aspects."

"I know the drill, Sergeant Detective Rogers." Lily gave the detective a mock salute, "Why can't you admit that they mistook Megan for Amelia?"

"We don't have any of the facts yet, Ms. Kelly," replied Detective Rogers.

"What about Amelia? Is she in any danger?" asked Lily. "If I were to speculate, I suppose that could be a possibility," Detective Rogers answered non-committally.

They both watched as the technicians gathered the evidence and blood samples and took pictures before the body was taken away.

"Will someone be assigned to guard her and keep her safe?" Lily asked getting exasperated.

"That's in motion, Crown Attorney Kelly," Detective Rogers explained, trying not to sound annoyed that she's telling him how to do his job.

Detective Rogers and Lily turned as another cop swaggered into the store. Burly and well over six feet tall, his hair was dark like Detective Rogers. Unlike Detective Rogers, this man preened like a peacock; Lily was aware of the type. Guys like him smiled with their mouths and not their eyes. They thought all women should admire them and only them. She noted his smile went as far as his lips.

“What have you got here, Emmett?”

“Nothing you need to be concerned about, Brad,” Detective Rogers replied, obvious tension showing between the two.

“You should be able to get some great publicity out of this one,” Brad said loudly to Detective Rogers.

Brad then strutted over to the murder scene.

“It’s my case, Brad,” Detective Rogers insisted.

“I’m not trying to interfere,” Brad persisted walking around, “I just thought if you needed some help, I would lend a hand. It doesn’t look like something you could handle on your own.”

“I don’t need help, thanks, Brad. I don’t need you messing up my crime scene.” Detective Rogers declared “I’ve got it all under control.

“It doesn’t look that way to me. I would solve this case quickly. You could use me in your corner,” Brad continued.

"We don't need you. Now the Crown attorney is here, so I have it all in hand. Goodbye, Brad." Detective Rogers practically spat.

"Ah, the lovely Crown attorney Kelly is here. Can't go now," Brad exclaimed trying to sound charming but failing miserably.

"And you are?" asked Lily putting her full aristocratic chill in to her voice.

"I'm Brad Owens, at your service, Attorney Kelly. Sergeant Detective Brad Owens. I use to be Emmett's partner," Brad explained smiling and pointing to Detective Rogers.

Detective Rogers rolled his eyes. "Thank God you're not anymore," He stated under his breath loud enough for only he and Lily to hear.

"So, what do you think, Crown Attorney? Was it a robbery gone wrong?" asked Brad.

"I'm not sure. Why do I bother to tell you this? This isn't your case," Lily commented suddenly not willing to share with Brad.

She didn't know why. Something about his smile, and the way Emmett Rogers had reacted to him made her dislike him. Brad's smile was phony, like a used car salesman. It was slick and slimy. That wasn't fair to used car sales people. Lily was sure they were more honest than this phoney, Brad Owens. Lily had come across a lot of people in her job. She certainly felt she was a good judge of character. In fact, she could spot a phoney a mile away. Detective Emmett Rogers, unlike Brad Owens, appeared like he knew his job. She'd heard of him many times, but had never run into him on the job until today. Thank goodness for the Internet on her phone. He was a dedicated cop. He had done his time and had come up through the ranks, strictly on merit. Detective Rogers didn't seem to like Brad Owens and that was reason enough for Lily not to trust him.

Emmett Rogers had an exemplary record as a police officer; she trusted his instincts and knowledge over this smarmy, Detective Brad Owens. He'd get to the bottom of this. Lily wished he would let her leave soon and check on Amelia. They had spent their teen years together and were as close as sisters. She'd always felt responsible for Amelia, being two years older. She wanted to make sure Amelia was okay.

"Okay. If you don't need my help, I'm leaving because I have work to do. There are other crimes to investigate." Brad answered leaving, "See you around Emmett."

"Not if I see you first," muttered Emmett under his breath.

"So, am I free to go?" Lily demanded.

Emmett then offered her his pen.

"I have your address, so as long as you sign here in my notebook. "You are free to go," he said gesturing.

Lily glanced over at Detective Owens and watched him leave before reaching for the book. She then signed her signature with a flourish. Detective Rogers scanned the signature, thinking momentarily it was just as elegant as Lily. He shook his head, reminding himself to stay connected to reality.

"So, I am free to go, Detective?" Lily repeated.

“I’ll be checking in on your friend, of course, and I may need to follow-up with you later, but as of now, you are free to go.” he smiled, already exhausted.

“I would expect nothing else from you, Detective Rogers.”

As she got into her car, Lily breathed a sigh of relief she had finally been able to leave the store. She buckled up her seatbelt and put her car in gear.

Backing the car up, Lily pulled out into the street and narrowly missed getting hit by a car, she didn’t view. Luckily the other driver slammed on his brakes. She noticed the male driver shouting, “Stupid woman driver” as she read his lips in her rear-view mirror. He was justified in his anger. It had been her fault, but she didn't have time to dwell.

She headed down the road toward the hospital; despite her resolve her mind wandered. She thought about poor Megan’s mother getting the news of her daughter's death. It would kill Lily to get news like that about her adopted daughter, Rose.

What kind of monster kills a young woman? Why did, whomever it was, have to kill Megan? It wasn’t a robbery, she’d read in Detective Rogers' notes, when he gave his notebook to her to sign her statement. As Lily drove, more questions flooded into her head. Was Amelia the real target? Megan certainly appeared like Amelia from the back.

Amelia didn't appear too hurt. Maybe she suffered a concussion? Concussions could be serious; she knew from her readings. The EMT hadn't said Amelia was in serious condition though. Not that the EMT could explain before Emmett Rogers got on his case. Revving the engine, she waited impatiently for the light to go green. Once Lily reached the hospital, she could reassure herself, Amelia was all right.

~0~

Excerpt from Love's Labour's Won

Preface:

Love's Labour's Won

Sarah sought a job,

Biting back a sob,

Her love and life,

All constant strife,

And filled with unbroken sorrow,

Like there was no tomorrow.

She thought her future,

Safely to be assured,

Instead of that Sarah found,

Many wonders to astound,

The world changed forever,

Yet the pull of a tether,

For the prize she sought,

And the joy and pain it wrought,

And all that she had done,

Was "Love's Labour's Won"

Written by S.G. Lee

Chapter 1 - Want Ads

Life was getting Sarah down. She was twenty-one years old and what did she have to show for it? Did she have a career? No, she didn't. Did life produce a boyfriend, husband or children? Another no! Or even a significant other? She had no one, no one to care if she lived or died. She had worked so many dead-end jobs; too many to count.

She had once been a Wal-Mart Greeter and even spent a winter as a telemarketer selling lawn services for the upcoming spring. She failed miserably not making that job a success either. Numerous hang-ups ensued and no sales.

They kept her for a month and then said… "I'm sorry you're not working out."

Like, duh. She didn't complete any sales. She had to make a living somehow.

She scanned the want ads. There remained lots of jobs for coffee servers, but she was so tired of smiling and serving food to people. Then she spotted the ad, the ad which made her sit up and take notice.

Companion wanted.

Must be young presentable and personable.

Apply by phone at 555-5555 only serious inquires need apply.

Must have two references

What was this some kind of weird scam luring young woman to their peril? Really, how dramatic was she being?

Sarah normally ignored such an ad, but she was getting short on cash and the rent was due next week.

She didn't have the eight hundred and fifty dollars the landlord wanted for this dump…err…wonderful furnished apartment. She'd be out on the street if she didn’t earn some money. It wasn’t like she had a lot of friends, which she could ask to crash on their sofas. Melanie would have let her, but she was off on a modeling job in France. Melanie had sublet her apartment to a yuppie couple that obviously didn’t know Sarah.

Should I or shouldn't I call? Sarah thought. I mean was it safe? What if the employers subsisted as white slavers? The people Gran were always warning her about growing up? Gran’s notions bordered on the ridiculous, of course. So, I should just seize the opportunity. Sarah thought. Gran was gone and so were her worrisome and outdated ideas. Sarah looked at the ads again.

Barista wanted must have previous experience and two references.

Must be prepared to clean and carry up to 40 pounds of product.

The ad’s specifications were a new take on the job. They were warning people that they would be heavy lifting. Hmm, generally they told you this when you started the job. But forty pounds, what the heck?

Were they having the baristas carry coffee beans? There had to be another job offer somewhere in these online sites. She scanned the ads once again.

No nothing in the ads but a companion job. A companion job didn't sound so bad. Did it? She needed a job and jobs were scarce that she qualified for right now. She had to at least try to get the job, didn't she? She took a huge breath and dialled the number.

"Hello," the voice said on the other end of the line.

A real live person answered instead of the answering machine Sarah expected. Sarah took another deep breath.

"Uh I'd like to apply for the job; you placed in the Free Press." She replied with all the enthusiasm she could muster.

“I see… and what makes you believe you’re the person we are looking for?” Asked the voice on the other end of the line

“I like people and people like me. I am often stopped by strangers and they always seem compelled to tell me their complete life histories,” Sarah replied.

“Uh huh, and how do you respond to these indignities to your peace and quiet?” asked the voice.

“I am aware not everyone would listen; I find it fascinating to hear the stories people tell and to just listen if that's what they need. In some way I feel I can help them. It's not an intrusion,” Sarah answered without even thinking.

“I comprehend one such as you, may have led a very difficult life. People do not always return the kindness to that you seem to offer so freely. You are an old soul,” replied the voice sounding distinctively male, and little too familiar.

“Well…I don’t know if this is odd or what but a long time ago, I decided I liked me. If others find me a Pollyanna; a person who is too kind, too naive for the world, that’s their problem. I like being different even if others think me odd, I can only be me. Oh, I can't believe I'm telling you this, in a job interview no less. Now you'll never hire me and I'm sorry I've wasted your time, sir." Sarah responded embarrassed and about to hang up.

"Miss, please don't hang up. I think you are an excellent potential candidate for this rather unique job."

"You think I might be the person you want?" asked Sarah incredulously.

"Well clearly my employer would have the final say, but you sound as if you might make my short list of candidates."

"Not to make you mad or anything and lose my chance at this job; but don't you think you should know more about me?"

"I am a very good judge of character. That's why my employer trusts me in this manner," stated the man with an almost mesmerizing voice. Sarah felt herself believing every word he said.

"Wow, you must be in a prestigious job," replied Sarah without thinking again.

"The only possible drawback to your employment might be your tendency to forthcoming with your thoughts. Do you do this often Miss?"

"Miss Sarah Dexler and no I don't usually blurt out everything. There is simply something about you."

Sarah realized her blunder. "Sorry I'm doing it again I don't know what has come over me. I promise I'm not typically like this and would guard myself with your employer."

"Never fear Miss Dexler. I'm a good judge of character and you seem to be nice and kind. My employer needs kindness, and someone who will listen most of all. You said you do that with strangers. You listen and help others, so that makes you a candidate we simply must see."

The man suddenly sounded very interested and in the next second he surprised Sarah with, "So would you be available for an interview tomorrow at 3 PM?"

"Yes, of course," Sarah became tentative. "I guess I could."

"Obviously given the generalities of our ad some applicants have been taken back and would like assurances of our trust worthiness. My employer, though he wishes to remain anonymous until the candidates are found, will be quite happy to provide references for himself.

Confidentiality agreements are signed as well. These, of course, will be provided at the interview stage. Interviews will be conducted at our temporary office at 1000 Park Street. We look forward to seeing you, Miss Dexler. Goodbye," the man ended the call abruptly.

Sarah closed her cell phone and thought… how strange this man appeared so mesmerizing on the phone He even seemed to snatch thoughts from her head. It was all a bit odd. Then as she thought some more, she realized even stranger he had forgotten to share his name. Had she distracted the poor man? Why had he forgotten to share his name? His English upper crust accent sounded so prim, proper and professional it seemed even peculiar to her now that he did not reveal his name. Still, she hoped this job would pan out or in a few days she'd be begging on the street corner.

363
S. G. Lee

~0~

Chapter 2 - Venimus, Vidimus, Vicimus

Sarah was in a hurry. She tried on every outfit she owned for this interview. Most of her wardrobe now lay strewn across her bed or floor. She finally settled on this black pantsuit. The tailored jacket was flattering and her pants that went with the jacket sculpted her rear end. Not that was necessary in an interview but it gave her a lift. She felt like a model in this outfit. A tall shapely model, because of these four-inch heels on her black sandals. They had cost her quite a fortune when she was pulling in a paycheque, but they were worth every penny. Sarah felt beautiful and hope her confidence would translate into a job. She really needed this job.

She entered the door at one thousand Park Street. The building was one of those non-descript glass buildings without about forty floors. She entered the building and realized the man on the phone had not given her the office number only the building number address. Without the office number she was lost. She could take the elevator but to where?

Sarah was in near tears thinking maybe the whole conversation with that man was a joke, a terrible joke on her. She spent her last five dollars to take a cab, so she wouldn't be late. She was lost…. the job was lost. Oh no even worse she'd be out on the street in a few days.

No, she couldn't let that happen. She had told the man on the phone she was good with people. That she could charm total strangers into telling their stories, so here was the time to prove it. She'd find the office. It might take a little talking; asking people questions that would lead to the office number. But surely being late would be excused when he realized he forgot to tell her the office number. Sarah began by talking to the receptionist at the desk in the hallway. She approached the young woman and she was almost taken aback. The receptionist appeared gorgeous her hair a beautiful honey blonde and cascading down in corkscrew ringlets. The receptionist's bright blue eyes were like diamonds and red lipstick finished the face that could launch a thousand ships. She was dressed in a very tight red dress. It didn't seem quite appropriate for the office, but who was Sarah to judge? Sarah couldn't help but wonder if this was the type of beauty that they hired here if so, she was in trouble. She couldn't compete with someone so incredibly lovely, or wear those oh so revealing clothes.

"Hi, my name is Sarah. I have a little problem I'm hoping that someone as knowledgeable and as intelligent as you are, could help me with," Sarah began.

"That's so flattering you think I can help you. People tend to treat me like a bit of an airhead because I'm a receptionist it's my job to assist people. I guess my parents didn't do me any favours by naming me Brandy," babbled Brandy breathlessly while snapping her gum.

“Oh, your name is Brandy? You know, some say Brandy is better than fine wine,” Sarah piled on the charm.

“I’m not... you know…. so, if …you know if that's what this is all about you can stop right there. Nothing against your preferences, but I’m seeing a guy,” replied Brandy awkwardly misunderstanding.

“Oh no….no …. Really, there’s nothing to worry about. I am straight too. I’m here trying to get a job. You see, I applied for this job, but the man on the phone forgot to tell me the office number where the interview is,” explained Sarah.

“That’s difficult because there are tons of offices in this building. Do you know what the guy looks like?” asked Brandy looking at her red painted fingernails and sliding a nail file over them.

“Sadly no, you see I talked to the man on the phone. He had an upper crust British accent though. Does that help you identify him for me?” begged Sarah.

“Oh, you are so in luck today.” Brandy replied, “We have only one guy who talks like that here. Mr. Poundstone. He’s conducting interviews today too so he is probably your man."

"Thank you so much Brandy, you don't know how much this means to me. Wait a minute I have a coupon for a free coffee, here this for you," answered Sarah digging the coupon out of her purse.

"But if you're looking for a job you must need the coupon."

"I wanted to let you know how much I truly appreciated your help," Sarah insisted sincerely.

"You are a really nice person, Sarah; I hope you get the job. Maybe we can share a coffee break when you do. You know... if you end up working in this building. Now the office number for Mr. Poundstone is 304. And just because I want you to get the job, if anyone asks for the number because he forgot to tell them I won't tell them," Brandy insisted winking.

"Oh no, that wouldn't be right," asserted Sarah, although delighted. "If they ask, please tell them. If this job is meant to be I'll get the position."

“Did anyone ever tell you Sarah, you’re too nice for your own good?” asked Brandy, as Sarah walked towards the elevator.

“Yes, people do say I’m too nice. But I can’t be any different than I am,” Sarah answered turning back to Brandy. Sarah then entered the elevator waving goodbye to Brandy.

The elevator reached the third floor and Sarah glanced at her watch, she realized she wasn't late at all; it was only 2:55 p.m. She was early, how amazing. She stepped off the elevator to find a room full of women of varying ages, shapes, sizes and colours. Sarah couldn’t help but noticing the other women appeared all extremely attractive.

Oh, so I’m not the only one up for the job, Sarah thought as she entered into room. If she had it her way when she left today, she’d have the job despite all these beauties. No second interviews, or third interview. This wasn’t a beauty contest after all. She would win this job. She was as sure of it as she was that her name was Sarah Dexler; Sarah thought proudly as she remembered the family Dexler motto.” *Venimus, Vidimus, Vicimus”*. It meant “We came. We saw. We conquered!

Sure, her ancestors had blatantly borrowed the saying from Caesar, but it was a good motto to live by and inspired confidence. Of course, if you could use your God-given charm and win the day why shouldn't you? She didn't think you had to use your attitude violently or cruelly, like a sword. A charming disposition worked as well or better than the sword and without drawing blood.

Sarah steeled herself marched up to the receptionist and confidently said… "Sarah Dexler, I have appointment at 3 pm."

"Yes, Miss Dexler, your name is here. Please take a seat. Mr. Poundstone will be with you momentarily," the receptionist said hardly looking up from her desk.

The office door opened and a congenial looking man came out. If Sarah were to describe him, she would describe a dignified Santa, maybe an Edmund Gwenn style from Miracle on 34th Street. His appearance was stylish and dignified, like an upper crust Englishman, suiting his voice on the phone.

His suit was a gray Burbury throughout. His hair trimmed short and he had a tiny white moustache. He seemed to be in his sixties.

“Miss Dexler, I presume?” Mr. Poundstone looked straight into her eyes.

“Yes, I am Sarah Dexler,” Sarah stood tall and threw her shoulders back, holding out her right hand which he clasped firmly with both his hands.

“I am Harry Poundstone. What a great pleasure to meet you in person. I worried I had steered you wrong as I remembered not giving you my office number. But I can see you are as good as your word and you obviously found me. Please do come into my office so we can discuss the particulars of this job and your qualifications for the position,” said Mr. Poundstone, while still smiling.

“Certainly, I would be happy to Mr. Poundstone,” replied Sarah while stepping into his office.

Mr. Poundstone continued to smile even more broadly, almost unnerving Sarah.

“Miss Dexler, I didn't want to tell you in front of all those job applicants, but we decided to give the job to you," Mr. Poundstone declared with great flourish.

"Me? But you didn't even interview me? Are you sure?" Sarah was shocked but rambled on, "Well, of course if you are sure or you wouldn't have said so. Oh, I'm doing it again. There's just something about you that makes me do that. Did I just say that aloud. Sorry," Sarah, blurted, and then blanching, asked… "Do you still want me for this job?"

Mr. Poundstone couldn't help but be amused.

"Miss Dexler. Or may I call you Sarah?" asked Mr. Poundstone.

"Please do, Mr. Poundstone," Sarah replied

"Please, would you care for some of this freshly steeped tea? Or, would you prefer coffee?"

"Yes, I would love some tea, two sugars and a little cream please," answered Sarah

"Huh, exactly how I made your tea. Most people prefer milk rather than cream. It's Harry actually. Please call me Harry. Mr. Poundstone is so formal," expressed Mr.

Poundstone, and then followed quickly with, "Where do you see yourself in five years Sarah?"

"I could lie and say I see myself in an executive position but the truth is I want it all. I want a career that fulfills me and I want children and a husband."

What a weird start to the interview, Sarah thought. Why, oh why, had she mentioned she desired a husband and children? Was she sharing things that were too personal? Were there bounds that were being overstepped? There had to be something in the tea, a truth serum perhaps? What was it about this man? What caused her to blurt out exactly what she was thinking? What possessed her?" He would think she didn't want this job and would leave at the first opportunity.

Sarah continued thinking knowing she needed to reassure Mr. Poundstone her priority was this job. "Oh, but I can tell you I see this position as a real opportunity to gain experience…"

Sarah wanted to continue but could not. She could not hide her suspicion and was suddenly compelled to ask "Did you put something in my tea to make me tell you only the truth and in fact say everything I am thinking?"

"No, but I'm finding this conversation absolutely amazing," Mr. Poundstone replied smiling and Sarah suddenly found his constant smile slightly creepy.

"What's amazing?" asked Sarah bravely, "That for some unknown reason, I believe that you have the power to mesmerize and draw words from people?"

Mr. Poundstone just grinned even wider like he knew a secret, a secret that Sarah didn't know but needed to uncover.

"Holy cow, I can't believe it. That's it isn't it? You have some unusual power and I can feel it. You can get people to tell you what they are really thinking," Sarah exclaimed while truly surprised by her own words.

Mr. Poundstone reached into his jacket and pulled out a pocket watch which he proceeded to open. The watch was gold and attached to a long chain.

"This is truly amazing. I have never encountered anyone with such acuity. Two minutes, that's all it took for you to perceive the unusualness of our conversation. Most people who have any ability require days to detect my power, but you became aware it within less than two minutes."

Mr. Poundstone's next words shook Sarah to her core.

"He said you would be the one. I heard glimmers of your abilities in our phone conversation, but he was absolutely right. This is so truly, truly astonishing." His voice became high pitched with excitement, almost maniacal, and belied the dignified image he had shown earlier.

"Uh…Ok… I'm going to leave now." Sarah had become slightly frightened of the nature of Mr. Poundstone's behaviour, "But no harm, no foul."

"Oh, please my dear lady, do not be frightened of me or my employer. I know I am not explaining this well but we've looked so long for one like you…"

Sarah found this last statement even more disturbing.

"That's okay but I think I'm going," Sarah replied reaching for the door handle.

“Please Sarah, I beg of you, give myself and my employer another chance. Wouldn't you like to find out the real reason why we chose you? Don’t you want to be aware of the untapped power that you alone hold?” Mr. Poundstone begged again with his voice once again deep and compelling.

“No! If you have some deep dark plan for me, you can just forget it,” Sarah turned the doorknob and continued to try to make her escape. “Quit trying to compel me. I know you're doing it. I don’t understand how you’re doing it but I can grasp you are doing it.”

“I apologize but it is sometimes hard to turn off one’s gift,” Mr. Poundstone stated calmly. “Did you ever wonder where you came from? Who your parents were? Who were your other relatives? Sarah, we know you started life in Foster Care.”

Sarah retorted, her fear changing to anger. “How dare you? That…has nothing to do with a job interview. How did you access those records? You didn't even have my social security number?”

"I know a lot about you Sarah Marie Dexler. For instance, I know your real last name is Maidenstone. The Dexler's adopted you when you were four years old, and isn't the truth, before they adopted you, you did not speak."

Tears formed in Sarah's eyes and her anger grew. "I'm going to report you and your agency to the Better Business Bureau, the police, and a lawyer; in that order. You have absolutely no right to snoop into my life."

"I've hurt you and that was not my intention. I know your grandfather and if he could have found you, believe me, he would have. He would have taken you from that foster home. It really wasn't his fault. Your parents disappeared without a trace in America. They were British citizens, born in Coventry, England. Your grandfather was not even aware of your existence. He found out six years after they had perished, that his beloved daughter and her husband had died. He went crazy with grief, and we despaired that we would never get him back again. But he did recover over time, albeit never to the same contented state. He discovered by searching through numerous records that she had a given birth to daughter; that daughter was you. And he asked me to find you."

"This was all a ruse? There is no job? Of course, there is no job! Why…why am I still here? Did you hypnotize me? All this because you say my so-called grandfather wants to meet me?"

Sarah was going to tell Mr. Poundstone, he was a very bad man, but he cut her off.

"Needless to say, your grandfather waits anxiously to meet you in person. Moreover, he is well aware of your current predicament and has an exciting job…mmm…opportunity, he wants to discuss with you. But I'm afraid, I have been forbidden to share the particulars with you at this time."

"I don't know about this. None of this seems right. A strange man tells me I possess a grandfather, a grandfather who didn't come forward to me when I was young? And now he wants to meet me? And then he expects me to just take a job from him?" Sarah composed herself. "I just don't know. This is a lot to take in."

"Think about meeting him. Please," begged Mr. Poundstone. "You won't be sorry if you agree to this meeting. Your grandfather is a wonderful and wise man."

Mr. Poundstone couldn't help but smile slightly at the corners of his mouth but he kept his eyes penetratingly fixed on Sarah's own deep gaze.

Mr. Poundstone mused out loud, "What if I go tell the other applicants to come back another day for an interview for the actual job, I brought them here for?"

"Please don't keep them waiting. If there's an honest job for them at least interview them. I can wait in the lobby," Sarah replied, relieved the other women were not being duped. And, she realized, she was not surprised Mr. Poundstone sensed her concern for those who unwittingly helped him in his duplicity.

"No, please, I have another office here, I'll interview them there. Just please… take your time. Have a cup from the freshly steeped pot of tea and I hope you'll make the decision you will see your grandfather," begged Mr. Poundstone while leaving the room.

“Fine… I'll wait…but I'm still not sure,” Sarah exclaimed with exasperation to Mr. Poundstone’s departing back.

In a room next to the one where Sarah waited, a man watched through a two-way mirror. From his side he could see her seated in the chair in front of Mr. Poundstone’s desk. The man was mature, his hair greyed at the temples and sides but with a shock of black hair that ran through the middle of his thick mane. He was tall and stood over six feet, possibly as tall as six feet six inches. He was broad shouldered and lean looking while surprisingly well muscled.

He looked to be about sixty, or maybe sixty-five years of age, but he moved with the ease of a much younger man; as he paced back and forth with his focus on the mirror. Dressed in a suit tailored perfectly for him, he exuded confidence. He seemed mesmerized as he intently surveyed Sarah though the glass. He appeared somewhat amused, that he knew Sarah was unaware that she was being watched.

The door opened to the chamber, where the tall man stood watching. Mr. Poundstone walked into this room with a much different demeanour, than the one he displayed when he had earlier greeted Sarah. Mr. Poundstone lowered his head and seemed hesitant to approach. He moved forward cautiously as if any misstep could trigger an explosion like bomb in a minefield.

"This is the one? This is she? No mistakes this time?" the man demanded harshly while taking a seat.

"Yes, my lord, this is the one. I promise there has been no mistake this time. As promised, I supervised this one myself," replied Harry Poundstone, his voice very subservient.

"Good. What did you tell her?" asked the tall man.

"I told her you were her grandfather and you kept looking for her, just as we rehearsed. I told her you grieved for her mother and searched for her as soon as you knew she existed."

"Marvellous Harry, a falsehood that is so close to the truth is always so much more believable," said the tall man pleased.

"I hope this makes up for the failure of my operatives last year?" asked Mr. Poundstone meekly, obviously seeking approval.

"It does if this is truly her!" replied the tall man, Sarah's grandfather. "Does she show any essence of her mother? Or is she only tainted by him?"

"The taint is there my lord. I am sorry my lord…but if there is any of you in her I see none of it." Mr. Poundstone cowered as he said this, expecting to be castigated. He was all too familiar with the consequences of failing to please his master, through words or deeds.

"I'm sure you are mistaken. She is of my line after all. I think I have seen glimmers of myself. If not, while then it is decided," pronounced the tall man, dismissing the matter.

"Must we, Lord Ecclestone?" Mr. Poundstone dared to ask.

"Are you questioning me? You dare to question me?" demanded Lord Ecclestone.

The tall man's face turned purple and his rage consumed the entire room. To Mr.

Poundstone it seemed as if darkness surrounded him, only broken by the fierce glower of his lord's penetrating eyes.

"No sir, of course I am not questioning you. I would never dare," replied Mr. Poundstone submissively, mollifying him.

The pair continued to observe Sarah unbeknownst as she waited anxiously in the adjoining office. Sarah found herself consumed by many thoughts that raged incessantly through her mind. A grandfather searched for her? She had family, but a family that took this long to come forward? Could the story really be true, that he just couldn't find her until now? What an incredible story, much like a fairy tale. Those usually didn't end well.

What of Mr. Poundstone? He was to say, a very unusual man. True. Still there was something not quite right about him. At times she felt he seemed a jovial Santa Claus, but could it just be a false persona? If Mr. Poundstone wasn't who he pretended to be, then how could she trust that this man would put her in touch with her real grandfather?

Maybe she should just leave. But if he did know her grandfather and he could put them in touch maybe she should give him a chance? Mr. Poundstone was distinctly odd, almost chilling with this strange power he had. He actually eluded she might have one as well, a power. That, of course, was ludicrous stuff and definitely nonsense. Then there was the fact that he had snooped in her personal business.

He had found out facts that she had never told anyone. It was like stripping her bare. She wasn't happy about that. What did she really know about these people? Only what he, Mr. Poundstone, had told her? She had already found out he had a power that made people believe and do what he wanted them to do; so why was she sitting here waiting for Mr. Poundstone? Or waiting for this man that claimed to be her grandfather?

How trustworthy was a man who manipulated people with some spellbinding ability and made them do what he wanted? She suddenly became afraid again. There was something definitely not quite right about this and she felt it down to her very bones. If her grandfather had truly wanted to meet her there was no need for this deception. And why were so many people interested in a companion job? And why were they all attractive young women? These thoughts had just entered her mind. What had prevented these thoughts before? There were just too many things that didn't add up here.

What was wrong with her, that she hadn't bolted all ready? Mr. Poundstone had used some of his power on her; that was the only explanation. The power that she was starting to believe he really possessed. Was it some kind of hypnotism? She was leaving now, this very minute, before something bad happened.

Just then the door opened to Mr. Poundstone's office and Sarah watched a man enter. He was tall, dark haired and mysterious looking. His hair was raven coloured, his eyes blue and piercing and his gaze centered on her. He was muscular and dynamic looking and he just seemed to be one of those people that drew upon all eyes upon them. Simply put, this man radiated power and one could not help but put all focus on his presence.

It was odd though when he came in the room it was like time stopped. She looked at the clock on Mr. Poundstone's desk and realized that it wasn't as if time had stopped, it actually had. The circumstances were getting more bizarre for Sarah the more she went along today. Had she really gotten up this morning, or was this all a dream?

As she gazed upon the man, he spoke… "Come on then, we have to leave now." he requested of her.

"We…we have to leave now? I don't think so. I have had enough you are very weird people. I don't understand what is going on but I'm not going anywhere with you," Sarah reacted, annoyed.

"I don't have time to explain this to you. You deserve explanations, but we definitely don't have time. This only lasts so long. It takes so much power and energy, that it's very draining. We have to go now. We have to be away from here before I lose my power, which could be at any moment," said the man urgently.

"Again, with the power? I'm getting out of here but not with you. I don't want to see any of you weirdoes ever again," replied a disgusted Sarah.

"Fine, just come with me now. Let us leave and get away now!" pleaded the man.

"I don't even know your name. I'm not going anywhere with you. I'm going home," Sarah's anger grew and she was very determined to get away.

"They know where you live. They want something from that you don't even know you have," The man then said cryptically "They are not nice people. You don't understand the lengths they will go to or the things they have done."

"Enlighten me then," Sarah demanded.

"I told you there isn't time. Please I beg of you, come with me now."

"And you are? And I should come with you because? I'm tired of this. You and all these other people just come into my life making impossible demands."

"You can do things that aren't possible or real. Oh…just go away and leave me be"

"My name is Demetrious Blackstone and we are sort of related. I promise I'll tell you more once we are away from here." Then seeing her face, he added, "I know all of this is difficult for you to understand and I will explain when we get away from here but we must get away now."

He then took Sarah's hands and pulled her to her feet. Moments later they are out the door. Sarah wasn't sure how they got to the waiting room so fast. Or even why she didn't fight back and resist but here they were. In this room Sarah saw all the people she had before, but there was still not a ripple of movement. Time was stood still and it seemed as if only they moved through it. It was all so unreal and peculiar. Demetrious opened the front door of the building and they passed out into the street. Cars were stilled, not moving at all as time and space stood still. Not even a breeze blowing. Sarah was amazed and frightened all at once. What was going on?

"How long will this last?" asked Sarah.

"Not much longer. We must be long away when it stops. He will know it was I and come after us," warned Demetrious ominously.

"I'm going home," insisted Sarah, afraid but determined.

"Do you not understand their fierce abilities? Don't you understand the danger you are in?" Demetrious asked, staring at Sarah. Then slowly searching her face he sighed and said… "No, of course you don't. How could you know that there is a great peril to you here? This man, who is your grandfather, is kin to a vampire. He finds power from innocents, from those who are not aware of their power. He then takes their power from them and not in a pleasant way, I assure you. What he leaves of these people is a nothing but a zombie like creature; a creature that only exists to obey their lord and master; your grandfather. Or, if he chooses, they are left a broken soul whose mind is completely stripped, so they function only on a basic primitive level."

Sarah did not believe her ears and denied everything the man was saying.

"This is all so utterly ridiculous. I'm starting to think that Mr. Poundstone drugged me, so I'm very glad you got me out of there Mr. Blackstone. I thank you for everything you have done so far but I'm going home. Now!"

"I am sorry I have to do this to you. I wouldn't if it wasn't necessary to protect you. But you don't even realize the great power you hold and how and what could happen if someone as unscrupulous as your grandfather got a hold of that power."

Demetrious gripped the back of her neck gently with the fullness of his hand and Sarah began to feel light headed. Slowly the world seemed to fade away and she fell into a deep unconsciousness.

~0~

Excerpt from Dreams Can Kill

Chapter 1- Survival

The rain pelted down on me, as I struggled to come to my senses. My head felt like it had split in two, as if little lumberjacks had taken up residence. I opened one eye. The world spun sideways like a ride at the fair. I tried shutting one eye, then the other. I nearly fell back to sleep. I opened my eyes again, fighting the sleep which wanted to overtake me. I shuttered my eyes again, as my stomach protested. My whole body manipulated, bruised, bent and broken like some old rag doll discarded.

Sleep...sleep would solve my problems, my brain protested. No! I had a reason I needed to stay awake and alert...A little sleep, a part of me protested again. No, I must stay conscious. But I remained so tired. I dragged myself across the pebbled ground. My right leg stuck out at an impossible angle, obviously broken. I saw by lifting my head slightly and turning it that there appeared to be a road up ahead. I had to get to the road. If I dragged myself that far, surely, I would be rescued?

But it was oh so hard, to drag yourself backwards, when you couldn't perceive where you were going. Oh no, what if he came back. He would finish me off...finish what he had started.

He who? Who was this person, who left me to die? Why couldn't I remember? Don't panic… the thing to do is right now is to reach help; then and only then would I be safe. I caressed large pieces of gravel which cut into the back of my head. I sensed I was close to the road. I reached out with my good hand and touched a paved surface.

I knew I didn't have much strength left. I experienced the energy drain quickly leaving my body. I tried to fight the drain, but the world faded to black.

~0~

Chapter 2- Time Flies When You're Having Fun

I opened my eyes slowly. A tube appeared to have been inserted in my arm, feeding me intravenously, another tube down my throat as well. The lumberjacks in my head had been replaced by a dull achy sensation, as if I wasn't quite there. I suffered from weakness all over, but my body didn't have the same sensation, as when I had blacked out on the road. My leg felt whole again and yet my leg didn't appear to be in a cast, or slung up on a tripod. How much time had passed? This definitely looked like a hospital room. The walls were pale white and I lay in a single bed. I rested in a private room how about that?

A nurse in a white cap entered the room. She grabbed my wrist and she proceeded to take my pulse. Alarmed, she stared straight into my face, "Well! Look who is awake. Welcome back to the real world," she proclaimed.

I tried to speak and realized the tube in my throat prevented that. Why was a tube in my throat I wondered? How long I been here? I assumed I looked scared because the nurse explained in a soft voice, "There, there honey, you take deep breaths, easy now."

"Why don't I go get the doctor? He can come and have a look at you and remove the tube from your throat."

I tried to nod my head in agreement but my head moved like lead. It seemed like eons before a man in a white doctor's coat appeared at my bedside. He appeared tall and lanky; with dark curly brown hair and warm deep blue eyes. Without any preamble he announced, "We will now remove this tube. Take a big breath now."

The tube came out as I gagged. Now I could ask the questions which plagued me.

"How did I get here? And where am I?" I tried to ask, croaking out the words, as if my voice hadn't been used in a while.

"Speak slowly. Here, have sips of water," answered the doctor.

"How did I get here?" I repeated, sure that I had been speaking clearer because I had taken a sip of water.

"I don't know who found you, but an ambulance brought you here in critical condition. You had a broken leg, some broken ribs, and a fractured skull."

"I came here in critical condition? So, I've been here awhile?" I asked shocked.

"Yes, you've been here awhile. You were at a different hospital first. You are in Andrews' clinic now."

"Your condition appeared to be perilous there for some time. They lost you twice. We had placed you in a coma to let your brain swelling go away. Then we didn't know if you would ever come out of the coma."

He continued to explain like he couldn't quite find the words. But why would a doctor have trouble explaining a medical condition?

"I guess time flies when you have fun," I stated flippantly, hiding fear I didn't quite understand and becoming puzzled.

Why did he say first they then we? Hadn't he been there?

"I would like to examine you to see how you're doing now and get an update on your condition."

"I'm good. As you can see," I answered in response.

"I don't know if you even realize, but your speech isn't as clear as you think. You're slurring your words," he stated. "I'm sure the words will come easier in time, but I'd like to check your reaction time and some other physical reactions."

What could he be talking about? I wasn't slurring my words. Was I?

The doctor began his examination. A flashlight flashed deep into my eyes. I blinked in response, as the light, so bright, made my eyes hurt. His response seemed to be to write down something on the chart, and pick up my wrist to take my pulse and blood pressure. He then listened to my chest with his stethoscope.

I moved my head and tried to sit up, but the effort zapped all my remaining strength. I surprised myself at how I felt like a newborn baby. He continued his examination. I grew tired but fought the sensation. If I closed my eyes for a moment, would the feeling would go away? I closed my eyelids and fell fast asleep.

I ran over hills. The night appeared so dark, and ink black; I could barely view two feet in front of me. My feet stumbled, as I tried to see the uneven ground in front of me. My palms clenched with sweat, as my heart pounded like the organ would jump out of my chest. I turned around, my eyes darting from side to side searching for my pursuer. No sign, but I knew he wasn't far behind.

My hair in a high ponytail, whipped at my face, as I picked up the pace in my flight. He seemed close enough, that I had the sensation of his breath on my neck… so close he might reach out and touch me. I turned again to see if I could glimpse him near, and I saw a man. But what puzzled me was what materialized in the man's face. Where his face should be, a gaping black hole yawned.

How could this be? The thought plagued me only for moment, as fear gripped me and survival instinct kicked in. Realizing if he caught me, I would be killed, I ran stumbling over rock and uneven ground. When the inevitable happened, I tripped falling to my knees. He had me. There was no escape from my fate. I would die now. I struggled as he grabbed my left wrist twisting my arm.

This appeared no dream, I might awake from; he had me now and he would kill me. I twisted slightly trying to free my wrist but he grabbed my other wrist and shook me slightly saying…, "Quite a dream you were having, but a dream none the less. Nothing can harm you now."

I stared into his face and slowly his look changed, from the faceless man, to another face entirely. This wasn't the man in my visions; the demon in my nightmare. I knew in my heart this remained an altogether different kind of man.

This face with smiling blue eyes radiated warmth, and kindness. His face stayed gentle, not violent. I had been dreaming and had mistaken his touch for the man in my dreams. I flushed with embarrassment.

"You are quite awake now? I won't harm you. Now, do remember me?"

I stared at him, slowly waking up, and realizing where I was.

"I'm your Doctor, Doctor Andrews, at your service, my lady. We met before when you awoke from your coma," he continued speaking softly, and gently, bowing at the waist and smiling.

Shouldn't I have recognized him immediately? Heat rushed to my cheeks, as I turned red in embarrassment.

I was a fish out of water. I didn't like the way I reacted; like something had happened and all was a secret to me. I liked to be in charge of my life every aspect, and right now it seemed like I appeared in charge of nothing.

"How long have I been here?" I whispered, trying to speak louder.

"I would have said it's a lot longer, than you think," he replied cryptically.

"Do you always answer a question with a question? I want an answer for my query," I demanded angrily.

"What do you remember?"

"I believe I asked you to stop making this an interrogation. If you must know, I remember waking up a little while ago the nurse came in and then you came a little later," I answered exasperated, wondering what could be wrong with me. I didn't get angry so easily. Did I? Why did I behave this way? Everything he said seemed to make me angry.

"Your little while ago was two days ago...," he explained, breaking off as if afraid to say more.

"But that's impossible..."

"You fell into a restorative sleep. It is not uncommon for patients who have been in a coma to do so."

"Two days? I slept for two days?" I commented incredulously.

"Yes," Doctor. Andrews stated.

"How long was I in a coma?" I asked worried to hear what he might say.

"What month do you remember?"

"You have to be in charge, don't you? Questions! Questions!" I replied, delaying the answer. I was suddenly afraid that I'd been in this coma far longer than I realized, and grew angrier.

"I know you're scared. Are you sure you want to know? The information can wait," he insisted.

"I'm not scared," I lied with false bravado, "I remember quite clearly the month is March."

"It is the eleventh of September nineteen hundred and seventy-one. Do you remember what happened the day of the accident?" he asked.

"That's not possible. I can't have been in a coma for six months. Why do you lie to me?" I spat at him.

"I know it's hard to assimilate but time has passed and it is September," he insisted softly, but firmly.

"Why do you persist in a lie? What do you have to gain with this preposterous story?" I demanded; still not ready to believe this.

"Exactly what do I have to gain? Sharron, I'm not lying to you," he stated sadly.

Until that moment I hadn't given any thought to my name, but as Doctor Andrews called me Sharron, I realized I wasn't even sure if that was my name. I didn't have a clue what my name was. My name might be Sharron, but I didn't recall the name. My name could be Mary, or Angela, or any other name in the world. If I had a surname, I couldn't remember it either. A huge blank spot stood where any recollection should be.

How could my last memory be of March, but I still had no recollection of my name, er names? This was normal after a long coma. I decided.

Perhaps my memory had been so underused, and only had temporary gaps? Or I was hungry? Yes, it had to be one of those things. A temporary aberration of the mind... No need for me to worry. No, need to share any such information.

My memory was only hiatus. That had to be the answer. Give it a few days and my memory would all come back. There was no need to tell the doctor, especially since my recollections would all come back. Absolutely not, I reasoned.

After all what good would it do to tell him? He'd look at me either with sympathy, or call in a shrink. I wanted none of the sympathy, and whispered glances which would follow. So, I had a few memory gaps, nothing to worry about. It was perfectly normal after a coma, I reassured myself.

“What will you do with all this information Sharron?” asked Doctor Andrews suddenly concerned.

“I must admit the information was a bit of a shock to find the month was September and not March, but I’m over the surprise. “I’m hungry what does it take to get food around here?’’ I demanded, quickly changing the subject. Besides I was ravenous.

“I think you can start some light foods, some soft foods, Jell-O soup etc.,” Doctor Andrews spouted. Turning to the nurse he commanded, “Nurse get a light meal for my patient.”

“Certainly Doctor,” the nurse replied, coming into the room rather quickly, at his summons.

Just when I thought I had successfully gotten rid of the doctor, he turned around and said... “I know you are rather tired and hungry right now, but I’m sure you to want to discuss these revelations later today.”

How could I get him to change his track? I didn't want to discuss my memory loss with anyone. I wasn't ready for anyone to find out, I didn 't know who I was. If I told him, would he treat me like a mental patient?

No, I wasn't going to tell him, or anyone. I needed to fake what I remembered. They'd never know, I couldn't remember. I would then have the time to accept this myself, and hopefully everything would come back. No one would ever have to know.

Wait a minute, did he know, I didn't remember? He talked about the fact I'd been in a coma, but had he given me any knowing glances? I gave him a sideways glance. Deciding he didn't have a clue about my memory problem. I plotted to keep it that way.

"There is not a lot to talk about; but if you want to, we can discuss my medical condition we can get to that later," I replied, hoping he would take my response as an agreement and leave.

Luckily for me he took the hint. Maybe he would even forget to come back and discuss this later? No, I hoped for too much, but he did look convinced that I'd talk to him later. Good then he'd go away.

"I will return later, Sharron."

He then left taking his questions with him. I breathed a sigh of relief. Now alone with my thoughts, surely, I'd conjure up a memory or two. First, I would eat and refuel. That would help the memories, as well as my stomach.

I stared at the food the nurse had brought in. I'm starving to death and the nurse gave me not enough food to feed a rabbit? I tried to pick up the spoon and found my hand wouldn't cooperate.

"Would you like some help?" the nurse asked kindly.

"I can do it myself," I responded stubbornly.

Although I had found it difficult to raise my hand to my mouth, that soon became easier. I found by clamping my hand around the spoon I could manage to feed myself. It was then I realized how much work I had ahead of me. The nurse watched, so I smiled at her like everything was fine. She smiled back and left.

I soon made short work of the food and wanted to move on to the therapy I recognized I needed. I would set the memories, or lack of them aside, and working on building up the muscle tone and abilities I'd lost. When the body restored itself, I would begin to remember. I understood without being told, that I had to begin like a baby to exercise my limbs and I wanted to start immediately. Let's be honest. I realized I could remember something. I grasped now that I was an impatient person, at least when it came to doing things I had to be doing. I called the nurse on the call bell to ask about therapy and exercises.

"Yes?" I heard a disembodied voice somewhere over my head say. Momentarily puzzled, I then realized the voice came from an intercom.

"Sorry to bother you but when can I start therapy? I need to get my limbs moving," I explained.

"Dear, you are barely out of coma. I'm sure your doctor would want you to build up your energy first. Or wait at least until you started solid foods."

She sounded surprised and had a hint of censor in her voice. No support there. I wanted those six months back, but clearly that wasn't going to happen. Move on, I told myself. I'd wasted six months sleeping, time to fight back and get back into fighting form as they said. But who had said that?

I somehow knew I was a fighter. I'd have to do everything myself; something I knew I always did. But how did I know that?

I thought about what would work, and what limbs need to work. My hands needed to a work out. Okay, they need to grip. How do you make hands stronger?

You give them something to grip. Squeezing something soft, medium soft, would work. Where to get something to work my grasp? I couldn't even get out of bed. My limbs were useless, absolutely useless.

My hand shook in weakness, from forcing the stupid thing, to do its job and feed me.

All of this began to feel hopeless. No, I wasn't some stupid helpless female. I had to figure out a plan. You're on your own, I told myself, nothing new. You can overcome any odds. Think, Sharron, think!

How about some finger exercises? Slowly working each finger, and then in tandem, I would get back movement. I began the exercise I devised. It sounded so simple when I had thought of how to exercise the hand, but painful and tiring. Work through the pain, I told myself. Isn't that what you've always heard?

I forced myself to do the exercises for what seemed like hours, until I couldn't take the pain any more. Then I decided to exercise my arms. Gripping well enough to pull myself up to the bar over my bed, I reached I'm with my right hand to grab the pole. My fingers won't cooperate. My fingers are weakened and my grip slipped. Damn it! Even simple exercise was impossible.

"Nothing is impossible," a voice spoke loudly in my head. But whose voice did I hear? My memory had fled, if it was ever there. I only comprehended the voice had been someone I loved, and respected. Was this a father, or a father figure? I knew I was bone weary, and a great sea of lethargy stole over me. It would be counterproductive not to take a nap, I reasoned. Surely a short nap would restore my energy and I would begin again.

I closed my eyes soon I began dreaming. At first the dream appeared happy. I viewed myself in a beautiful home and grinning at someone I couldn't see.

I smiled and felt great joy, but the sky grew dark and I found myself outside on a field. The moon overhead slowly covered by clouds, and I grew terrified. Something was wrong. The faceless man chased me once more. I ran over rocks and streams and more rocks. He kept coming and coming. I knew he'd soon be on me. He nearly had me when I willed myself to wake up saying… This is a dream and I want to wake up now.

I awoke gasping for air like I had been running a marathon. A strange man sat by my bed. His hair appeared dark, practically black, greasy, and slicked back. He had black thick glasses that he peered over like they were a prop.

An oversized suit coat in plaid and matching pants completed the picture. Despite his harmless appearance, he struck terror to my heart. What gave me the idea he put on this persona, like a piece of new clothing? I think it was his face which seemed to give it all away, like he tried too hard to portray someone he wasn't.

As I gazed at him, he jumped from the chair he sat and exclaimed, "About damn time you woke up out of the coma Sharron. I thought you laze there forever."

He then continued, as if choosing his words carefully, "Oh Sharron, this is the most wonderful day of my life." Then he pulled me to him, fiercely.

"Let go of me, this instance. Who do you think you are? I said don't touch me! And quit acting and looking around there's no audience for your play," I blurted out, before I stop myself.

"Sharron that's not funny. Quit joking. You always had a wicked sense of humour, but I'm not laughing." the man stated, sounding annoyed and grabbing my wrist.

"I said let me go, and I meant every word. Now kindly take your hands off me," I demanded at the top of my lungs, struggling unsuccessfully to free myself of the grip, he now had on my wrist.

Taken back by my yelling, he let me go, but he still continued to treat me, like a bug under a microscope. Suddenly switching gears, his face changed. It was if a curtain went down over his face. He took on a concerned look and then a hurt look. I admit he nearly had me fooled.

I started thinking I had forgotten a boyfriend, but surely, I wouldn't suffer from such bad taste.

He wasn't my type. He seemed quite violent too. I wouldn't have been so foolish to get mixed up with a weirdo like him! Would I?

"Sharron quit staring at me that way you're making me uncomfortable. I'm not amused here...Wait a minute you're not kidding. You don't recognize me at all. You don't recognize your fiancé?"

I recognized somehow that he was put on an act. No, I wasn't engaged to him. If I had been it would boggle my mind. He had to be lying, I decided. Why I didn't know, but I knew he lied.

I had no sparks with him. In fact, something about him gave me the creeps. He repulsed me and made my stomach hurt. He certainly didn't sound sincere. He put on an act ... but why? He grabbed my wrists again, once again in a vice grip. I struggled valiantly, but his grip tightened and I couldn't handle his fierce clutch in my weakened stated.

"Let me go you, caveman. I don't know you and what is more, I don't ever want to know you," screamed at him fighting frantically.

"Sharron, you cut me to the quick. Why do you say such things to me?" he whined, letting go of my wrist, but gripping my arms even tighter.

Maybe it was because of my dream, but suddenly I was terrified. Why did they leave me all alone with this crazy man? Where was everyone else? Couldn't they hear me shouting?

"Let me go. Let me go.... Don't touch me," I yelled at the top of my lungs, and then screamed, hysterically "Help me someone help me."

As I started to pull harder frantically to be free, he stilled held fast. What kind of evil demon had me in his grasp? I tried to bite him, but that was impossible; finally in the answer to my screams were footsteps running. Seconds later a nurse and Doctor Andrews entered.

"Let my patient go immediately. I said let her go," Doctor Andrews growled, pulling the man's arms behind his back.

I breathed a sigh of relief. I was safe. Doctor Andrews had saved me.

"I wasn't hurting her! What kind of a man do you think I am? Gee, I have more bruises than her. She acted crazy, so I grabbed both her arms to calm her," the man explained, sounding plausible.

Surely Doctor Andrews and the nurse who followed him in, didn't believe his act?

"Your technique doesn't seem to have calmed her, but it certainly frightened her," Doctor Andrews said, checking my blood pressure and heart rate.

"You can't tell me what to do. She's my fiancée I can speak to her anyway I want," complained the man, loudly.

"You've upset my patient. Her blood pressure and heart rate are elevated as well. This is not good for my patient, so I can tell you what to do. What is your name?" demanded Doctor Andrews.

"Titus Brown is my name and Sharron is my fiancée," the man replied a little too quickly.

Doctor Andrews consulted his clipboard. He pointed to it and then announced, "This is the approved register and you're not on the list. Leave now, Mr. Brown, or I'll have security escort you out of the facility."

"I'm not going anywhere. Who do you think you are?"

Mr. Brown showed his true colours, I thought. They would trounce him faster than you could say Jack Robinson.

"Mr. Brown, so far, I've been pleasant. The nurse has already called for a security guard. I suggest you leave now and don't come back, or you will find yourself with a trespassing charge and jail time," Doctor Andrews said through his teeth.

"I'll be back with my lawyer and you'll be sorry," Mr. Brown menaced.

Two security guards entered and forcefully removed Mr. Brown from my room. I began to shake like a leaf. I tried to stop, but I grew frightened. Someone had tried to kill me and that is why I was in the hospital. What if it was Him, Mr. Brown?

They wouldn't let him take me when he talked to his lawyer? Would they? Words I hadn't wanted to share, spilled out of my mouth, first in torments, and then at a screeching level.

"I don't know who the heck he is, but I do know I don't know him. I'm not his fiancée. Don't let him come back lawyer, or no lawyer. I don't want to see him. Someone did this to me! I wouldn't be surprised if the person was him!" I guess I appeared a little too hysterically and forcefully, because the next thing that occurred was Doctor Andrews plunged a needle into me.

"Please, please don't. It's not necessary, really. I'll be good," I pleaded too late.

"It's a little sedative. I don't like your colour, your blood pressure, or your heart rate. You've had a nasty scare and your body isn't able to cope with this right now. Calm down now," he said comforting "Go to sleep."

"I think I hate you," I replied vehemently.

"That's okay, you can hate me if you need to," he answered, smiling.

Damn him and his handsome smile! Something about the grin, made me want to smile back and tell him all my secrets.

"Don't leave me alone. He might come back," I pleaded as I drifted into a deep drugged sleep.

~0~

If you enjoyed *London Bridge is Broken Down ~A Tale of Two Londons,* please consider leaving me a few words at your favourite retailer and if you liked the excerpts and would like to read more of my books, please check out one of my other books listed on the next page at Amazon and other retailers

Sincerely S. G. Lee.

~0~

List of Books by S. G. Lee

Murder Mysteries:

The Kelly Murder Mysteries:

1.) A Penny Saved A Murder Earned

2.) A Diller A Dollar A Really Dead Scholar

3.) Betty Blue Lost Her Holiday Shoe

4.) What Will Poor Robin Do?

5.) This Little Piggy Had None

6.) This Little Girl Had A Little Curl

7.) London Bridge is Broken Down-A Tale of Two Londons (this book)

8.) Coming 2024- The Butcher, the Baker, The Candlestick Maker

The Kelly Murder Mysteries-Book 1-3

The Kelly Murder Mysteries Book 4-6

A Stitch in Time-Prequel to the Kelly Murder Mysteries

The Sheriff Bullet Murder Mysteries:

1-Stray Bullet

2~Untraceable

3~Dead Center

4.). Coming 2024 - Cloudburst

Stand alone murder mystery~ Dreams Can Kill

Paranormal:

Love's Labour's Won

A Tiger's Heart Wrapped in a Player's Hide

Reborn – a novella~ prequel

Short Story Books:

Murder Most Fowl

Jack be Nimble

Day of the Dead

Legends, Folktales and other Stories

The Stuff of Nightmares

ObsessionX2

422
London Bridge is Broken Down
A Tale of Two Londons

<u>Christmas</u>

Christmas is Calling

The Christmas Card

The Christmas Angel

Visions of Sugarplums

<u>Poetry-</u>

A Poetic Touch - The Human Condition

Poetry in Motion~ A Forest of Feelings

<u>Children's Books</u>

Mare the Hare

Henrietta and the Donor Eggs

The Magical Life of Me

Hello. Baby, I'm Your Big Sister

~0~

424
London Bridge is Broken Down
A Tale of Two Londons

www.ingramcontent.com/pod-product-compliance
Lightning Source LLC
LaVergne TN
LVHW010628110826
845149LV00014B/2808